BLUE

Farmhouse

FLOWERS

BLUE

Farmhouse

FLOWERS

TERI HARMAN

Mirror Press

Interior Design by Cora Johnson
Edited by Lisa Russo Leigh and Lisa Shepherd
Cover design by Rachael Anderson
Cover Image Credit: Shutterstock #1393235996

Published by Mirror Press, LLC
ISBN-13: 978-1-947152-73-1

Dedication:

To my sweet sister Maren. As you create your own path, remember this advice from a cranky, old miser ghost: *All work has critics. Only fools listen to what they say.*

PART I – PLANTING

Autumn Island, Oregon
June 2018

THE FLOWERS WERE all wrong. Edith Daniels sat three rows back from the shiny oak casket of Simone Cuthbert. Pastor Bill droned on about Simone's contribution to the town. Edith couldn't hear him over the loud buzz of her annoyance.

Wrong. All wrong. So wrong.

Simone would die.

Edith felt the snort-laugh start before she could stop it. To cover it, she coughed into her hand. Only a few people looked sideways at her.

Oh, wow. That was inappropriate. Sorry, Simone.

But Edith wasn't really sorry, because Simone would have laughed too. The thought sobered Edith. A rush of emotion pushed tears out of the corners of her eyes. Edith had missed her last Sunday phone call with her old neighbor. At ninety-three, Simone was more than sixty years Edith's senior, but Edith had never had a closer friend.

And I forgot to call. Wasn't even busy. Just binging Supernatural on Netflix. Curse you, Netflix!

Simone's peeling-paint white Victorian farmhouse with its wide yard and wooden rail fence lived more vibrantly in Edith's memory than her own childhood home. In the Daniels' yard there had been half-dead grass and some struggling lilac bushes. But in Simone's yard there had been flowers *everywhere*—in the ground, on vines, in planter boxes, old milk cans, clay pots, hanging baskets, and even an old claw-foot bathtub.

Simone's husband died the same year Edith was born. To Edith, Martin Cuthbert had been merely a smiling, round face in pictures on Simone's mantel. Simone had been fond of saying, *The day you toddled into my yard—reaching those pudgy baby hands out for the poppies—I smiled for the first time since I lost my Martin. I knew right then we were gonna be good friends.*

And now Edith sat at Simone's funeral scowling at the flowers. *Flowers brought us together, Simone. And now look at this!* Sunflowers and zinnias. *Too happy.* Carnations dyed colors never found in nature. *Too ugly.* Tasteless, cheap ribbons and stiff wire frames. Simone had told Edith several times that she wanted her to do the arrangements at her future funeral. *No tacky florist sprays, you hear me? I'll come back from the grave and gag on those inappropriate carnations and stiff, uninteresting greenery. I want tragic, drooping flowers. Enchanting, but sad. Things that have drama! Like chocolate cosmos with their dark petals and staghorn ferns, all airy and weepy. Snowberries and thistles. Love-lies-bleeding amaranthus, for obvious reasons. Can you picture it?* Simone had stopped to sigh contentedly. *And you, Edie—you're the only one who can do it right. Because, of course, I taught you how.* Simone had laughed heartily at her own joke.

Simone's daughters didn't feel the same about flowers. Edith had mentioned Simone's request on the phone with

Kate, the oldest of four daughters, the day after Simone was found dead in her bed. But Kate had quickly clipped her off with, "We'll just go with the normal stuff from Better Blooms in town. It'll be fine. Everyone else uses them. And I've got too many other things to worry about."

"But it's important to her," Edith had answered shyly. An awkward pause followed.

"I know, Edith," Kate said stiffly. "I know all about Mom and her flowers. But it's expensive to do fancy custom stuff. And we aren't exactly wealthy. Thank you for the offer, but this is a family affair."

Edith's face had flushed with shame. "I didn't mean to— I'm sorry. I'm happy to pay for—"

"No, thanks. I'll take care of it. See you Friday."

Now, Edith looked at a sagging sunflower in one of the largest sprays and felt a sob constrict her chest. Replacement floral designs filled her head. She knew exactly what she would have done. White cyclamen, delicate and mysterious. Dusty miller, silver and skeletal. Ranunculus, astilbe, stems of borage, and, of course, those crimson weeping amaranthus. All arranged in old tarnished silver teapots, glazed stoneware crocks, and vintage blue mason jars. And on the casket, a single white peony. Simone's favorite.

You deserve better, old friend.

Simone had been there when Edith planted her first flower seeds. She'd bandaged thorn cuts and bike crash road rashes. She'd been at Edith's ninth grade promotion and high school graduation. Simone had been there with open arms and hot chocolate the bitter morning Edith discovered her mother left. The old woman had been there in the hard, lonely years that followed when Edith became mother to her younger brother, Milo. Simone kept Edith going by distracting her with flowers and plants. Simone cheerfully waved good-bye

3

when Edith moved away four years ago to accompany Milo to Los Angeles for him to play football at UCLA. *You'll hate it,* she'd said, a whisper in Edith's ear as they'd hugged. *But I'm proud of how you're helping him. When he's done, please remember to do something for you.*

Edith folded her hands in her lap and gripped hard. Simone had been right: Edith hated L.A. The noise, the people, the smog—everything about it felt wrong. She missed Oregon's fresh, wet air and the abundant green. She missed the mystical beauty of the San Juan Islands. She missed being surrounded by flowers and living things. Everything and everyone in L.A. felt dead, fake. And the owner of the flower shop she worked for was one of the worst.

But Milo is thriving. He's living his dream. And that's all that matters.

Simone's voice spoke in her head. *Is it, Edie?*

Edith shook the thought away and took a long breath. She sat up taller in her seat and fixed her eyes on the casket.

I should have called on Sunday. I should have made you a thousand enchanting, dramatic, mournful flower arrangements for this terrible day.

The choir sang a melancholy hymn. "I'm sorry, Simone," Edith whispered under her breath.

Noah Winters leaned against the rear wall of the chapel, arms crossed, and a deep frown on his bearded face. Simone Cuthbert lay dead in her casket, surrounded by hideous, stiff floral arrangements. Noah's sharp gaze swept over the crowd. The four daughters sat rigidly in the front row with damp tissues wadded into their hands. Their grown children sat stoically behind, handing snacks to their toddlers to keep them quiet.

"None of this is right," he mumbled to himself. The Simone he knew would have wanted a party, a celebration. A room dripping with flowers, loud with laughter, and tables heavy with pies. But this proper, solemn affair—that was the work of her daughters, the snobbish children who did not understand their free-spirited mother. Not one bit.

He moved his gaze off the family. A head of radiant rose gold hair caught his attention. Sun spilled in through the arched windows to pour over the woman's long waves. "Stunning," he whispered. She reminded him of someone, but he couldn't place it. He sat with that nagging feeling, watching her for a few moments. She turned her head to look in the family's direction. Her skin was romantically pale, and her profile dignified, like the movie stars of old Hollywood. She wore a floral print top of cream, pastel pink, and soft green. Her eyes were pinched in thought. Or grief. Or . . . something complicated and interesting. Noah shifted to see her better. On her face he saw the depth of emotion of someone who loved Simone, someone who knew her well.

"Who are you?" he whispered.

The choir launched into song, the sudden noise jolting Noah from his contemplation. The woman's mouth moved with whispered words. *What did she say?* She tucked her hair behind her ear, dropping her eyes to her lap. Noah thought of moving closer to study her further, but the tug of home had become insistent. He shifted, ready to leave. The woman lifted her eyes and found his, an instant lock. A tremor moved through him.

Can she see me?

Noah immediately faded away.

"Edith Daniels, is that you?"

Edith turned toward the vibrant voice, searching the crowd gathered in the church gym for lunch. She spotted her high school art teacher slicing through the mass, a stout tugboat of determination. Instantly, Edith could smell the scent of oil paints and hand soap. "Hello, Mrs. Blair."

"Oh, my goodness. It *is* you! How are *you*? It's been years." Mrs. Blair, only about five feet tall and round with extra pounds, opened her arms wide. Edith, at five-eleven, hinged at the waist to accept her old teacher's hug. Mrs. Blair squeezed tightly and then pulled back. Her face had more wrinkles, the skin thin and dry looking, but her smile was still wide and warm. "You can call me Bessie. I'm not your teacher anymore."

"Of course." Edith smiled, knowing it would be much too weird to call the teacher by her first name. She was and always would be Mrs. Blair. "How are you?" Edith asked.

"Oh, good, good. Retired. Which is just another word for bored." She waved her hand between them, dismissing her comment. "But what about you? How's the big city? You running your own flower shop yet?"

A pulse of embarrassed regret moved through Edith, tightening her chest. "No, I work for a florist though. We do some of the big Hollywood weddings."

"How exciting! That must be so glamorous. Flowers and movie stars."

Edith smiled tightly. It wasn't at all glamorous. It was tedious and thankless. Her boss, Rhonna, had a unique way of sucking all the joy and creativity from flower arranging. But she paid well and every aspiring florist in L.A. wanted to work for her. Edith had tried to feel grateful, but it never fully formed. Edith answered, "It's interesting. And big budgets make for some really magnificent arrangements."

Mrs. Blair nodded. "I can imagine. So fun. And Milo? Did I hear right—is he going to the pros?"

Edith smiled genuinely, glad the conversation had moved away from her life. "He is! He was just drafted and moves out to Buffalo, New York, soon. He's worked so hard."

"I can't believe our little Milo, from our little Autumn Island, is going to be famous. Just so cool."

"It really is. It doesn't feel real yet, but I'm so happy for him."

Mrs. Blair patted Edith's hand. "He's so lucky to have you as a sister. You really stepped up after Phoebe left. Phoebe was so bright and beautiful and kind. Everyone loved her. It still surprises me that she—" Mrs. Blair's cheeks flushed as she pressed her lips closed. "Oh, sorry, sweetie."

Edith's pale skin heated with embarrassment. She shrugged. "It's okay. And I didn't really do that much."

Mrs. Blair raised her eyebrows. "Don't sell yourself short, sweetie. You did a million little things to help Milo get to where he is. You helped your dad too. I watched you. We all did."

Edith forced herself to smile. Her mother, Phoebe Daniels, had walked out of their home and lives with only a short note to her family, written on the back of a junk-mail envelope and tacked to the fridge with a strawberry-shaped magnet.

Edith and Milo—

I have to go. You'll be better off without me. I'm so sorry.

I love you,

Mom

The note and the raw change had left all of them blinking at the front door, wondering, questioning, and waiting for it not to be true. Waiting for their mom to come back. Edith's dad, David, had walked around the house as if he were lost in a vast, dark forest.

The note had still been on the fridge a week later. Edith had stood in the kitchen, leaning her hip into the sink, reading her acceptance letter to the horticulture program at Oregon State University. She wanted to feel happy; she'd worked hard to get that letter. She had plans, dreams of flowers and farms, and a life of growing things. But her mother was gone. Edith's eyes moved from her letter to that scrawled note. There was hurry and panic in the slant of her mom's letters.

Why? Why did she feel she had to run away like that?

And what do I do now?

Milo, eight years younger than Edith, had wandered into the kitchen, hungry for dinner. Her parents had struggled to get pregnant again after Edith and had eventually given up. Milo had been a welcome surprise a few years later. He opened a cupboard behind her and pulled out a can of SpaghettiOs. He dragged opened a drawer and found the can opener. Edith stared at the college letter. *Congratulations. You've been accepted . . .* Behind her, Milo struggled with the can opener. He'd been born a gifted athlete, amazingly coordinated and agile, but his fine motor skills had always lagged behind, as if all his energy had gone to developing bigger muscle movements. Edith heard him grunt in frustration.

David came into the kitchen. Milo asked, "Dad, can you open this?"

Edith looked up at her father. David Daniels blinked at his son, the circles under his eyes sickly dark in the pallor of the florescent lights. He opened the fridge, eyes moving over the note. "You gotta learn how to do it, buddy. Figure it out." With a fresh beer in hand, David went back to the couch in the family room.

Edith turned to look at her brother. Milo looked like their mother: dark brown hair, dark brown eyes, and olive-toned skin. Edith looked like her father's mother, all pale skin and strawberry blond hair. Most people would never have guessed that she and Milo were related, let alone brother and sister. Milo's face scrunched into a tight mash of frustration as he tried to latch the can opener into place. She set her letter on the counter. "I got it," she said. Milo sighed with relief and moved the can to her, setting it on top of her letter. She opened it easily and handed it to him. He smiled, his ten-year-old face fresh with relief. "You want some?" he asked, lifting to his toes to reach into a cupboard for two bowls. Edith looked back down at her letter, at a red splash of tomato sauce over her name.

I can't leave him. Mom left him.

Selfishly.

My mother is selfish. So I can't be.

I can't leave him too.

Who will help him?

Her heart thudded hard in her chest. She took a shaky breath and looked over at Milo. "Yeah, football boy, I'll take some. Thanks." Milo had smiled, his teeth adorably crooked. While he had put the soup in the microwave, Edith had gone to the fridge, taken down her mom's note, and tossed it and her acceptance letter into the garbage.

Edith brought herself out of the memory, blinking at the crowd around her. Mrs. Blair narrowed her eyes, noticing Edith's drift away. "You okay, Edith?" Her voice was low and sweet.

"Yeah, yeah. Sorry."

Mrs. Blair patted her arm again. "Funerals are hard."

She nodded, smiling as normally as she could.

"Is your father here?" The older woman lifted her chin to

look around the room. "Oh! There he is, coming this way." She lifted her hand to wave. "Hello, David."

Edith turned to look at her father. She hadn't seen him in the chapel. Had he come in late? "Hi, Dad." David Daniels stood six foot three, thin as a flagpole and shoulders hunched slightly forward. He had light coloring, like Edith, but his hair was dusty blond, and significantly thinned now. They shared the forget-me-not blue eyes.

"Hi, Edith."

Edith wished he didn't look so uncomfortable. And was that a stain on his striped tie? Mrs. Blair said, "Edith and I were just talking about Milo. You must be so proud."

"Yes. It's really something," David said evenly. "Second-round, pick thirty-two. He's doing really well." Edith knew he was proud of his son—David Daniels was a big football fan—but he had an odd way of showing it. Or, not showing it.

Mrs. Blair nodded vaguely; Edith was certain the older woman didn't know what the draft numbers meant. "That just means he did well in the drafting process. Like getting picked first for a team in gym class."

Mrs. Blair laughed lightly, while David frowned at the comparison. Edith pressed her teeth together, unsure why she was so annoyed by him. Mrs. Blair said, "I'm sure Milo *always* got picked first in gym class. So athletic! And it'll be so fun to watch him on TV, won't it?"

"Yes, it will." Edith glanced over at her father.

David added, "That team has struggled the last few seasons. Just hope he can help them get some wins."

Edith furrowed her brow. She expected a little more enthusiasm from him about Milo's draft. The man she remembered from her childhood had been quick to laugh, easy to please, and always ready to hand out praise. And though it'd been over a decade since Phoebe left, David's sullenness still surprised Edith.

Mrs. Blair looked between them. "Well, I'll let you two catch up. Edith, good to see you!" She hurried away, chugging away between the circles of chatting mourners.

An awkward moment of silence followed. Edith mentally rolled her eyes. *Why is it so hard to talk to my own father?* She fumbled for something to say. "How's work?"

"Fine," David nodded. He'd had the same job for all of Edith's life: a mechanic at the local auto shop. She'd never seen his hands without grease under the fingernails. "We're having some trouble getting Volkswagen parts in, but things are good. Same old. "You?" he asked.

"Fine," she repeated, wanting to sigh in frustration.

He put his hands in his pockets. "You still planning to go with him to New York?"

The question plucked a string of nerves. "Yeah, I'm planning on it. Already gave my notice to Rhonna." Milo had to be in New York in two weeks to start training. Honestly, the move felt forced, and a little weird. She'd spent the last twelve years helping Milo, being there for him in ways their parents never were. Did that change now? Should it change? She was pretty sure most professional football players didn't bring their adult sisters along. But what else was she supposed to do? She certainly wasn't staying in L.A. alone.

David frowned, fueling her anxiety about the move. "It's cold there," he said. "Not like California, or even here."

"Just in the winter." Edith let out a quiet sigh. "Will you come visit? Go to some games?" He'd only made it to two of Milo's college games over the last four years.

David shrugged. "Maybe. Shop is pretty busy. Might be hard to get away."

A flash of bitterness moved through her. *Still not*

interested, Dad? Still hiding out on the couch with some beer? You have no idea what Milo's life is like. The pressure, the hours of training, the watchful microscope of coaches and media. You have no idea what my life is like. Did you even notice the horrible flowers?

"Hey, Edith," David cleared his throat, "there's . . . uh . . . something I'd like to tell you."

Edith raised her eyebrows. "Okay."

"Edith!" Kate, Simone's daughter, sliced through the crowd in a rush. "Edith, there you are! Before I forget—there is a package for you at the house. I put it on the porch. Will you stop by and grab it before you go? Thanks." Kate didn't give Edith time to acknowledge; she went hurrying back to the kitchen.

"What do you think it is?" David asked.

Edith shrugged. "Don't know. I guess I'll go get it now. I've got to hit the next ferry to get back to Seattle for my flight. But what did you want to say?"

David shook his head. "Never mind. It's nothing."

Edith was pretty sure it wasn't nothing. David drove his hands into his pockets and looked away. "You sure?" she pushed gently.

"Yeah, yeah. Good to see you. Say hi to your brother."

"Okay, Dad. See ya."

David nodded once and left. Edith let out a long sigh.

Two

EDITH STOOD AT the edge of Simone's narrow pebbled driveway and drank in the chaotic perfection of the yard. There were so many plants it was hard to see them all at first glance. A hundred colors and shapes and textures. *Layers,* Simone had said, *a garden should have depth and layers so it can surprise you every time you look at it.* Edith lifted her face to the warm summer sun, closed her eyes, and pulled in a long inhale of fragrant air. It smelled like home.

The two-story, Victorian farmhouse stood a champion to the Queen Anne style. Complete with a charming turret room, gingerbread trim, mermaid scale siding under the eaves, and flourished gable decorations. Edith had never seen its equal. The white house sat proudly at the center of the floral pandemonium. Though it had seen better days, somehow the peeling paint and missing roof shingles only added to the charm. Everything was old and loved. Everything was perfect.

Except that Simone was dead.

A heaviness settled in Edith's chest as she made her way up the creaking steps to the wide wrap-around porch. Simone's wooden rocker sat achingly empty to the left of the front door. And beside it was a large wooden box. Edith gasped, her hand coming to her mouth. "No, no she didn't," she mumbled against her fingers. She sank slowly to her knees in front of the box, oblivious to the thick layer of dust now covering her gray maxi skirt. The box was as wide as the rocking chair and sat as high as Edith's chest. It was made from oak, nearly white with age, and had a hinged lid. Carved into the top lay the image of a spray of peonies. *Simone's favorite.* In a tiny font, the date had been stamped under the peonies: December 25, 1943. Martin had made this box for Simone as a gift for their first Christmas together.

Edith ran her fingers over the carvings, her pulse quickening. A folded note was taped to the top with her name written in a shaky scribble. She tugged the paper free, unfolded it. The same rickety writing greeted her—Simone's writing.

To my fabulous Edith—

Let's be honest: I'm stinkin' old and can't possibly last much longer. So, I'm getting things ready. Like early-spring in the garden, preparing for change and growth. And let's hope death is a type of growth, a moving on to something else and not just death. That'd be too boring. I believe there is more. I have faith in the Universe.

I give you my seeds. Don't be surprised; you know no one else is worthy of them. I know it'll be tough, but you'll find a way to use them. I think, maybe, you need some change and growth too. I think it's time we both move on. Don't be mad. I'm asking you to trust me one last time. Please trust this. I love you, Edie. Now grow something pretty and spread it around the world.

With love and hope, Simone

P.S. Don't listen to that cranky old miser, Noah Winters.

Edith blinked through a mist of tears. Her heart twisted with grief, familiar shame, and confusion. Simone's gift was one last push of encouragement. A final signal to move forward and start that farm Edith had talked Simone's ear off about for years. The precious seeds were the grand gesture Simone hoped Edith couldn't ignore.

"Oh, Simone, you know I can't," she whispered. "That dream died a long time ago." She thought of the tomato sauce stain on her college acceptance letter. Her eyes moved over Simone's note again. "And who is Noah Winters?" She was certain she didn't know anyone—cranky or otherwise—by that name. Yet, it did feel annoyingly familiar, like she *should* know and just couldn't remember. A noise to her right brought her head up.

Just a breeze shuffling some dried leaves into the corner of the porch railing.

With a shuddering sigh, Edith turned back to the box. Carefully, she flipped down the brass clasps and lifted the lid. The smell of dirt and dried lavender floated up to her face. Edith towed her fingertips over the bumpy edges of the tops of the seed packets, all carefully labeled and divided. "Simone's seeds," she whispered.

Memory flooded into her, bringing with it the feel of summer skin and the smell of roses on the morning breeze. Edith had been ten years old that record-hot summer. She'd wandered into Simone's kitchen and laid down flat on the cool tile. Seated at the kitchen table, Simone had laughed without looking away from her wooden box. "It's not *that* hot," she teased.

Edith scoffed. "I think my brain has melted." She pressed her palms to her damp temples. "Guess that means they can't send me back to school next week, right?"

Simone laughed, hands busy in the box. "Nice try."

"Whatcha doing?" Edith asked, slowly lifting an arm to feel her skin peel away from the tile like sticky tape.

"Making sure my seeds are in order."

"That whole thing has seeds in it?"

"Yep. Every year I keep the seeds from my favorite flowers and veggies. I put them all in here to plant next time. It's better than a treasure chest. Coins and jewels can't grow over and over. And they don't smell good or taste good."

Edith had smiled, her eyes watching the ceiling fan swoosh through the hot, humid air. Everything Simone said sounded like something from a story. "Can I have some seeds to plant?"

"Of course. It's too late to plant anything now, but in the spring, I'll give you a little space in the back garden and you can plant whatever you want. Only rule is you must take care of it. Not me, *you*. That means watering *every* day and pinching and dead-heading and feeding and weeding. Think you can do all that?"

"Sure, I can." She'd been helping Simone for years, watching and learning. She felt connected to plants and secretly thought she could *feel* what they needed. Like a small fairy-whisper meant just for her. *Please give me a little more water. Please clip off this dead flower so I can grow another. There's a pesky caterpillar hiding in my leaves, take him off, won't you?* Flowers were always polite and light-hearted.

Simone smiled as she slipped a seed packet into the box. Edith was certain Simone heard that little whisper too.

Now, kneeling on the dirty porch, Edith felt Simone's loss like a punch to the face. She shook her head at the seeds, tears floating across her vision. "Why would you give these to me? You know I don't have anywhere to plant them. That's just . . . *mean*, Simone." She turned to look at the trumpet honeysuckle vines growing up a trellis on the side of the porch. A tiny velvet blue hummingbird dove into the scarlet blooms and took several deep gulps of nectar. Edith had helped train the vines; the smell of honeysuckle had always lingered on her hands for a week after the work. Her gaze moved around the porch to the row of peonies in front of the spindled railing. All white and all blooming, their parchment-thin petals spreading open like round books. In the front beds, surrounded by vibrant green grass, were happy daises and elegant irises. The two magnolia trees showed off their pink and white blooms, only just starting to drop to the ground. She could hear the buzz of the bees as giddy as toddlers on a playground.

It was all so gorgeous that Edith found it hard to breathe for a moment.

What will happen to this place now?

Edith shuddered at the thought of it in Kate's unfeeling control. She imagined it shriveled and neglected by a new owner or, worse, torn down for something stark and modern. Simone's house had been one of the first built on Autumn Island. Simone had loved that about her house and knew all the history. She'd told Edith about it, but she was having a hard time remembering the details now. Edith was certain a man with no family had built it, and it'd been a big farm of some kind. When he died, the land had been chopped up into smaller pieces and sold off. Simone and Martin bought the original house with four acres and watched as others, like the Daniels' house, were built for new families.

Her gaze dropped back to the note. "Noah Winters . . ." *Isn't that the man who built the house?* Edith gasped. How could she forget? Noah Winters was somewhat famous on Autumn Island, or at least he had been once upon a time. A bachelor farmer who built a fairytale house, avoided social situations, and wrote best-selling mystery novels. Simone had all the paperbacks lined up on a shelf in her living room. Edith frowned at the words of the note.

But Noah Winters died decades ago.

Edith flipped the note over, looking for more information. "What did you mean, Simone?"

Edith turned back to the seed box. The first part of Simone's message was clear and familiar. Every Sunday she had asked Edith, "So when you gonna get out of that dead city and come grow things?" The question had become a familiar tease, but the truth behind it always pinched Edith's emotions. Her answer had become automatic as well. "Milo needs me. I've gotta be here for him."

Some things couldn't be changed. Edith couldn't change the fact that her mother had walked out and never contacted her family again. She couldn't drag her father out of his hole of self-pity. And she couldn't let Milo take the massive leap into his career without support. Edith folded Simone's note in half again. "I'm sorry, Simone," she whispered, her throat constricted with too many emotions.

Edith closed the box and carefully latched the locks. She pushed herself to standing and brushed away the dirt on her skirt. A powerful flash of possibility rocked through her mind. *I want this place.* It was so easy to picture herself living here, fixing up the house and planting rows of flowers in the fields. Selling those flowers and building a business. So easy. Edith put a hand to her throat and suppressed a groan. It was exactly what she could *not* do. "So mean, Simone," she whispered. "Why did you have to be so mean?"

A breeze rolled through the porch, sweet with honeysuckle. Edith thought of the upcoming move to New York with Milo. He'd be instantly busy with training and practices. He'd enter a whole new, exciting world, and what would she do? Find another soulless florist to work for? Live in another apartment with a few flowerpots on the balcony? Freeze to death in upstate New York winters?

Edith shuddered and took a deep breath. She turned her

back on the seed box. Her feet and heart sagged as she went back to her rental car. Turning the ignition, she repeated the familiar words, "Milo needs me. I won't leave him." The words didn't stop the tears as she drove away from Simone's house.

Noah watched Edith drive away with tears pouring down her face. He looked over at the seed box, confused as to why she'd left it. He remembered her now. The skinny little elf who used to run around Simone's yard. The bright-eyed child Simone took under her flower-growing wing. The lovely young woman whose mother left in the middle of the night with one duffle bag tossed into the back of the car. The young woman who became a selfless caregiver to her younger brother.

Noah had been there for it all, watching from afar.

He walked over to the rocker and glared down at the carved peonies on the box lid. Something about the box being left behind bothered him deeply. Perhaps it was just worry over what would happen to his house. Simone and Martin had been hard enough to get used to, even with how well they loved the land. He couldn't stand the idea of anyone new coming in and making changes. Although it would be nice if someone put up some fresh paint.

He touched the peeling clapboard, remembering the effort of nailing each one into place. Remembering the ache of building this house for a woman who would never live in it. For the woman who loved a turret room, gingerbread trim, and the snap of a screen door. He'd never have built those things for himself—a log cabin was as fancy as he'd ever desired—but he'd found himself alone and building a

Victorian farmhouse. Then living in it, writing in it, day after day, the empty rooms throbbing with bitterness.

Noah shook his head, withdrew his hand from the box. He looked back to the empty road beyond the house. He was certain Edith Daniels loved this place. So why would she, Simone's equal in growing things, leave a box of heirloom seeds sitting in the sun? He found he didn't hate the idea of Edith living in his house, tending his land. Although, that might be torture of a whole new kind. The image of her sitting in the church, head bowed and haloed with sunlight filled his mind.

"Stop it, you cranky old miser," he told himself. Why did emotions and yearnings have to follow him after death? He gave the seed box a last look and then with a huff Noah vanished from the porch.

Edith's phone rang as she merged onto L.A.'s parking-lot freeway. She pressed the button to accept the call, her phone in the hands-free device. "It's rush hour," she complained, depressing the brake to come to a full stop.

"Bad timing," Milo answered. "Sorry. How was the funeral?"

"As good as a funeral can be, I guess. The flowers were all wrong."

"Sorry about that. Kate should have let you do them. You see Dad?"

"For a minute. Same old Dad. He says hi but *without* any enthusiasm."

Milo sighed. "You doing okay?"

Edith pressed her teeth together. No, she wasn't okay. Simone was gone, and she gifted those glorious seeds. The seeds Edith had left behind. She' d almost turned around but was too proud, or too stubborn, or too stupid. She couldn't decide which. "I'm all right."

"Liar."

"Yeah, well . . . everyone is starstruck by *your* success."

Milo clicked his tongue. "As they should be," he teased.

"You train today?"

"Of course. Weights and some foot drills. Gotta keep those feet moving."

"Always. The secret to success as a free safety." Edith smiled, a tiny portion of her tension slipping away. "That, and ball intelligence. Have to play smart." She loved to throw football speak at him.

"We only use the smartest balls."

She laughed loudly and felt more of her tension snap off and fall away. A pause in the conversation. Her car moved forward one foot. Someone behind her honked. Edith rolled her eyes. "Why do L.A. drivers think honking will help *this?*" She gestured at the sea of cars. "These people all need some yoga."

Milo laughed. "They all do yoga, but only to look cool with their mats, coffee cups, and athleisure name brand clothes."

"Totally missing the point."

"That's L.A. for ya." He gave a short laugh. "I'll pick up dinner. Burgers and fries okay?"

"Sounds good. Thanks."

"Sure." Another pause. "Edith, you *sure* you're okay? Simone was . . ."

"Yeah, she was, but I'm okay. She was ninety-three; it's not a surprise."

"That doesn't mean it's not hard. She was your replacement mom and your only friend."

"Oh gee, thanks for pointing that out."

"That's not what I meant, although I'm not wrong."

"I have friends."

"No. You have work, co-workers, and me. And the random guys you date once and then forget about. Like Hal, the running back. He still asks about you, by the way."

"Not my fault they are forgettable. Who is Hal?"

Milo laughed. Then serious again, said, "She was really important to you."

Edith's stomach tightened. "Yes, she was."

"It's okay if you're not okay."

"The flowers were all wrong, Milo." Her voice broke with a new round of tears. "They were hideous, and Kate wouldn't let me make them right. She wouldn't let me do that for Simone. And I hate her for that. I hate her. And I *hate* that Simone is gone." Edith swiped at her wet cheeks and tried to slow her breathing. *I hate that she left me her seeds. I hate that I left them behind.*

"I'm so sorry, Edie."

Edith nodded, fighting to regain composure. Her head throbbed, a crying-headache roaring to life. After a long, quiet moment she said, "Better get some shakes with those burgers and fries."

"You bet, sis."

July
Orchard Park, New York

"WHAT'S THIS? WHAT are you doing, Edith?"

Edith looked up from her worktable at her new boss, Faye Lender, owner of Faye's Fine Flowers, in Orchard Park, New York. Faye always wore perfectly fitted skinny jeans, a crisp T-shirt, and a tailored blazer. Behind her stylish, sexy librarian glasses, she stared at Edith with raised eyebrows. Edith gripped a single craspedia stem in her hand and felt under-dressed in her not-so-fitted jeans, baseball T, and canvas apron. She meekly answered, "I'm adding some of these to the table arrangements." It came out more like a question than a statement, and she hated that.

Faye frowned at the small, bright yellow, sphere-shaped blooms. "I like craspedia too, Edith, but this is the *Randolph* Wedding. The Randolphs, who own like thirty bottling factories and have more money than you or I can even comprehend." She made a broad gesture with her hands as if these people owned the whole world. "We have to keep things *classy*. Upscale, you know?"

Edith looked at the arrangements. The whimsical craspedia was the perfect complement to the stems of lavender delphinium and white lysimachia. They added shape, texture, and contrast. She had also been considering sticking in some succulents or maybe cabbage. *How is that not classy? Is classy the same as boring?* She put down the yellow flower. "So, no craspedia?"

Faye shook her head, her perfectly waved chestnut hair swishing around her face. "Please, take it out. It's much too . . . *California.*" She said it like she was saying Ebola. "And in the future, please ask me before you add things to the arrangements. I love how creative you are, but we have to meet certain standards. Okay?"

"Sure. Sorry."

"No worries. You're new."

Edith scowled at Faye's back as she retreated to the front of the shop, leaving Edith alone with the flowers. "New? Hardly," she murmured under her breath. "I'm older than you and have been doing this since I was a baby." Dejected, she started carefully pulling the yellow blooms out of the glass vases. "I'm not even from California." Edith rolled her eyes. She laid the craspedia in a pile. "So sorry, my dears, not this time." She leaned down close to the flowers. "Faye of Faye's Fine Flowers obviously has no taste." She half-smiled to herself, but then quickly frowned. Faye actually had great taste. She was a talented florist and savvy businesswoman. *This is about me, not her. Why am I still working for someone else? Still taking orders and pulling out flowers I love from arrangements that could be better?*

Her phone buzzed in her apron pocket. Stepping back from the table, she pulled it out. An unknown number. Normally, she ignored numbers she didn't know, but an odd feeling had her answering the call. "This is Edith."

"Hello, Edith. It's Kate. Simone's daughter."

Edith flinched. An image of the seed box left forlornly by

24

the porch rocker flashed in her mind. "Kate, uh, hi. How are you?"

"Fine, thanks. I'm calling about Mother's will. It turns out there's a strange clause in it about her house."

"Okay . . ." Edith's hand tensed on the phone.

"She wants *you* to buy it, or at least to have first pick before anyone else buys it."

Edith blinked at the now boring arrangements on the table. "She wants me to buy her house?" Her first gut-reaction was a resounding *I'll take it!* But, how could she?

Gee, thanks, Simone. The seeds weren't torture enough.

"Yes," Kate went on. "And why did you leave the seed box behind? Those are yours. She also left you all her ratty Noah Winters paperbacks. That's the weirdest thing. Who wants those?"

I do. "I don't have anywhere to plant the seeds."

Kate hummed her understanding. "Well, buy the house and you will."

If only it were that easy. "I . . . uh—I can't. I just moved to New York with my brother. His football, you know. I . . ." A lump of regret and desire clogged her throat.

"We are about to put the house on the market. As is, of course. I cleaned out her things, but any repairs or updates would be up to you. I left the seed box and books in the house. You're *sure* you can't buy it?"

No, I'm not sure. I want it. But, how? "Yes, sadly, I'm sure. I can't buy it."

Kate sighed. "Okay. Well, the will says we must inform you of any offers. Think about it some more and let me know if you change your mind. Otherwise, I'll call you when we have some interest."

"That's not really necessary."

"Yes, it is. The will says it is. And if you don't buy the house, I'll ship you the seeds and books. Okay?"

"Okay."

"Good luck in New York, Edith."

"Thanks, Kate."

The call ended. Edith stood unmoving, her eyes gazing at the mess of clippings on the table, not really seeing any of it. Instead, she saw herself sitting on Simone's porch on a cool fall evening, hoodie and yoga pants, and a cup of tea. Earl Grey tea, of course, just like Simone used to drink. Simone drank it for the simple, ridiculously endearing reason that she had a crush on Captain Jean-Luc Picard, and Earl Grey was his tea of choice. Edith had watched every episode of *Star Trek: The Next Generation* with Simone at least three times. Every time the old woman wanted a cup of tea she would shuffle into the kitchen and announce, loudly, using Captain Picard's words, "Tea. Earl Grey. Hot." As if her kitchen could conjure a cup of tea out of thin air like the machines on the starship *Enterprise.* And Simone would laugh at herself, *every* time.

Edith started to smile, the vision of what could be growing brighter.

Sitting there on the porch with her tea, hands cupping the mug, she'd admire the mums in full bloom, crimson, and yellow, and pink, lining the path to the porch like dollops of ice cream. She'd swoon over the big leaf maples, sentinel trees on either side of the driveway entrance, showing off a candy-apple display of green, yellow, and orange. She'd breathe in the crisp, clean, smog-free air and watch the sun swim into a lavender and pink cashmere horizon. She'd feel peaceful and content.

Is that a real feeling?

The question made her flinch. "Stop being dramatic," she

mumbled to herself, reaching for the pile of outcast craspedia. She plopped them into a bucket of water.

My life is great. Everything is fine.

Faye burst back into the workroom. "I just remembered I have some white cornflowers. We can add those for a round element."

Edith flinched, nearly dropping the bucket.

"Oh, sorry. You okay?" Faye reached out to her.

Edith kept her face turned away, swallowed hard. "Yeah, yeah. I'm fine. Cornflower will look great. I'll get it."

"Also . . ."

Edith paused at the refrigerator room door. "Yes?" She looked back at Faye whose cheeks were flushed an attractive pink.

"A man is here for you." Her eyes pulled wide behind her glasses. "And he's the new free safety for the Bills." Surprised Faye knew anything about football, Edith turned all the way around to get a better read on her reaction. Faye was looking at Edith as if trying to decipher what a hunky football player would be doing here for a girl in a baseball T and ponytail. It was also clear that Faye was schoolgirl crushing. Not an uncommon reaction where Milo was concerned.

"Yeah, that's my *brother.*" Edith almost laughed at the look of relief on her boss' face. "He's picking me up. He's early though."

"Milo Daniels is *your* brother? He played at UCLA, broke like three school records. And now he plays right here, for the Bills. For *my* team." The declarations came out quickly, excitedly. Faye stopped to take a breath and adjust her glasses. She smiled self-consciously. "I *love* football. I know it's kind of weird, but I get it from my dad. That's our thing. We still go to most the Bills games together."

Edith nodded. "That's nice." Faye looked at her with an

expression that was both desperate and giddy. Edith held back a sigh. "Let me introduce you."

"Really?" Faye clasped her hands together. "Yes, please!"

Edith hurried to put the flowers away in the fridge, grabbed her purse, and then led the way back out front. The customer area was bursting with pre-made bouquets and bunches of flowers in tall metal buckets. The buckets were arranged on painted antique tables of different sizes and styles—no cold, industrial refrigerators in Faye's Fine Flowers. The walls were painted a soft cream to let the flowers pop and shine. Faye had hung chic sheer curtains on the front windows. And there were fancy mints at the checkout table. Edith found it perfectly lovely, and so did everyone who walked in.

"Hey, Milo," she said, spotting her brother fingering a stem of blue China aster. "You're early." Milo was the same height as Edith at five feet eleven inches. Edith was thin and athletic; Milo was solid and muscular. Those two hundred pounds of muscle and expert skills had earned him his spot on the Bills. His short, dark brown hair, dark brown eyes, and square jaw had earned him plenty of attention from the media and women. *If only they knew about his extreme goofiness and that he leaves socks and water cups all over the house.* Edith smiled to herself as she watched Faye's face bloom with adoration.

"Yeah, sorry," Milo answered. "We finished sooner than I expected." His eyes went to Faye hovering behind Edith. "I can wait, though, if Edith's not done."

Faye waved her hand. "Oh, no, it's fine. Totally fine."

Edith smiled. "Milo, this is Faye. She owns the shop."

Milo stepped closer and held out his hand. Faye's cheeks flushed two shades deeper. "Nice to meet you, Faye. Great shop."

She smiled, touched her glasses again. "Thanks. Nice to meet you too. I'm a *big* football fan."

"Really?" He stepped a little closer. Edith moved out of the way.

Here we go.

"Oh, yeah," Faye said, tucking her hair behind her ear. "Die-hard Bills fan. I also

saw you play for UCLA. My dad and I hit some NCAA finals games two years ago. I've never seen such tight deep pass coverage."

Edith looked between them. *Oh boy, she can football-speak. He's sold.* It'd be good for Milo to date a nice girl. He'd only had one serious girlfriend, sophomore year of college. Tami Miles, a barista from his and Edith's favorite coffee shop near campus. But Tami didn't really understand or even like football, and didn't appreciate how much of Milo's time and attention it required. So, the relationship had fizzled out after six months.

Milo's grin widened, his eyes warming. "Awesome. Thanks. Those were good games." He folded his arms, his biceps straining his plain black T-shirt. "I'll have to get you some tickets."

"Really? That'd be *amazing.*" Faye's eyes predictably went to Milo's biceps and chest.

"Of course." Milo stepped even closer and the two beamed at each other like teenagers.

Edith felt like she'd been sucked into the meet-cute of some romantic comedy: two gorgeous people, surrounded by flowers, their instant chemistry sizzling in the air. And she was the out-of-place, pathetic third wheel. Suddenly the whole thing soured for her.

Just another way Milo's life will progress while I stand

still. He has his dream job and now there's a dream girl. While I just said no to Simone's house.

Edith blinked quickly, surprised by the stinging bitterness. *What was that?* She needed to leave, now. "Okay, well . . ." she said breaking their moment. "Thanks, Faye. I'll see you tomorrow."

Milo turned to look at her like he'd forgotten she was there. She frowned back at him. He said, "Oh, yeah. Umm . . . nice to meet you, Faye. I'm sure I'll see you again." He held out his hand for a second time.

Faye took it, her smile coy. "I hope so. Come by anytime."

"Cool. Thanks."

Edith ground her teeth together. "Let's go," she whispered. Milo reluctantly followed her out the door.

"Hey, what's wrong with you?" he asked.

"Nothing."

Dropping into the passenger seat of Milo's blue F-150 Lariat, Edith added, "I need a mocha and the nearest bookshop."

"Uh oh. What happened?" Milo pulled out into the street.

"I put craspedia in the table arrangements for the Randolph wedding." She couldn't bring herself to mention the phone call from Kate or her abrupt bitterness, so she dumped all her emotions on the floral mishap instead.

Milo gasped dramatically and slapped a hand to his chest. "How dare you!" He paused, narrowing his eyes thoughtfully. "I have no idea what craspedia is . . . *but* it sounds evil. So again, I say, how dare you!"

Edith half smiled. "It's a perfectly lovely flower and it looked amazing."

"Of course, it did. I keep telling you to open your own

shop. You gotta stop working for these inferior florists. Although, I think Faye seemed really nice."

"Oh, yes, I'm sure you did. I think you got a little drool"— she lifted her hand toward him—"just there." She swatted at his face and he dodged her hand, laughing. Edith's smile grew.

"Shut up, flower girl."

"*You* shut up, football boy. You and Faye should just announce the wedding now. Get on with it. Why waste time?"

"Har, har. Real funny."

Edith adjusted in her seat. "Do you know where a bookstore is? One with coffee, of course. Or, near coffee. There must be some form of chocolate added to espresso."

"Use your phone."

Edith pulled out her phone and tried to do a search in her Google Maps. She grunted. "It's not working. It's still thinking about it. I think it's confused. Or brain dead." She shook the phone, as if that would help.

He scoffed. "You and technology. You should have been born in the thirties."

"I agree. Technology is evil, unlike craspedia, which is awesome." Edith tapped the screen, scowling. "Can you look it up, please? I'm blind and wandering in the wilderness."

"We can't have that. There are bears in the wilderness and since I prefer that you are not eaten by bears, yeah, hold on." Milo shook his head. They stopped at a red light and he pulled out his phone. Which, of course, worked perfectly the first try. "There's one two streets over from the house *with* a coffee shop next door. Your dream come true."

She frowned at the phrase. "Then go. Hurry up!" Edith pointed like a general calling her men to arms. Milo turned right. "Hey, how was practice?" she asked, relaxing into her seat. "Still feeling like the awkward, acne-covered new kid? Anyone shove you in a locker yet?"

"Like these shoulders could fit in a locker." He flexed his right arm and raised an eyebrow.

"Gross. Save it for Faye."

Milo returned his hand to the wheel. "Actually, today was a good day. I like these guys. It's gonna be a successful team."

Edith started to smile but a tinge of jealousy cut it off. She did not appreciate this new hostile awareness. This pesky voice in her head telling her things were not right with her life. Her brother's voice revealed just how happy he felt. All was right in his world. She couldn't say the same.

I blame you, Simone. Making me want things I can't have.

"What's wrong, Edie?" Milo leaned toward the steering wheel to try to catch her gaze.

She glanced at him with a false, nonchalant smile and then turned to the window. "Nothing. Just getting used to all the new stuff. It's exhausting."

"You sound weird. You sure there's not something else bothering you?"

"No, no. I'm good. I just want a mocha and a pile of garden books."

"Okay, I'll wait. Tell me the truth when you're ready. 'Cause I know you're lying," he said, unconvinced but experienced enough to know when to drop something.

"I'm not lying." Even she could hear how weak that sounded. *Just tell him.* The thought of saying it out loud made her hands sweat.

Ugh. Why? What is wrong with me?

"Maybe the coffee shop has a super-size option," Milo offered. "A McMocha. Or maybe a gallon bucket. Even better." With an exaggerated Brooklyn/valley girl mash-up accent he added, "'Cause you is *cranky,* girl!"

Edith slapped his shoulder. "Just drive, you jerk."

"My pleasure, you nerd."

Noah stood in his empty house listening to the crickets hum. Stuffy Kate had come, crew in tow, and dragged out all the pieces of Simone and Martin's life. Now there were only faded squares on the gray paisley wallpaper and empty echoes. Over the years he'd longed for his house back. He'd cursed Simone and Martin for invading his personal space and wished them gone. But now . . . the emptiness only reminded him of his pain. He hadn't realized how much their presence helped drown out the whine of his broken heart.

The broken heart that not even death could cure.

Scowling, Noah shuffled through the rooms. Kitchen, dining room, living room. Up the stairs to the three bedrooms. He stopped in the master bedroom. The room he built for Maggie, but she never set foot in. Dead a month after their wedding and a month before they planned to start work on their homestead.

Noah quickly left the room and went back down to the living room. He stood at one of the tall twin windows. Simone's seed box sat quietly at his feet, moonlight brushing the carved peonies. Beside it, another box with all his books. Edith's face filled his mind. He still didn't understand why she had left the seed box and now why Kate had left it with his ragged paperbacks as companions. Was Edith coming to get it? His gut tightened in anticipation. It shocked him to find he hoped she did.

"What for?" he asked the room. "So I can haunt her too?" He touched the box. "No, thanks." His eyes lifted to the full moon outside the window. A few stray clouds lay across its white belly. "Maggie, come get me. I'm done here. I've waited long enough."

He listened to the crickets and felt the emptiness of the house like a wound in his soul. Of course, Maggie wouldn't come. It'd been forty-six years since his death, sixty-six since hers. There'd been plenty of time to pull him from this suspended after-life. Why would anything change just because Simone was gone?

Getting left behind seemed to be his lot in life—and death. When his B-42 nose-dived into the Pacific Ocean in 1945, he'd been the only man left alive. Both his brothers had died in Germany. Maggie had died. Now Simone.

Where was his escape, his relief?

"Why am I still here?" he whispered to the moon.

November
Orchard Park, New York

EDITH SAT CURLED up on the couch under a heavy blanket with the TV set to the Hallmark Channel. The townhouse Milo had purchased was moderately sized, clean and cozy. Only a few minutes from the stadium, it was located in the quaint town center of Orchard Park. The family room was attached to a decent sized kitchen with creamy marble counters and dark walnut cabinets. She and Milo each had their own room and bathroom. The furniture was all new and modern. The TV was huge.

Milo enjoyed his NFL paychecks, and Edith couldn't help feeling like a guest.

She was on her second Christmas movie, too tired to keep her eyes open, but also too tired to get up and get ready for bed. She didn't want to sleep yet anyway. Milo would be home from his game soon. He'd want to tell her all the things he could have done better, and she would tell him that he was a brilliant free safety.

Normally, she attended every game, but Faye had begged Edith to help do the set up and take down for a swanky charity event. It'd been a night of wading through glamorous people and laying out dull, predictable arrangements. Her feet still hurt, and she kept redesigning the arrangements in her head. *It's November—there shouldn't be roses and lilies. There should be the last of the dahlias, coral-like celosia, grasses, and branches with changing leaves. Autumn things with darker colors of orange, yellow, red, brown. Not flashy, springy pink and violet.*

Her eyes had been closed for a few minutes when the apartment door opened. She jerked out of her half-sleep. Milo's gear bag hit the floor, followed by his tired feet moving down the hall.

"Hallmark *again?*" he asked with a groan. "Christmas movies *every* night since Halloween. I seriously think you have a problem."

She smiled, her eyes only half open. He smiled back. "How was it?" she asked.

"Good. A win. 21—7. Started snowing in the middle of the third quarter. You should be glad you weren't there." He dropped down on the couch by her feet. "Man, it's so cold here." Milo ran a hand back through his shower and snow-wet hair, leaving it spiked up off his head. "I missed the angle on the first hash. I'm still so nervous, and my hands were freezing, even with gloves. Takes me the whole first quarter to calm down and warm up."

"But you got all the other angles, right?"

"Well, yeah . . ."

"And prevented any long passes?"

"That's the job."

"And you moved your feet."

"Of course. Fast feet, always."

"And you don't smell half as bad as most of those guys."

Milo laughed, leaning his head back against the couch cushion. "Gee, thanks. That makes me feel much better." They fell quiet for a moment as the main characters in the movie kissed in a winter wonderland of peacefully falling snow. "If that were here, their lips would freeze together," he said, mock serious. "They'd have to call the fire department, like on *A Christmas Story.* That'd be seriously awkward." Milo stuck out his tongue and said, his voice mashed in a funny way, "Ha-whoa, 911? We hab a French kissing e-mer-gencee." Milo pulled his tongue back and leaned toward her. He imitated the sound of static and spoke into his fist like a walkie-talkie. "All units respond. Hot kiss turned ice cold."

Edith rolled her eyes and playfully kicked his thigh. "Nerd," she mumbled. Milo gave her a self-satisfied grin and settled back into the couch. They watched the end of the scene, the couple smiling and walking hand in hand through lighted Christmas trees.

"Who put up all those lights? I mean, good grief! That'd take forever," Milo said, shaking his head. "But was the kiss good? I mean, was all that work worth this scene? You're the expert here."

"It was a good kiss. Totally worth it." The long antici-pated kiss scenes always made her ache deep in her stomach. She'd been on lots of first dates, a few second and third dates, but never anything beyond that. Milo was currently trying to set her up with one of the kickers. *Bill or Randy or . . . something that sounds like a cowboy. What was his name?* As if she needed another football boy in her life. Although, it would be nice to get that winter wonderland, swoon worthy kiss. Orchard Park had plenty of charming snow.

Milo's head rolled in her direction. "We need to talk about something."

His tone forced her eyes open all the way. She shifted to see him better. "What's wrong?"

"I was going through that pile of mail this morning and I

opened a letter. I didn't realize it was addressed to you." He lifted his body and turned to face her, leaning forward. "Why didn't you tell me Simone's house was for sale?"

Edith's body went stiff, her gaze dropping away from her brother's sweetly concerned expression. She didn't know what to say. Milo went on, "You *love* that house. No—you're *obsessed* with it. Why are you here with me in this frozen football town when you could be *there* in flower fantasyland?"

"I can't do that," she answered weakly.

"Why the heck not? We have the money, and if you haven't noticed I'm not ten anymore."

She grimaced. "That's your money."

"Don't do that. It's *our* money."

"But you'll be here alone. What if you get injured or—"

Milo grabbed her ankle through the blanket. "Edith, you are the most amazing sister in the history of the world. I can't believe what you've done for me. I didn't really get it until the last couple years. I didn't realize *how much* you gave up for me. And for that, I love you so, so much. You did what Mom and Dad wouldn't or couldn't." He frowned, his eyes reflecting the hurt that would never really go away. "You got me to the NFL. But I think it's time for you to go."

"You don't want me here?"

He scoffed. "Of course, I do! I hate the idea of you living across the country. But I'm not sure it's right for *you* anymore. I'm not sure it ever really was, but I'm forever in your debt for the sacrifices you made."

Edith pushed away the sting of tears and started to shake her head.

"Uh uh. Nope. Don't do that. You're a freakin' saint, just admit it. And because of that I'm good now. Your services are no longer needed. At least not right here, right now, like this.

It's time you go after *your* dream. I've got mine, thanks to you. I'm going to help *you* now."

Edith pushed herself up, her pulse raced at the look on his face. She pushed her hair away from her eyes. "What did you do, Milo?"

"I bought the house."

Edith's mouth dropped open. "That was your signing bonus, you jerk!"

"Yeah, and I can't think of anything better to do with it, you idiot!"

"But what about—"

"Stop it, seriously." He smiled, a soft, knowing expression. "Edie, you gotta go now. I want you out of my apartment and on a plane ASAP. There are these things called cell phones with which we can still stay attached at the digital hip." He gave her shoulder a little shove. "You hate it here. You hated it in L.A. And someone with your talents should be living on a farm or building her own business. You can put *crap*-seia in every bouquet."

"Craspedia," she corrected, smiling.

"That too." He pointed to the black shape of the balcony door. "A few pots aren't enough. Working for hot Faye is not enough. And you know it."

"Did you just call Faye hot?"

"Just stating a fact." He grinned, a little embarrassed flush on his cheeks.

"It's going well then?"

"Very well." He winked.

Edith shook her head. Her stomach tightened. "Is that why you want me gone? Because of your relationship with Faye?"

"Man, I think too many chick flicks has ruined your brain." He rolled his eyes. "No! That's not it. I'm trying to *help*

39

you, not kick you out. I'll miss you like a football misses the end zone." She groaned at the metaphor; he pressed on. "Yes, it'll be nice to have Faye for company once you're gone, but I bought that house so *you* could be happy. You are not happy here, Edith."

She shook her head again, looked at her hands gripped in her lap. It wasn't enough—not the balcony pots, not the jobs working for other florists, not feeling alone all the time. Milo was right about everything. It shocked her how astute he'd become, how well he knew her though she rarely talked about what she wanted. "You bought Simone's house?"

"Yes, I did. Her daughter Kate wrote the letter. It said they finally had an interested buyer and she wanted to give you one more chance. Said it was her official proof of informing you before it was sold. Very serious. Why would she send you a notice like that?"

Edith sighed, embarrassed she hadn't told him earlier. "It's in Simone's will that I get first option to buy."

Milo scoffed and threw up his hands. "Why didn't you tell me?"

"You've been a bit busy."

"But this was a *big* deal. I may be busy, but I want to be there for you as much as you've been there for me. Can we do that, please?" He took her hand. "Please?"

"Yeah," she nodded shyly. "That'd be nice."

"Yeah, it would."

"She left me all her seeds too."

Milo's jaw dropped. "Once again—ya coulda told me!" He shook his head. "How many times did you turn down Kate?"

"Three."

"You're insane."

"But what am I going to do with that house? Just wander around and grow flowers? Live off your football money?"

"Oh, come on. I know you've got a plan in there somewhere." He lightly pushed a finger into her head. Edith bit her bottom lip. She *did* have an idea. A perfect, terrifying idea. The fantasy of it had been growing in her head since she opened that seed box. "Out with it!" Milo prompted.

"I want to be a farmer florist."

"Awesome! What's that?"

She laughed. "I would grow all the flowers I arrange and sell. I'd sell bouquets at farmer's markets and grocery stores, also do weddings, events. That stuff. It's kind of a thing now. I follow a bunch of them on Instagram."

Milo grinned. "Yes! Awesome. That's the *perfect* job for you. Do that, *for sure.* You'd be amazing at it."

A rush of fear pushed aside her enthusiasm. "I've never planted anything on that big of a scale. I'd need a green house and equipment. And how do I get clients? And the house is a wreck; it needs a lot of work. And then—"

Milo lifted a hand, palm out. "Those are all problems you can solve along the way. You have to start before you're ready because you'll never actually be ready. You just have to go for it. Just do it!"

"Are you trying to get a Nike endorsement?"

"Of course. Agent's working on it." Another sly grin. "But seriously, I never know exactly what an offense is going to throw at me. Even if I watch all the game tape and study every player, that moment after that ball is let loose is always a surprise. I work it out as it comes at me. You can do the same thing. But you can't keep sitting around here, depressed and watching Hallmark movies . . . as great as they are." He smiled and then grew serious. "You've changed since the funeral. Gone quiet. I feel like it's getting worse. The coffee shop is going to run out of mocha, and I'm going to have to buy more bookshelves." He shifted his eyes to the shelves surrounding the TV, mostly filled with garden and flower books. "You *have* to go. You *have* to try."

Tremendous excitement and weighty fear mixed in her gut. "But what if . . ." Her voice trailed off, unsure which potential problem to name next.

"'Clear eyes. Full heart. Can't lose!'" Milo chanted, lifting a fist in the air dramatically.

"Seriously? You're quoting Coach Taylor now?"

"*Friday Night Lights* wisdom is *always* appropriate."

Edith half scoffed, half laughed. She squeezed her hands together. "You bought me Simone's house?"

"The house and four acres—all yours, Edie. And I put some start-up money in your account. You're welcome. I expect you to spend it and then when it's gone ask me for more. As far as I'm concerned, I owe you half of everything I earn. Think of it as the"—he lifted his hands to do air quotes—"our mom left us and you're an awesome sister tax."

A rush of emotions pushed the hovering tears out of her eyes. She reached for

Milo and he pulled her into a hug. He whispered to her, "Thank you for staying all these years."

"Thank you for making me go now."

"My pleasure. Now, keep in mind, you'll have to be neighbors with Dad."

Edith winced. "Never mind, I'll stay here."

They both laughed, collapsing back into the couch. Edith laid her head on Milo's shoulder. "Watch the next one with me?" A new movie had started, swelling music setting the scene of a snow-covered mountain town.

"Only if I can make popcorn. And make hilarious, sarcastic, mocking commentary through the whole thing."

"Deal. Though you really should just admit you like these shows as much as I do."

Milo smirked, "Never! My manhood prevents such a confession."

Edith sighed. "You're so weird."

"Weird and proud, baby."

"I changed my mind."

"No, you didn't."

"Yep, totally did. Let's go home."

"*Your* home, Edith Daniels, is on Autumn Island, Oregon. In a dumpy old farmhouse. With a box full of seeds." Milo took Edith by the shoulders. Busy travelers raced past them to catch flights. Edith was sure she was going to vomit onto the scuffed tile floor. Some unsuspecting businessman would slip in it and get sent sprawling, along with his roller suitcase.

She took a shaky breath. "The house is not *that* dumpy."

"Pretty dumpy."

She let the smile come. "I hate the smell of planes."

"You'll survive." He shifted his hands to her upper arms. "You're *sure* you don't want me to come with you? I could miss a couple days of practice and be back in time for the Sunday game."

Edith shook her head. "Thanks, but no. I'm okay. And you shouldn't miss practice. You're still the new guy."

"Text me. Call me. Messenger pigeon me. Although, I'm pretty sure a pigeon would die trying to fly from the San Juan Islands to New York. I guess there's always the message in a bottle option. Oh, wait, no ocean. Let's see . . . are we telepathic?"

43

She punched his rock wall stomach. "I get it." She took another unsteady breath, still worried about revisiting her breakfast.

"First and foremost: Don't throw up. Okay?"

"I'm trying." She swallowed hard. "This is weird. We've never lived apart."

"Well, don't we sound pathetic?"

Another punch, harder. It only hurt her hand and hardly fazed Milo. She shook her fist. "What do you have in there?"

"Thor-like muscles. In fact, Thor is jealous of this." He rubbed his stomach and grinned. "You are going to grow flowers. Tons and tons of flowers. Just keep telling yourself that." He lifted his chin and yelled to the crowd, "Flowers for everyone!"

Edith flinched, embarrassed by the people who turned to look. "Okay, I'm ready to get away from you now."

Milo pulled her into a hug. "Just go grow flowers," he repeated tenderly. "If, somehow, it sucks and doesn't work out you can always come back. You are not banned from New York. Although knock first 'cause Faye might be over and—"

"I'll text you," she said to cut him off. She smiled into his shoulder, her throat tight with emotions. He held her for a long moment. Finally, she was able to pull back. Milo's eyes were as wet as hers.

"Good luck, flower girl."

"Watch those angles, football boy." Edith stepped back, trying to calm her raging instincts that had spent years keeping her by Milo's side. *He's not ten anymore. I'm not leaving him like Mom did. I'm moving on. It's okay. It's totally okay.* It didn't feel okay. She thought of that SpaghettiOs stain. *This is different.*

Milo nodded, eyes astutely narrowed. "You're *not* Mom, Edith."

A sob slipped from her throat. She nodded back, her breath trembling. "I know."

"Turn around and start walking. Or I'll start singing *really* loudly to draw lots of attention this way. I feel like some Michael Jackson." He pivoted on his toes, dropped his chin and put his hand on his head as if to grab a hat.

She held up a hand, her sobs turning to laughs. "Save us all." She took those first steps away from him.

"Love you," he said.

"Love you back."

Milo waved and Edith forced herself to turn her back on him. She walked fast, dragging her carry-on behind her. "What am I doing?" Her legs shook, her jaw hurt from clenching back more tears. A surprising memory popped into her head. She'd been thinking about her mother and Simone, but her father came to her instead. For ninth grade promotion, she'd been asked to give a speech. The only student-given speech on the program. The pressure and the fear had her puking for most of the two days before the event. Her mom had fussed with ginger tea and cold cloths smashed to her forehead. Little Milo had handed her his stuffed football for comfort. But it wasn't until her dad came into her room the night before promotion that she got what she needed.

He sat at the end of her bed, elbows propped on knees. He folded his grease-stained hands and looked at her through the sleepy darkness. "It's okay to be afraid, Edie," he said quietly, in that still-lake voice of his. "Everybody is afraid. Big things, little things. Most of us are scared a lot of the time. But, being brave means you do it anyway. And that feels really good. After, of course. Still sucks before." He smiled and she'd smiled back, the twist in her stomach releasing a little.

She remembered the rush of standing at the microphone, looking down at the audience to pick out her cheering section.

Mom, Dad, Milo, and Simone. Four smiling faces. *My people.* The speech had flowed out of her with solid confidence.

Now, her stomach twisted in a similar way, Edith passed her I.D. to the middle-aged, overweight security agent. "You all right, miss?" he asked.

She nodded. "Yep, just a hard good-bye. You know?"

He nodded somberly, marked a place on her boarding pass. "Yep, I do. Good luck."

"Thanks."

Do it anyway.

I'm going to do it anyway.

Edith headed for the plane.

November
Autumn Island, Oregon

NOAH DIDN'T HAVE to hide; he decided if and when the living saw him. So, when the gray sedan pulled up well past midnight, he stood on the porch and watched Edith Daniels stumble out onto the pebbled driveway.

You're here. Did you come for the seeds and books?
Or something more?

Her hair and clothes were rumpled, her eyes red with fatigue. She hauled out a suitcase and large duffle, and then stood facing the car, her back to the house.

Ever so slowly, she turned around to look up at the house. A brilliant smile broke over her face, erasing the weariness. As quickly as it came the smile disappeared. She shook her head, snatched the handle of the suitcase and dragged it through the meandering pebbled pathway and up the porch steps. She planted her feet squarely in front of the door.

Noah stood right next to her, close enough to touch. He watched her closely, noting the tension in her shoulders, the smudges of mascara under her eyes. *She's here, but it seems to have cost her greatly.* His years as a mystery novelist had taught him to watch people for the layers of clues that revealed their thoughts. Edith Daniels had all the signs of someone who was afraid. Not scared, but deep-down, war of emotions afraid. Afraid to move forward, afraid to want, to need. Afraid of herself.

You bought the house, didn't you? Gonna plant those seeds?

Good. So why the fear?

A tendril of empathy snaked its way into his heart. He had the urge to stroke her hair. The impulse instantly made him angry. *Stop it, you lonely fool.* He took a silent step back.

Edith dug a set of keys from her purse. With a sigh, she pulled back the screen door and unlocked the bolt. Noah followed her into the empty entryway. The second floor stairs were the only thing there to greet her. She turned to the right to go into the living room. She crossed to the far wall beside the simple brick fireplace and put her hand on a large square of wallpaper, the shadow left behind by Simone's bookshelf. She smiled softly. After a stroll around the room, she went to all the others, methodically touching something in each one. It reminded him of his own lap through the house after Kate had removed Simone's stuff.

He found himself smiling at Edith and was uncertain how he felt about it.

Finally, she came back to the seed box under the living room windows. Her eyes misted. She squatted down and patted the wood. "I'm here, Simone. I'm finally here. Thank you." Shifting her attention to the cardboard box, she lifted one of Noah's paperbacks into her elegant fingers. She frowned at it. Noah peered over her shoulder. It was *Death Under the Wide Sky,* his twelfth book, and one of the Detective Anson Lake mysteries. In this book, his broody, damaged main character traveled to Montana to catch a serial killer. One of his better ones, Noah thought.

Edith caressed the cover, her eyes still narrowed in

thought. He whispered, "I, too, wonder why Simone left them for you." But she could not hear him. She pressed up to standing, taking the book with her. She dragged the duffle bag into the living room. She yanked out a flannel lined sleeping bag, a thin pad, and set up for a night by the cold fireplace. She turned up the heat, put on a long T-shirt, and brushed her teeth. With an exhausted sigh, she sat on the makeshift bed, legs tucked to one side. His book was waiting on the hearth. Noah's eyes moved over her creamy legs.

Beautiful and sexy.

A forgotten feeling tugged at his stomach.

He blinked in shock.

Edith pulled her long, bronze hair to the side. Eyes closed, her fingers moving gracefully with habit, she braided it. Noah put a fist to his sternum to push at the hot flare of pain there.

Maggie did the same thing. Every night, sitting on the edge of the bed.

Oh, no. This will not do. This living, breathing woman can't be here. I can't do this. I want my house empty, left alone.

Edith Daniels cannot stay.

Edith shimmied into the flannel-lined sleeping bag and tucked her travel pillow under her head. She lifted her phone to text Milo.

Edith: I feel like a hobo, but I'm here. Text me when you wake up.

Milo: Hobos ride the rails. You feel like a squatter. Please use the correct form of homeless situations in the future.

Edith smiled. The quick reply surprised her. It was almost four in the morning in New York.

Edith: And why are you awake?

Milo: I'm not. Totally asleep. I have special talents.

Edith: Weirdo. You'll be tired at practice.

Milo: Thor doesn't get tired. So . . . you're there. How do you feel?

Edith looked out over the empty room. Misty moonlight drifted in the big twin windows. They looked taller and naked without Simone's red gingham curtains tied back at the edges. Edith had hoped it would instantly feel like home, but all the things that had made it *Simone's House* were gone, stripped away. The antique furniture, the mediocre watercolors gifted to Simone by her grandma. The smell of baked bread and the bouquets of flowers everywhere. Framed photos of her girls as kids going up the stairway wall. The brassy triumph of the *Star Trek* theme coming from the old box television set.

The room felt too big, too empty, and strangely foreign. She shivered.

Edith: I'm re-thinking all those episodes of *Supernatural.*

Milo: There are no monsters on Autumn Island. And Simone is too cool to come back and haunt you. I think you're good.

Edith: It just feels weird in here. The walls have eyes. And Simone did say she'd rise from the grave if there were bad flowers at her funeral. So . . .

Milo: First night jitters. It's going to be awesome. And it won't feel so *House on Haunted Hill* once you have furniture and stuff.

Edith: I know. Still wish I had an EMF reader and a shotgun.

Milo: I'll talk to Dean and Sam. They have spares.

Edith: You know, most of those episodes start with pretty, young people, minding their own business, and then—WHAM—gruesome end.

Milo: There's always a salt circle.

Edith: I don't have any salt.

Milo: Well, it was nice knowing you.

Edith: Haha.

Milo: Everything is fine. I promise. Nothing bad could ever happen to you in Simone's house.

Edith: Yeah. I know.

Milo: Deep breaths and happy thoughts. Like how hot Dean Winchester is.

Edith laughed out loud.

Edith: Right. All better now. Go back to sleep.

Milo: You too. Night.

Edith plugged her phone into the charger, which was stretched across the room from the nearest outlet, and picked up the Noah Winters book. *Why the books, Simone? The seeds I get, but these? Is it just for light reading while I'm alone and bored?* She stared at the cover's enchanting grass field with thunderclouds in the distance. *Or is there something else?* She thought of the postscript in Simone's letter.

Don't listen to that cranky old miser, Noah Winters.

"So, should I *not* read them?" Edith scoffed. "Crazy old woman."

Edith ran her fingertip over Noah's name on the cover embossed in big silver letters. She flipped it over to look at his author photo. "Well, aren't you the broody cowboy type." Noah Winters stood in front of a wheat field—probably the field behind this house—looking away from the camera so he was captured in profile. His thick hair and trimmed beard were ashy brown, streaked with silver. He didn't smile, instead his heavy brow furrowed seriously, maybe even a little mysteriously, and his angled jaw was set. He wore a faded blue flannel over a gray Henley, the muscles in his shoulders and arms obvious even through the layers of fabric.

Lifting the book closer to her face, Edith tried to get a better look at his eyes, but the dim light and aged cover didn't help. "Are the stories true? Did you really live here all alone? A sad, handsome man in a beautiful house by himself. Why?"

The box of Winters' books tipped violently onto its side, sending the paperbacks sliding across the floor toward Edith. She jerked back, scrambling out of her bag and into a crouched position on the flagstone hearth. Her sharp scream echoed in the empty room. Frozen, she locked her gaze on the box.

Her heart pounded. The shock raced in her blood. The box had not crumpled or tipped on its own. No, that had been a violent fall, as if it'd crashed from a shelf. But the box had been sitting flat on the ground. Her eyes flashed to the windows. *No, closed tight.* The front door. *Locked.* Her ears strained. Her senses watchful.

A quiet house yawned around her.

Edith's heart rate would not drop, and her body grew stiff, perched and clenched for flight or fight. She waited for something else to happen. Something that might explain the scattered books in front of her.

The heater groaned into action, the vents ticking.

Edith forced herself to crawl toward the books, pick them up one by one, and return them to the box. She pushed the restored upright box against the wall under the windows. *Maybe the floor is uneven here.* She swallowed. Her throat was dry. She spread her hands out along the floor, checking for imperfections.

No floor is that *uneven. So . . . how?*

She stood, walking on unsteady legs around the room. Checking, listening. Fear churning in her gut.

"Just minding my own business when . . ."

Stop it. It's nothing. Too many ghost stories and Halloween movies.

So then why do I feel like there's someone in the room?
Because you're crazy.

Edith thought of calling Milo, but what could he do? A box had tipped over. That wasn't life threatening. It was just . . . unnerving and bizarre and impossible. Just like the things that happen to all those people in *Supernatural.* The lead up to the scary parts. The warning no one ever listened to.

Edith shuddered. "This is not a TV show."

She surveyed the box again.

Maybe I moved it without realizing it when I pulled out Death Under the Wide Sky. *Yeah, that's gotta be it. Somehow, I tipped it and the books shifted just right until it fell over.*

Several minutes later.

And with enough force to push the books across the floor.

Edith frowned. She grabbed her phone, turned on the flashlight, and walked from room to room. Inspecting every dark corner and closed closet. Every few minutes she felt the burn of eyes on her back and had to turn around. Every time she found only dark, empty space.

I'm imagining this. I'm alone and safe. But I swear . . .

As she came back down the stairs, she whispered, "This is a sign. A bad sign. This is a mistake. I should have stayed in New York." *And how pathetic am I that I can't stay one night in this house alone?* A flush of anger replaced her fear.

With determined steps, she went toward the living room, but all her fight drained away when she saw both windows wide open. She froze, gripping her phone so tightly her knuckles ached. Cold air filled the room, swirling around the space, as if excited to have access to the warm house. The pages of *Death Under the Wide Sky* rustled.

Edith's heart punched her ribs, her breath a shallow tug of war.

She wanted to move but couldn't.

She wanted to scream but had no voice.

The back of her neck prickled painfully.

"Simone," she choked out, "is that you?"

The windows started to close, so slowly and exactly in unison. A garbled scream escaped her throat. Edith turned and ran back up the stairs. She bolted into the farthest bedroom, and slammed the door, leaning back against it. Gray spots clouded her vision; her lungs burned. Frightened tears puddled in her eyes.

Nothing bad can happen to me in Simone's house.

Nothing bad.

Nothing bad.

She repeated it until her breathing calmed slightly. She looked out at the trembling light of her phone, still in flashlight mode. It upset her to find that her hands shook badly. "You have to go back down there," she told herself. "Get up and walk."

Using the door as support, she managed to get to her feet. Her legs shook as much as her hands. "Go down the stairs." She took one stair at a time, her phone held out like a sword. At the base of the stairs, she closed her eyes and gathered what pathetic strength she had.

The windows were closed.

Edith blinked quickly. She stepped farther into the room and scanned the space. Nothing. All normal.

Did I imagine it?

"No way. Not possible." The cold room was undeniable proof.

She stood listening over her ragged breath for a long time. So long that her feet started to ache. She waited for a clue or for something else to happen. But the heater ticked, the room warmed, and the house remained silent. She turned, checked the locks on the windows and then the front door. She checked the back door and then every window in the house.

Finally, she could think of nothing else to do but take refuge in her sleeping bag. She cocooned herself inside and opened Winters' book. "I can do this," she mumbled. "Stop freaking out. Read, calm down, go to sleep." She focused on the words on the page.

Just read.

Fifty pages later, she reluctantly closed the book. The descriptions of the beautiful land in Montana and the emotional way the opening murder scene played out had quickly eased her fear. She still flinched at every little noise, but there was some comfort in the words. She liked this Anson Lake, even though he was dark and damaged. But she couldn't keep her eyes open anymore; being scared was exhausting. Rolling onto her side, Edith tried to relax.

I'll never sleep.

Her eyes went to the windows, her body tensed. She tried to take long, slow breaths, like she'd learned in yoga. She ached with fatigue.

Everything is fine. I'm safe. Go to sleep. Just get a little sleep.

Soon her body gave in.

But her dreams were not kind. For the rest of the night, she dreamed that Noah Winters knelt beside her, whispering in her ear. "Go home, Edith Daniels. I don't want you here. Go home!"

As dawn woke the eastern sky, Noah moved away from

Edith. He took his books and carefully stacked them brick-layer style in a straight line in front of her sleeping face. Then he took the seed packets—*Sorry, Simone*—and scattered them all over the living room.

He stood in the entryway looking back at his devious mess. The initial grim satisfaction soured to a harsh self-loathing.

What is wrong with me?

Terrorizing this beautiful woman—it's cruel. I should let her stay. Leave her in peace.

His pride and years of solitude spoke louder.

Oh, no. She's gotta go. She makes me feel too much. I'm too tired of being dead to remember how nice it was to live.

"Go away, Edith Daniels," he hissed once more. Then he walked out the door to seek solace in the winter fields, and left Edith to wake to a disaster.

Six

EDITH'S BODY JERKED at the sound of knocking. Her brain took an extra few seconds to catch up and realize what the sound meant. The knock at the front door came again. Edith groaned and pulled her eyes open, blinking against all the sunlight. She blinked again, registering shapes close to her face.

She screamed, like all those girls in *Supernatural.*

Kicking out of the sleeping bag, she kept screaming as the rest of the room came into focus. *What the heck??* It was the only sentiment her brain could manage as she surveyed the deliberately stacked books and dispersed seed packets.

A woman came bursting in the front door.

Edith screamed louder and retreated into a corner; body coiled like a snake ready to strike. Instinctively, she yelled out, "Don't step on the seeds!"

"Edith, it's okay!" The woman held up both hands, one gripping a tall paper coffee cup. "I'm Cori, from next door." Her eyes did a quick sweep of the room. Her arms dropped to her sides and she rolled her eyes. "Oh, my gosh! Really, Noah? Not cool. Not cool *at all!* Are you here, you big jerk?" Cori cocked her head, waiting.

Edith's eyes pulled wide, her pulse racing. And her mind continued to repeat, *What the heck? What is happening?*

"Coward," Cori spit at the ceiling before bringing her attention back to Edith huddled in the corner. Cori looked like a bundle of blended wool roving. She wore a bright pink knitted cap on her head, pulled down over coils of blonde hair. A neon green knitted scarf circled her neck. Her bomber jacket looked vintage, the leather beautifully creased and the collar and lapels lined with cream shearling. Beneath it was a Led Zeppelin T-shirt and faded jeans. Edith squinted at the cheap, sunshine yellow flip-flops on Cori's tiny feet.

This is still a dream. Has to be.

Edith pulled in a breath. "I'm sorry. *Who* are you and who are you talking to?"

Cori stepped closer, carefully tip-toeing through the seeds. She held out the coffee. "This will help."

Edith eyed the cup and then the strange woman offering it. Edith realized Cori was much older than she looked from far away. There were deep creases around her golden brown eyes, thick parentheses framing her mouth, and a little gray in the blonde curls. "For real," Cori urged, "take a few sips, wake up your brain. It's good. In fact, it's the best."

Edith smelled the earthy sent of coffee and automatically reached for the cup. Frowning, she took a sip. "It's a mocha."

"I heard that's your drink."

She took another couple sips. "And it's seriously good!"

Cori beamed. "Told ya. I own the coffee shop in town."

"Wait, Autumn Island has a *real* coffee shop now? Not just Babe's Diner?"

"That's right. I opened up about two years ago and proudly offer brilliant beverages to the good people of Autumn Island." She knelt eye level with Edith. "And by the way, that crap at Babe's doesn't even count as coffee."

Edith laughed and then remembered the room. She

gripped the coffee in both hands, anchoring herself to its warmth. "You said you live next door?"

"Yeah. Well, mostly."

"But my dad lives next door."

"Right. I'm David's Cori."

Edith narrowed her eyes, shook her head. "I'm sorry. I don't—"

"Oh, you've got to be kidding me! He said he told you guys. He didn't tell you?"

"Didn't tell me—"

"Your father and I have been dating *for a year.*" Cori huffed. "That jerk. He promised."

Edith was now certain she'd slipped into some alternate universe during the night. She put a hand to her throbbing temple. "I think I might pass out."

Cori laughed heartily. "It's not that big of a shock." The humor left her face when she looked at Edith. "Is it?"

Edith scoffed. "I just . . . don't even know what to say right now. My house is a mysterious mess, and my hermit father has a vibrant, coffee making girlfriend."

"Oh, well, this mess isn't a mystery. It's Noah." Cori sat down cross-legged and unwound her scarf.

"Yeah, you've said that, but I don't know who that is."

Cori hitch-hiked her thumb toward the wall of books. "Yeah, you know, Noah Winters. He haunts this place."

Edith's mouth dropped open.

Cori frowned. "Simone didn't tell you? I thought for sure—" Her eyebrows shot up. "She didn't tell you! No way! Apparently, I assume too much about people communicating important details." She laughed, shook her head. "The screaming makes more sense now."

Edith brought her cup to her lips and took a long swig; she didn't know what else to do. This woman was obviously crazy. A ghost? That wasn't a thing, was it? For real? But the windows opening and closing themselves and that feeling on her neck as she searched the house. The mess in the room now.

A ghost, in Simone's house? How?

Why hadn't Simone ever said anything? Edith had spent hours and hours in this house and never seen or felt anything out of the ordinary. But the seed box note: *Don't listen to Noah Winters.*

"I see your head is spinning," Cori said softly. "Let me explain. Just keep an open mind. Okay?"

Edith nodded; her head felt heavy and foggy. She wished she were back in New York in her nice townhouse room with a bed and nightstands and flower books. Her un-hunted room, at home with Milo.

"Noah Daniels built this house for his dead wife. She fell off a horse a month after they were married and broke her neck. Died instantly, poor thing. Noah built her dream home anyway, just as they'd planned." Cori gestured around the room. "He was staunchly anti-social, like a serious recluse. He stayed holed up here, working his farm and writing his books. I don't think he ever left the island. Which was a true tragedy for the women of his time. 'Cause, I mean"—she reached back to grab a book and held up Noah's author photo—"look at this man! So hot! All broody farmer. It works, am I right?"

Edith smiled over her cup. "You're right but really . . . a *ghost*?"

"I know. But yes, really. I've seen him myself, walking out in the fields. And Simone talked about him. Just once, over a cup of tea about six months ago. I mentioned the man I kept seeing in the fields and she opened up."

"Did he do this kind of stuff to her?" Edith nodded to the room.

"A little, at first. But Simone always just laughed at him and told him to go outside to brood. I guess they came to some kind of understanding. Mostly, he left her alone."

"Why didn't she ever say anything? That's so weird." Edith tried not to feel hurt, but it didn't take. "Did she want this to happen to me?"

Cori pursed her lips. "I doubt it. Her memory wasn't great in the end. Maybe she thought she had told you." A shrug.

"But I grew up here, spent most of my childhood in this house. Why didn't I ever see him?"

"Simone said he chooses who sees him and when, and that she only actually saw him a handful of times. I've seen him maybe three times." Cori laughed at Edith's confused expression. "Noah isn't the first ghost I've seen, let's just say that."

Edith frowned. "Well, I didn't really plan for this. The house with four acres is a lot but a haunted house . . ." *Did I really just say that?*

Cori smiled. "Talk to him. Be firm. I'm sure he'll settle down once he understands you're not leaving. I don't think he's a big fan of change."

Edith bit her bottom lip. *Maybe I am leaving.*

Cori smiled knowingly. "Don't run. You got this."

The idea of running jerked her to attention. *I am not my mother. I'm not running away because it's hard. I'm staying. Get used to it Noah Winters.* "How could I leave when there is mocha like this?" She saluted Cori with her cup.

"Atta girl! And you come get a cup anytime. On me." Cori stood up, grunting a little when her knees cracked. "I'm right next to the bookshop, on Main."

"That's the best place for a coffee shop."

"I know." Cori grinned. "I like you, Edith Daniels."

"Wait—what about you and my dad?"

"I think you've got enough rattling around your brain for one morning. Come to dinner tonight and David can tell you about it like he was supposed to." She rolled her eyes as she wound her scarf back into place.

Edith resisted the urge to wrinkle her nose at the idea of eating dinner in her childhood home with her stoic dad and his quirky girlfriend. But she couldn't resist knowing more. "Sure. Thanks."

Cori teetered back through the seeds. "I've gotta get back to the shop, but I can help you clean up first."

"No," Edith stood, waving her offer away. "The seeds have to be organized a very specific way. It'll take a while. I got it. But thanks."

"Sure thing. See you tonight. And remember: Be bold, be strong. Noah Winters only respects strength." Cori gave her a double thumbs up, as if facing the ghost were a sporting event to win.

"Uh, right. Okay." *What does that even mean—he only respects strength?* "Thanks for the coffee."

"You bet. See you tonight." Cori waved, zipped up her coat, and breezed out the door. Edith watched her close it. *Didn't I lock that last night? Another part of Noah's tantrum?* She shook her head.

Facing the mess in the living room, Edith felt a chill skitter up her neck. She remembered her dreams of Noah whispering in her ear to leave. She shivered, her stomach clenching. "It wasn't a dream." She hugged her arms close and looked behind her. How could she stay here? She sprinted across the room and scooped up her phone. Her thumb hovered over Milo's number.

What do I say? He'll think I'm crazy.

She opened her camera and took a few pictures of the

room. "Yes. Evidence." She decided not to call Milo yet. She wanted this to sit in her brain for a while; she needed to explain it to herself before she could explain it to him. She dropped her phone onto the sleeping bag and went to her purse. Setting the empty coffee cup aside, she pulled out a spiral bound notebook. On the first page was a to-do list for her new life.

Stick to the list. Get things done.

First on the list was to buy some furniture for the house. There was an antiques warehouse a few miles outside of town. She'd start there. And, bonus, it would get her out of the house. She surveyed the mess once again. A sense of urgency to leave made her decide to clean it up later.

Later, when I can handle the source of this scene.

Edith dressed in dark wash skinny jeans, an ivory sweater, and grabbed her ruby-red pea coat and white scarf. She threw a protein bar and apple left over from her traveling food into her purse for breakfast and bolted outside to her rental car. A flood of relief washed over her as the cold November air hit her face. At the end of the path, she turned to take in the sun-bathed yard. Her breath caught in her chest.

It's so beautiful.

The sight resonated with her soul, warming her chest. Winter in the garden was all about texture. The magnolia trees' dark branches in crooked line patterns against the washed-out blue sky. The outer shells of the mums, the colors fading. The bare vines; exposed and proud. Leaves on the ground, swept into mounds and drifts at the whim of the wind. Simone's pots with dead flowers bowing their heads to the cold.

Edith took a quick detour and walked down the side of the house, eager to see the backyard and fields. The rear lawn had been cut short before it went dormant and looked like an expensive roll of wheat colored carpet. The big oak had lost all its leaves; the weeping willow kept its yellowed leaves. The old clawfoot tub planter held the remains of a mound of petunias. The birdhouses—there were about ten in a rainbow of colors— hanging from the oak branches swung gently in the breeze.

Edith smiled big, continuing her easy stroll. The huge garden plot sat clean and groomed behind the boundary of the grass. The soil dark, gorgeous. Edith thought of tomatoes and basil, pumpkins and peas. Her hands tingled with the longing to plant.

Beyond the garden was a weathered rail fence that divided the yard from the barnyard. The small barn was built in monitor style with a tall section in the middle and shorter wings to each side. The wide double doors were shut tight. It had been painted white to match the house with black trim and had also seen better days. Across the dirt barnyard was the old chicken coop, a miniature version of the barn.

Behind the barn were the fields. The three acres there had been long dormant. Simone had allowed the fields to go wild for the last fifteen years of her life. The tall grasses had dried in the sun and cold, now rustling like paper.

This was where Edith planned to plant her flowers. Neat, purposeful rows of snapdragons, dahlias, peonies, zinnias. Roses, coneflowers, and cosmos. Decorative grasses, weeping amaranthus, and strange celosia. Lilacs, snowball bushes, snowberries. Whatever she wanted. That was what thrilled her the most: the possibilities. But she wasn't used to getting what she wanted. Staring at this empty, forgotten field brought the enormity of the task pressing down on her shoulders. The hundreds of decisions she faced felt like a swarm of angry hornets around her head. How could it ever go from this barren field to thriving, productive, money-making flowers?

Edith leaned her forearms on the fence and let out a long, despondent sigh. "Just grow flowers. Just grow flowers." She repeated it over and over, hoping the mantra would dispel the irritating fear. But fear was loud and pesky. With a frustrated grunt, she pushed away from the fence, sad that her pleasant walk had been spoiled by anxiety.

Movement in the distance made her freeze. A man in a stone blue flannel shirt walked the far end of the property. Instinct had her dropping to a low crouch behind a fence post five times too small to actually hide her. Pride had her rolling her eyes at herself. *Coward.* She watched him for a moment. His hands plunged deep in his pockets, shoulders and head curved toward the ground. Edith felt a pang of sadness. If what Cori had told her was true, then this man had suffered for decades.

Is it him? The ghost of Noah Winters treading his land decades after his death?

Is it you?

His head lifted and he turned in her direction.

A thrill moved through her stomach. She wasn't sure if it was terror or anticipation. Cori's words came back: *He only respects strength.* Edith thought of standing up and yelling out to him. Screaming at him to leave her alone. But her courage ran away like a spooked cat. She decided to follow it. Once he turned away again, she bolted back through the yard to her car. Fumbling with the key fob, she unlocked the door and dropped inside. She reversed down the drive, sending pebbles flying behind her.

Noah kept his head turned away, but his periphery saw

Edith dart away. He felt compelled to run after her but didn't. *What, so you can whisper more poison in her ear and act like a fool?* He grimaced down at his dusty boots. What he wouldn't give for a beer on the porch and to lie down next to Maggie.

He didn't miss food or sleep so much, but those simple habits of comfort, he craved them fiercely. Even more so since last night when Edith Daniels stepped into his house with her shiny bronze hair and long, sexy legs.

Noah came to the oldest tree on the property, one of the original oaks; its trunk wide and canopy an impressive umbrella. He sat down, back against the base of the tree, feet planted and forearms resting on his knees. Leaning his head back, he looked up into the bare branches, a web of wood. Toby sat high up in the tree, as usual, swinging his legs and staring back down with wide blue eyes.

"Hey, Toby." Noah mumbled, out of habit more than a desire to talk.

"Hello, Mr. Winters." One hundred years ago, Toby had fallen from these branches and died. His ghost had refused to leave the oak. "Did you hear that screaming a little while ago?" the boy asked.

Noah stared at the swaying bottoms of Toby's black boots. "Yeah, I heard it."

"Who was it? I didn't recognize the voice."

"Someone new."

"In your house?"

"Yeah."

"Uh oh." Toby looked down through his knees, his mop of blonde hair falling over his eyes. His brown suit, oddly formal and obviously from another time, looked clean and neat. "You should be nice," Toby added.

Noah grunted, looked away. "It's *my* house."

"I share my tree with the birds."

"Well, you're nicer than me."

"You could be nice, if you tried."

Noah frowned up at the ghost-child. "Can't teach an old dog new tricks, Toby."

"You're a lot smarter than a dog, Mr. Winters." Toby looked at Noah like he should know better. And he did know better. Although Toby's spirit never wandered too far from the tree, the boy had somehow grown wise.

Noah furrowed his brow, looked at his hands.

"What is the new woman like? Old like Mrs. Cuthbert?"

Noah half smiled. "No, she's young. Late twenties, thirty, maybe. It's Edith Daniels, who grew up next door to Simone."

"The girl with white skin and red hair? I remember seeing her. Is she nice?"

Noah sighed, tired of the questions. "I think so."

"Then you shouldn't make her scream."

"I know, Toby!" Noah bit down on his anger. He took a breath. "Can we just . . . not talk about it, please?"

"Okay," Toby answered lightly.

Noah felt the boy's eyes still on him, but he didn't look up. A Maggie memory filled his mind. She'd always been after him to be more open to others, friendlier. Even before her death, all his life, in fact, he'd disliked being around a lot of people. Maggie was the only person whose company he preferred to being alone.

One afternoon, a week before their wedding, she found him in the barn with an ewe ready to give birth. He was bent over the sheep, pressing into her swollen womb when Maggie strolled in, vibrant in a yellow sundress, her thick, blonde hair loose around her face. She rested her forearms over the rail of the stall and grinned sunshine at him. "Hey, cowboy."

"Hey," he'd grunted, focused on the sheep.

"I'm trying to decide if you forgot . . . or got distracted . . . or simply like this sheep more than me?"

Noah had cocked his head at her. "What're you talking—" His stomach dropped. "Dinner with your parents."

"Yes, dinner with my refined, wealthy, always-on-time parents. Which you missed."

"I've been watching this ewe. She's due any minute and—"

Maggie started to laugh. "I never dreamed I'd love a man who loved animals and plants more than people."

"I'm sorry, Maggie." Noah searched her oval face for signs of anger, but she was still smiling.

"It's all right. *I* don't even like having dinner with my parents. But you will have to be nice to people at the wedding. Okay? Can you smile and talk and be nice for just one day? That's all I'll ever ask of you."

Noah's heart tugged. He stepped over the sheep and came to Maggie at the rails. He tugged off his gloves, took her face in his hands, and kissed her softly. "I think I can manage one day."

"Glad to hear it."

"As long as it's just you and me at the end of it."

"Guaranteed, mister." She smiled seductively and kissed him again.

Looking up at Toby now, Noah wondered what Maggie would say about his behavior last night. Would she understand his aversion or scold him for being antisocial? She'd never embraced or understood his introversion, despite her promise. Noah asked Toby, "So you think I should be nice to Edith, huh?"

Toby grinned. "You should at least try. You were nice to Simone."

"But I was used to Simone. This is someone new. What if she tries to change my house?"

"I think it's her house now."

Noah frowned, lowering his gaze to look back through the fields at his beautiful white house. "And that, Toby, is the problem right there."

Seven

EDITH'S PHONE RANG as she signed the receipt for her new bedroom furniture, kitchen supplies, and gorgeous 1960's green velvet couch. "I'm buying furniture," she answered.

Milo answered, "Sweet. Is any of it from this decade?"

"Not a single thing."

"Typical. So . . . sounds like you survived the night."

A flash of the living room scene and the panic at first seeing it sent a nervous tremor through Edith. "Yeah, I suppose." She decided not to tell Milo about the ghost situation. Not yet. She went for the more tangible gossip. "So get this—Dad has a girlfriend."

"What? No, that's not possible." He laughed. "Nice joke."

"No joke, man. Her name is Cori. I met her this morning. She's this rad hippie lady who owns a legit coffee shop in town. She had on a Zeppelin shirt and flip flops, even though it's freezing. But her mocha—oh, my gosh, Milo!"

"Okay, wait—for real? Dad hasn't dated anyone since Mom and certainly not someone that cool."

"I'm as shocked as you. But they've been dating *for a year*. I'm going to dinner with them tonight. I'll get all the details."

There was a pause. "I have no idea what to do with this information. I think it broke my brain."

Edith smiled. "Are you desperately lonely without me?"

"I nearly jumped off a bridge three times yesterday."

"Was it a tall bridge?"

"The tallest one I could find. People had to pull me back from the edge. There were police and news reporters and psychiatrists with notebooks and mustaches. There were *mustaches*, Edie! I'm a total mess. You better come back."

He was joking, but Edith felt a rush of emotion anyway. "Don't tempt me," she mumbled.

Milo heard something in her tone. "Is it that bad? It's only been one day. You gotta give it some time. A month, at least."

"I know. I'm fine. Really. It's fine."

"Such a bad liar."

"Yeah, well, at least I have good taste in furniture." Edith went outside the warehouse and watched two burly men load her things into a delivery truck. They planned to follow her home.

"That's debatable. Vintage is just code for used."

"How dare you! No, it isn't. Vintage is code for cool."

Milo snorted. "I refuse to fight about this again. Plus, you're just avoiding the real question. Come on, what's bothering you?"

Edith sighed and walked a few steps back from the truck. She didn't really want anyone overhearing. "I need you to believe me," she started. "This is not stress or delusion or too much *Supernatural.*"

"Umm . . . okay . . ."

"The house is haunted." She shivered, lowering her chin deeper into her scarf. She waited for Milo to laugh or crack a joke.

"Tell me more," he said evenly.

Edith quickly dumped the whole story onto him. She felt a small rush of relief, which was quickly stomped down by a mountain of embarrassment. "If it'd been just me then, yes, maybe I'd call the men in white coats, but Cori and Simone confirm his existence. It's not a rumor, it's fact. Noah Winters haunts Simone's—no, *my*—house. And he ain't exactly a friendly ghost."

Milo remained quiet for a beat. When he spoke his voice was thoughtful and void of humor. "I don't like this. It doesn't sound safe—windows opening, doors unlocking. Are you afraid for your safety?"

"A little, yes," she whispered. The movers waved at her, signaling that they were ready to go. She hurried to her car. "But maybe not. I mean, he had all night to hurt me and didn't. It's obvious he just wanted to scare me. I don't think he's violent."

"This is too weird. Why didn't Simone ever tell you?"

"I don't know. I wish she had. I've never believed in ghosts. Yeah, I'm a sucker for any book or movie involving them, but in real life? No. Never. How about you?"

Milo sighed. "Not really, no. Except there was this thing once."

"What thing?" Edith pulled out onto the road, the moving truck behind her.

"A few nights after Mom left I had a dream. In it Great Grandma Sue sat on the end of my bed. She smelled of lilac, like she always did, and told me not to worry because Edith would help me. She said everything would be okay."

Edith put a hand to her chest. "What? You never said anything before."

"It was a dream. I was ten. But looking back, maybe . . . *maybe* it was more than a dream. It felt *very* real."

"Grandma Sue was the best. So sassy and loud. To this day, I've never met someone who can laugh louder or bigger. I miss her scones and lemon curd. Remember those?"

Milo laughed. "Not really, but I remember that laugh. And her garish floral moo-moos. Those seemed to be imprinted on my brain."

Edith laughed back. "Yeah. I remember a purple and yellow one. Truly hideous." They both laughed again and then grew solemn. Edith asked, "So you think her ghost came to visit you?"

"Maybe. And that's a BIG maybe."

"That feels like something she'd do."

"But what about you and your ghost? A ghost wasn't really part of the deal. What do *you* want to do, Edie?"

Edith stopped at a red light. She flexed her hands on the wheel and looked at her phone in the hands free clamp. "I don't know," she whispered.

"I think you have to decide how hard you want to fight. If he's not really a danger, I suppose you can work through it. Are you going to figure it out and fight for your flowers or take the easy way out and come back here?"

Her gut clenched. "Ugh. Why can't it just be simple? As if building a farm wasn't complicated enough."

"Nothing worth anything is ever simple."

"Thank you, wise Yoda."

Milo laughed. "You know what I mean. I've fought every day to get where I am and still battle the fear and doubt *every single day*. Moving forward, *through* the tough stuff—not around it or over it but straight on through—is what it takes to do great things. You did it after Mom left to keep us going. You can do it now."

She let out a long breath. That reminded her of what their dad had told her the night before ninth grade promotion. *Do it anyway.* "You should be a motivational speaker."

"Thank you. I'll keep that in mind for when I'm too old

to play football. I'll fill stadiums and shout really loud and wear garish moo-moos."

Edith scoff-laughed. "Fight for the flowers."

"Fight, baby, fight. I'll make T-shirts."

"But what do I *actually* do about a ghost in my house?"

"Talk to him?" Milo laughed doubtfully. "That's all I got."

"Talk to the ghost. Right."

"Couldn't hurt."

"It probably could."

"Just tell him what's what. I know you're not big on social interactions, but he's already dead so you can't kill him with your awkwardness."

"Gee, thanks. Supportive."

There was another voice on the line, muffled. Milo said something to the voice Edith didn't hear clearly. "Hey, sis, I gotta go. Break is over. So good luck with the ghost." He laughed. "You can do it. Just do what feels best. Okay?"

"Okay. Thanks, Milo."

"I'm here to help, don't forget that. I can come punch the guy. These guns aren't just for football and impressing the ladies. Wait—can you punch a ghost?"

Edith laughed. "I guess I'll find out."

"Call me tonight."

"Yep. Bye." Edith ended the call. "How do I fight a ghost?" She scanned the world outside her windshield. She was driving through the main shopping area of town. Howe's Hardware had a big neon green poster on the front window with hand lettering announcing: Paint Sale!

Edith turned on her blinker and pulled over. She waved to the truck, told them she had to make a quick stop, and then ran into the hardware store.

Noah replaced the last seed packet in Simone's box. He knew her organizing technique and made sure everything was just as it should be. Exactly as it was before he decided to be an idiot. He put his books back in their box and neatly slid both boxes back under the front windows. He even rolled up Edith's sleeping bag.

The sound of approaching wheels on the pebbled drive brought his head up. He went out to the porch. Two trucks— a big moving truck and a pick-up with a bed full of ladders— followed Edith's sedan. Noah tensed. "She's moving in," he murmured. He tried to ignore the tremor of anger at the thought of her things in his house. "It's not my house anymore. Be nice." He repeated Toby's words to himself, hoping to calm his instinct to push Edith away.

Edith got out of her car. He didn't miss the way her coat fit her figure or how her jeans tightly hugged her long legs. The late-morning sun bounced off her rose gold hair. Noah frowned. Her eyes flicked to the house, nervous about him, no doubt. She lifted her chin and came up the steps. "You guys can bring everything in through here," she called back to the movers. "I just need to move some stuff out of the way." Noah leaned close as she passed; she smelled of coffee and chocolate. His eyes traveled to a bare spot on her neck just above her voluminous white scarf. Her hand came to her neck at the same moment.

Can she sense me?

Edith rubbed the skin as she unlocked the door. He followed her inside. She stopped dead at the entrance to the living room, jaw dropped. She took another step in, looking side to side. Her gaze settled on the replaced boxes. She hurried over to the seed box, knelt down and opened it. She checked the order of the seeds. "You know where they go," she whispered.

Noah decided it was time for proper introductions. "Yes, I do."

Edith spun around, lifting to her feet, quick and graceful. He watched the expression on her face morph from fear to realization to stubbornness. She took a step forward and lifted her chin. "This is *my* house now." She jabbed a finger toward the floor in emphasis.

Noah couldn't help his smile. "Well, that's where things get a little complicated, Edith."

Her eyes flashed at her own name. "What do you mean, *Noah?*"

"I built the house, lived in it, and now I haunt it. I can't wander more than a few miles away before the need to return is unbearable. I'm tethered here by whatever supernatural force exists after life. So it remains *my* house even if you own it by law."

"I'm not leaving."

"Are you sure about that?" He heard the tremor in her voice and stepped closer. So close he could see that her whole body trembled. "It would probably be better if you left."

"But you cleaned up the mess."

Her eyes were such an unusual shade of blue, like a robin's egg but illuminated. "That doesn't mean I want you to stay. That doesn't mean I won't do worse."

Her eyes widened, she swallowed. "You let Simone stay. She never even mentioned you to me. So are you really threatening me or just marking your territory?"

That one stung. He already felt utterly helpless, trapped. He took a beat to calm his anger. "Do you really want to stay here knowing I'll be here, watching?" Edith shivered. Noah

77

pressed the advantage. He stepped directly in front of her. She was tall for a woman, but he was a few inches taller. He looked down at her, his body almost touching hers. She gasped quietly, and went as rigid as ice. He stroked his knuckles down her cheek, telling himself it was to let her know just how real he was and not to feel the silk of her skin. "I will *never* go away," he whispered.

Edith shuddered, unable to breathe with Noah so close to her. His hand felt solid, his skin warm against hers. She'd expected cold or to feel nothing—as all those ghost stories claimed—but Noah Winters felt every bit human and all too real. A new type of terror settled like a rock in her gut. The solid realization that the man standing only inches away really was a ghost and she'd moved into his house. This wasn't a game or a joke. He was one hundred percent genuine.

His deep-voice whisper raised chills on her arms. All the fight drained out of her. She wanted to run, screaming like a banshee from this house she'd always loved but now didn't recognize. She stumbled back several steps, slamming into the wall between the windows and catching her calf roughly on the seed box. Noah lowered his hand to his side, watching her, staring at her with an odd expression.

Why does he look so sad?

"Miss Daniels?"

Edith flinched. She turned to the voice, one of the movers stepping into the doorway. He narrowed his eyes at her. "You okay, miss?"

Her gaze flashed around the room. No Noah. *Did I imagine him?* Her hand came to her cheek where he'd touched her. *No way I imagined that!* She pushed away from the wall and straightened her coat. "I'm fine. Yeah. Fine."

He frowned, doubtful. "Where do you want this couch?" He gestured to the door and then hitched up his pants, which struggled to stay in place under his sizable belly.

"The couch. Yes. Umm . . . right here. In front of the fireplace, please." She forced herself to refocus. "And the bed goes upstairs, first room on the right. Thanks."

He nodded and went out the front door. Edith let out a shaky breath; her hands wouldn't stop shaking. She gripped them tightly together. *Fight for the flowers. Fight for the flowers.* She set the refrain on repeat and forced her breathing to slow. *Be bold. Be in charge.* She rolled her eyes at herself. *What am I doing?*

Stepping into the foyer, she put her hand on the open door and looked out at the two crews. A portion of her resolve returned. "I'm staying." She said it for Noah and herself. "I bought a bed and a couch. I bought three overpriced yellow-ware bowls and a rolling pin. I'm moving in. I'm putting granite counter tops in the kitchen, a new roof on, and a new soaking tub in the master bathroom. I'm painting walls and hanging curtains. And I'm going to plant a ridiculous amount of flowers." She looked over her shoulder at the empty foyer. "Get used to it, Noah Winters." She moved to walk out but then stopped. "Oh, and I'm painting *my* house *blue.*"

Blue! What? No.

Who paints a house blue?

Noah moved to stop her, but Edith was already out the door. She went to the porch rail and yelled, "Painters, where do you want to start?"

Two men, one young and scrawny, the other older and pot-bellied, carried paint buckets to the porch stairs. The potbellied one looked the house over with a trained eye. "Sanding will take the whole day. But once that's done, we move fast. We'll start here in front and work around."

Edith nodded. "Sounds good. I want the barn done too, please. Same colors." She went down the stairs to wait for the moving men. Noah followed, keeping himself unseen. He noticed Edith looking over her shoulder right toward him anyway.

You can't paint my house blue, woman.

Edith smiled.

The first item they pulled from the truck was an emerald green velvet couch. Noah gasped. "Is that . . . ? No, not possible." But the modern lines, low profile, and button-tufted cushions were the same. His gaze went to Edith. "You bought my couch." He flinched when she turned his way again, her eyes narrowing.

Maybe it was just the same style, and not actually *the* couch he'd spent the last ten years of his life sitting on, reading on late at night, and editing manuscripts in the morning, a steaming mug of coffee at his elbow. Not the exact same couch he'd slumped down on, cold beer in hand, after a long day in the fields. The couch he'd slept on when his bed felt too empty.

Noah followed the movers, couch, and Edith into the front room.

"Yep, right there," Edith said as the men settled the couch in place in front of the fireplace. The same place Noah had arranged his couch. He circled around it. If this really were his couch there'd be a few pen marks on the cushions. He bent over the seats. No pen. He straightened, unsatisfied; any savvy antiques dealer would have cleaned the pen. He remembered banging it on the front doorjamb the night he lugged it in by himself, having refused help from the store. There should be a dent in the frame on the right side. No damage to the fabric, just a notch in the wood.

He squatted down to run his finger along the frame and found a small divot in the wood about half way up. Noah shook his head. *How is this possible? Of all the couches in the world . . .* He looked over at Edith who stood at the opposite end of the couch running her hand over the aged-soft velvet. She smiled, a genuine, adoring smile. Something in Noah's chest twisted tight. The movers had gone so he allowed her to see him. She flinched but not as badly as before. "This is my couch," he growled.

She scoffed. "Seriously. Are you *five*? Just 'cause you see something you like doesn't mean it's yours."

"No, I'm serious. This is the couch I owned when I lived here. The *actual* couch."

Edith's brows pulled together. "I don't understand."

"Where did you find it?"

"The antiques warehouse at the edge of town. The big one with all the vendor booths."

Noah frowned.

"Wait—you mean . . ." Edith narrowed her eyes at him. "I bought the *same* couch you bought? The same one that sat in this house when you were . . . alive?" She pulled her hand away from the couch.

"Yes, that's exactly what I'm saying. And it's even in the same spot I had it."

Edith grimaced, looking at the couch now as if it were a rotten piece of fruit. "I don't . . ." She started but didn't finish. "I just saw it and loved it. I loved the shape, the color. I didn't know . . ." She huffed and folded her arms.

"Well, of course you didn't."

"But . . . does that mean something?"

He scoffed. "It's just a piece of furniture." That's what he told her, but he didn't really believe that. This was not a coincidence.

She leveled her eyes on him. "Yeah, and you're *just* a ghost."

Apparently, Edith didn't believe it either. Noah strode forward. "You can't paint my house *blue.*" He spit the word at her. He couldn't do anything about the couch, but maybe he could stop this crazy idea. "It's white. It's always been white. It needs new paint, but it must be white."

"It's time for a change." She stood her ground. "The house *and* barn will soon be a glorious robin's egg blue, with crisp white trim."

Noah didn't like that he'd thought of that color earlier when noticing her eyes. "That's ridiculous."

She shrugged. "Maybe. But I once saw a house that color in a *Country Living* magazine and fell deeply, and completely in love. Plus, I adore the idea of calling my farm Blue Farmhouse Flowers." Her eyes lit up. "I'll use blue paper to wrap my bouquets and blue Mason jars for small arrangements. It's memorable and marketable."

Noah couldn't help admiring the passion leaking into her hand gestures and expression. He'd once felt that way about his novels. The realization made him frown. He started to come closer, to say something else insulting, but the movers interrupted again. Noah instantly disappeared.

"The first door on the right, you said?" The guy in charge asked.

Edith answered, "Yes. I'll follow you up." Once the movers were halfway up the stairs, she turned back to where

Noah had been. Lowering her voice, she said, "I can feel you when I can't see you, so no more lurking, please. Show yourself or go away. I've got work to do." She pounded up the stairs.

Noah huffed and stomped his way out to the fields.

Eight

EDITH STOOD ON the small, dingy porch of her childhood home. The overhead light buzzed slightly, and the crack in the concrete under her feet looked exactly as it had all her life. Like the western outline of California, as Milo had once pointed out. The only difference was the wreath of fake daises on the front door. Edith blinked at it, fighting the urge to flee. But all she had to run back to was an ornery ghost and an unfamiliar bedroom. Facing her father seemed like the better option.

She rang the doorbell. The door flew open almost immediately. "You're here!" Cori sang. "And you look *gorgeous*." She waved a hand at Edith's simple tan wrap dress and bright pink cardigan. "Those long legs! Like Vera-Ellen— minus the eating disorder, of course."

Edith answered with a tense laugh. "Thanks. I wasn't sure what to wear. I'm never sure what to wear."

"Oh, nonsense. You have natural chic and you look great."

Edith looked at Cori's multi-colored peasant skirt and black ribbed tank top. Her smile warmed. "Thanks."

"Come in, come in. It's cold out there."

Edith followed Cori through the narrow entrance hall and into the living room, which sat off the kitchen. Edith swept her eyes over every detail. The corner fireplace with gray slate tile, the olive-green carpet, the faded beige couch and love seat—all the same with a few splashes of Cori here and there. Colored afghans and a bowl of crystals. Were those Tarot cards sitting on the coffee table?

This is the Twilight Zone. My new house may be haunted, but this is far more bizarre.

She wanted badly to text Milo a play-by-play but resisted taking out her phone.

"Your dad's in the kitchen. And I already poured the coffee. I'm not really a wine person, I hope that's okay."

"Coffee is great, thanks."

The round dinner table sat unassuming under an eighties era domed chandelier of garish gold and dusty glass. And there at the stove, in a simple white apron, was her father. He smiled shyly, looking up from a steaming pot. "I made my broccoli and cheese soup. Remember that?"

Edith kept her face neutral. She remembered she loved it as a kid and that he hadn't made it once after Mom left. "Sounds great," she managed.

He nodded, face solemn as if he, too, realized that small but meaningful fact. Cori looked between them, studying every nuance in their faces and body language. Edith started to take off her coat to cover her awkwardness. "I'll take that," Cori opened her hands and took Edith's coat and scarf. "Sit, honey."

Edith sat, relieved by the sturdiness of the wooden chair. Cori slipped out of the room. There was a yellow tablecloth on the table and hothouse daises in a small clay vase in the center. The plates and utensils were all laid out nicely. Edith picked up her mug, held it between her hands, and finally let her eyes move to the fridge. It wasn't the mustard yellow giant she remembered. A new, sleek, stainless-steel machine sat in its place. But that didn't stop the memory of the junk mail note or the smell of SpaghettiOs from invading her mind.

"I know this is weird." David had turned to watch her. He wore slacks and a navy polo shirt. Whatever clothes he wore, he always looked too thin, too long. But his face didn't look as gaunt as she remembered. His blue eyes had the smallest of a spark. She hadn't noticed it at Simone's funeral, but it was obvious now. Cori had brought life back into him and the house. So why hadn't he shared the joyous news with his children? Is that what he'd started to tell her at the funeral? Why had he stopped?

Edith pressed her teeth together to temper her rising anger.

"Yeah, it's pretty weird," she answered, not looking at him.

"Cori is great."

"She really is, so why didn't you tell us?" And there it was, out before she meant it to, landing like a quick jab to her dad's jaw.

David frowned as he turned back to the pot. He stirred. "I didn't know how."

The words broke her heart. She gripped the mug tighter and wished she hadn't come. Cori breezed back into the room. "I saw the trucks earlier—did you get some furniture for that big empty house?"

"A few things," Edith murmured. *Yeah, just the same couch that Noah Winters used and a gorgeous four-poster bed I'm afraid to sleep in.*

Cori looked between father and daughter, pursed her lips. "You guys have to figure this out."

"Coriander . . ." David started.

"Oh, I know—it's *complicated.* But good grief, David, she's your daughter!"

Edith looked up. "Your full name is Coriander?"

Cori raised her eyebrows at her. "That's what you say to that?" She laughed, shook her head. "Yes, my full name is Coriander, like the spice. My mother was a vegan chef."

"It's lovely."

Cori laughed again. "You guys are the champions of avoiding reality, aren't you? Blows my mind. Just *talk* to each other. That's what people do. That's what *families* do."

"Soup is ready," David said with a small, apologetic smile. The grim reality was that they didn't know how to talk to each other; it wasn't as simple as Cori made it sound. Words had a way of getting wedged underneath the years of grief and distance, never quite making it through.

Cori scoffed. "Well, bring it on. I'm so excited to eat in awkward silence."

Edith smiled into her mug. She decided to be on Cori's side and attempt to help things along. "How did you meet Cori, Dad?"

He smiled as he ladled soup into white bowls. "I went into her coffee shop on my lunch. Everyone was talking about the amazing coffee at the new place on Main Street. So, I decided to give it a try. All I wanted was one small coffee, black and simple. But this insane woman with the craziest hair I've ever seen dragged me to a table, brought me coffee, but then also insisted on reading my cards." He put a bowl in front of Edith. "You know, Tarot cards?"

"Yeah, I know it."

"Oh, she also put maple syrup in my coffee, which is strangely good."

"And calming," Cori added. "He was a knot of tension."

David smiled warmly. "I had no earthly idea what she was talking about with those cards, rambling on about being stuck in my life or broken or something like that."

Cori rolled her eyes. "I never said you were broken. Blocked. I said blocked and sad."

David gave her a bowl of soup and nodded. "Right. Well, I ran out of there as fast as I could and planned never to return. Even if the coffee was amazing." He tossed Cori a grin. "But the next day there I was, asking for coffee with maple syrup, and hoping to talk to her. Still took me a year to officially ask her out." He laid his hand on Cori's shoulder.

"It was worth the wait." Cori put her hand on his and beamed up at him.

Edith looked away from the loving gesture. Shocking anger rose sharp and foul in her throat. She knew she should be happy for her dad, but all she felt was resentment. A sour bitterness came with the anger. Why hadn't he been this happy, relaxed man for her and Milo when they needed him? He'd pushed them away and now there was a canyon of distance yawning between them, so wide she could barely sit at the same table. Her bitterness spawned irritation and jealousy. She realized that she was jealous her father had found happiness while she was still floundering to make a life for herself.

Edith set down her mug, the boxing match of emotions stealing all her strength.

"I'm sorry, Cori, but I'm really tired. I gotta go." Edith stood quickly and headed for the door.

"Edith, wait." Cori came after her. David didn't, which only added to Edith's anger.

Edith scooped her coat up from the back of the couch. Her eyes caught on a framed photo of her and Milo as kids, sitting on the swings in the backyard. Tears filled her eyes. "I'm so sorry. I just . . ."

"I know." The softness in Cori's tone stopped her. Edith turned, the first tears sliding down her cheek. Cori came up close and lowered her voice. "You got here. That's all that matters tonight. Every step forward counts. Okay?"

Edith nodded, surprised by Cori's empathy.

"Go home and get some sleep."

Edith nodded again, feeling dazed and exhausted.

"Come to the shop in the morning. We can talk."

"Okay."

"Sure thing, honey." Cori opened the door, smiling tenderly. "These things take time. Don't rush yourself."

"Thanks," she mumbled and sniffed. "I'm sorry."

"Nope, don't be. Good night."

"Night." Edith waited until the door closed and then she sprinted across the frozen grass and up the porch steps. She threw open the door and slammed it behind her. The tears came hard now. She dropped onto the carpeted stairs and buried her face in her arms. She felt Noah's presence almost immediately. "Go away!" she hissed through her sobs.

"She ruined him."

Edith looked up through bleary eyes, confused. Noah sat a few steps above her. "What?"

"Your mother. She ruined your father. Cori is healing him."

She shook her head, exasperated that she couldn't cry in peace and that Noah made perfect sense. "I know that."

He leaned toward her. "No, you *don't*. You don't know what it is like to have the woman you love torn from your life."

Edith stilled. The house felt suddenly so quiet, as if leaning in to listen to this conversation. "You know what that's like," she whispered.

Noah looked away. After a tense moment, he said, "David didn't want to be useless to his children. He didn't mean to do that. You and Milo had each other; David didn't have anyone. Stop your dramatics and forgive him."

She flinched at his harshness. "This is *none* of your business. And I know very well what it means to be left behind. She left me too."

"It's different."

"Leave me alone."

He scowled. "With pleasure." He stood up and stomped down the stairs past her. She watched him head toward the kitchen at the rear of the house. Several cupboards opened and slammed shut. She rolled her eyes, sniffed. Her stomach groaned with hunger and guilt.

He's right. Stupid Noah Winters is right about my dad.
Did I ever really think about how he felt?

Edith ran back through her memories. She'd known her dad was depressed, sad. Sometimes even angry. But she'd never really thought of the depth of his pain. She hadn't known how to as a teenager and young adult. But now? Now, she could imagine more empathically what his life must have been like. She didn't actually know, as Noah had rudely pointed out, but she knew she hadn't given her father enough space to grieve. She'd been critical instead of loving. She'd been so focused on making sure Milo survived the aftermath that she'd allowed her father to drown.

The tears returned. Another cupboard slammed.

She growled. "Stop it!" she yelled.

"No!" Noah yelled back and slammed two more cupboards.

"You are a child!"

"So are you!"

With a huff, Edith got up from the stairs. Maybe she could find peace outside on the porch, despite the cold. She yanked opened the front door and found her father standing with his hand raised to knock and his eyes wide. "Dad!"

"Who are you yelling at?"

91

Edith sighed. "Uh . . . just myself."

"What?"

"Never mind."

David frowned, cleared his throat. He lifted a Mason jar of soup toward her, a cheesy peace offering. "I'm sorry, Edie. I'm sorry I didn't tell you and Milo about Coriander."

Edith took the hot jar and waved him forward. "Come in out of the cold." She led him to the couch.

"Cool couch," he said, sitting on one end.

She sat on the other, the soup warming her lap. "Thanks." She swallowed. "I think I'm the one who needs to apologize. I didn't really know what you were going through. I got so focused on Milo—"

David lifted his hand. "You have nothing to apologize for. It wasn't your place to help me. What you did for Milo . . . I am forever in your debt and so is he. I wish I'd done better. It was just so . . . hard." He shrugged, knowing his words fell short.

Edith's chest tightened. "It's okay, Dad."

David sighed. "It's not okay, but it can't be changed. You're here now and I want to get to know you. I can do that, if you'll let me. What do you think?"

Edith nodded. "Yeah, good idea."

David nodded back. "Good." He stood, nervously rubbing his hands on his apron front. "I better get back. That's all the emotions I can handle for one night."

Edith watched a smile break on his face and realized he was joking. She let out a burst of laughter. "Daniels aren't really made for tender moments," she agreed.

"That's for sure."

Edith walked her dad to the door. "Thanks for the soup."

"Yeah, yeah. Enjoy." He stepped out onto the porch. "And for the record," he looked back over his shoulder, "Cori did *not* make me come over here. I did that on my own, and she's over there bouncing up and down with joy like some crazed puppy."

Edith laughed again. She'd forgotten her dad was funny. *That's where Milo gets it.* "Well, good luck with that," she said.

"Goodnight, Edith."

"Night, Dad."

Edith shut the door and turned around. Noah stood leaning against the newel post, arms crossed, face wide with a self-satisfied expression. She glared back. "No one likes a smug ghost."

He laughed, which surprised Edith. It was a deep, full laugh that spread warmth through her belly. The sadness left his eyes for just a moment, and she felt a hard pull of attraction. *He really is handsome. How did Cori put it—sexy farmer? Yep. That fits.* She smiled back. Their gazes met and held.

A wave of heat moved through Edith.

At the same moment, they looked away.

"I'm going to eat this soup and then I'm going to bed," she said, her throat a little dry. "You are *not* allowed in my room."

Noah's eyes darkened. "I may be a jerk, but I do have manners. I'll stay on the couch."

Edith gave him a curt nod. "Wait—do you sleep?"

Another small laugh, rimmed with a weighted exhaustion. "No, I do not."

She looked around the empty foyer. "So . . . what do you do all night?"

Noah frowned. "What all insomniacs do: read, watch TV, stare at the wall and wish for sleep."

Edith nodded. "I'm sorry my books and TV aren't here

yet. It's all being shipped. All I have are . . ." Her gaze moved to the living room, thinking of the box of his own books.

"I've read those ones, thanks." He gave her a small smile.

Edith thumbed the lid of the jar, unsure what to say next. "Okay. Well, goodnight."

Noah grunted, his eyes on her. He half blocked the hall to the kitchen. She slowly stepped past him, all too aware of his body, so solid and *there*. How could a ghost feel so real? He leaned toward her as she came to his side, and she thought he might say something. His intense, broody eyes were a contradicting soft blue, almost gray. His gaze moved over her face, and then he turned away.

Edith quickly retreated the rest of the way into the kitchen, fighting an odd sense of disappointment. *What do I care? I hate him. I wish he'd disappear.* She tried to shake off the heat of his eyes. And tried not to think of going to sleep with Noah Winters in her house.

Noah sat on his green couch, hands absently stroking the velvet. He couldn't decide if it felt comforting or disconcerting to sit on it again. He wished Edith had brought home his old typewriter too. He had the urge to write a murder scene. Maybe it would kill the irrational longing in his chest to go upstairs to Edith.

What are you doing, old man?
You're dead. She's alive.

It was hard to admit that he'd never felt like this about any other woman after Maggie. Not that he'd given himself much opportunity. There were, however, a few women who'd tried to pursue him over the years, but to be honest, they'd bored him to tears. Edith . . . she infuriated him and challenged him and made him want to stop her rebuffs with his kisses.

So stupid. So very, very foolish.

I'm dead. She's alive. How can I even feel attracted to her?

He looked up at the ceiling. The floorboards groaned as Edith walked across the room. He followed the sound with his eyes. He heard her voice and assumed she was talking to her brother on the phone. *Young Milo, football star.* It was nice that she had a close sibling. A brother. Noah had lost both his brothers to World War II. It would have been nice to have their company after Maggie died. Trusted confidants to help him navigate the storm of grief and anger.

He laughed quietly to himself. The trouble the three of them had gotten into as boys. Noah's smile grew as he recalled the time they'd snuck into Mrs. Clump's chicken coop every day for a week and taken all the eggs. The old woman had thought she, or the chickens, had gone insane. When his father found the pile of eggs hoarded in the hayloft, there had been a lengthy lecture and punishment in the form of cleaning Mrs. Clump's coop for a year.

Aiden and Roger.

Noah's smile slipped away.

Too young to die. Especially from German bullets in their heads.

His loneliness reared its ugly, shadowed head.

Noah focused on the sound of Edith's voice drifting through the warm house. Words of how he would describe her if she were a character in his novels filled his mind. She was definitely Anson Lake's type and would make a thrilling love interest. This part of Noah—the writer—had also been dormant for so long, and he felt heady with the drug of the words and thoughts of the woman only a floor away.

Noah lay down on the couch, propped his hands behind his head, and let the words swirl in his head. He knew it was dangerous to give into thoughts about Edith, but he didn't have the strength to fight it. He knew in the morning he'd regret it. But for now, in the silent darkness, he chose to give in.

Nine

EDITH WOKE TO the sound of ladders unfolding and men shouting. Startled, she grabbed the sheets in tight fists. It took a few seconds to remember where she was and why there was so much noise at seven in the morning. Her eyes traveled around the bare room, her black-walnut, four-poster bed was an island in the middle. The new sheets—which she released from a death-grip—were a bit stiff but the mattress perfectly soft. And she'd slept deeply.

Energized, she hurried to dress so she could get out to see the painters. Rushing into the hall, she collided with the brick wall of Noah's chest. "What—"

"You cannot paint my house blue!" he growled.

Edith stepped back, flustered. Her first instinct was to cower to the confrontation, to give in, but Milo's mantra came to her aid. *Fight for the flowers. This is my house, my farm. Noah is not my boss.* She put her hands on her hips. "I can and I will. There's no more to discuss."

His eyes narrowed. "I just saw the color and there is *no way* I'm going to allow it. This house has always been white and will always be white."

"It's time for a change." Edith moved to walk past him, but he hooked her upper arm in a tight grip. She gasped, and reflexively brought her hand to his chest. "Let go!" She tried to pull away.

"I will sabotage it," he said, putting his face in hers. "Think those painters will want to stay if ladders keep falling over and paint brushes go sailing through the air?"

Edith's heartbeat pounded in her ears. *This man is insane. Civil and wise one moment, angry and violent the next.* She pushed her hand into his chest, trying to find the courage to stand up to him. "Noah Winters, let me go *right now!*"

He looked down at his hand on her arm and quickly released his grip. His eyes flickered with something that looked like regret. She stepped back several steps, her upper arm throbbed. She resisted the urge to rub it. Neither of them spoke for several moments. Edith's breath sounded loud in the narrow hall. Noah wouldn't look at her.

Finally, she forced herself to speak. "The house needs to be painted. It needs a lot of things; I'm trying to take care of it. I love it as much as you do."

"No, you don't," he mumbled. "You can't. I built it with my bare hands. I built it for—" He clenched off his wife's name. Edith wondered what it was and wished he'd tell her about this legendary woman.

She waited a beat and then asked, "Then why have you let it fall into disrepair? You're a ghost, but you can touch and move. You could have done repairs, even painted the house yourself. Isn't that better than playing the angry, wandering ghost?"

Noah blinked at her several times before his eyes narrowed. He opened his mouth to speak, but then snapped his jaw shut.

An idea came to her. "There's an old tractor in the barn. Is it yours?"

"Yes," he answered slowly.

"Do you know how to fix it, get it working?"

"Of course."

"Go do it then. I'll use it to clear the fields. If it needs parts, make a list. I'll have my dad get it all."

"You want to put me to work? Like some farm hand?"

"Just do it, Noah." A tremor moved through her stomach as she used his name. She swallowed hard. Would he listen to her? She recognized herself in him. She'd been diligent about keeping herself busy over the years because otherwise the sadness would creep in and feed her resentment. Noah needed something to do, something to accomplish.

He didn't say anything else, only watched her. Edith left him standing in the hall, too nervous to say anything more and risk him noticing how badly she was shaking. She grabbed her coat from the stair railing and shoved her arms in the sleeves as she went outside.

"Morning," she said to the painter in charge, Mr. Halls.

"Morning, Miss Daniels. We just opened the paint, if you'd like a look before we start spraying."

"Absolutely." She followed him to the truck. One of the large buckets sat in the pebbles, lid removed. She gasped. "It's perfect." The blue, a delightful mix of robin's egg and thunderstorm sky, thrilled her. She turned to look at the house, imagining the finished product.

This is the first big step. This will make it mine.

How much will Noah fight me?

Noah came out the front door, hands in his pockets. She froze, side-eyeing Mr. Halls to see if he saw the ghost. The painter was busy pulling plastic draping from the bed of the truck. Noah held her gaze as he thumped down the stairs. He stopped next to one of the ladders. Edith gritted her teeth.

Don't do it! Don't you dare, Noah Winters.

He gave her a smug grin and gleefully pushed over the ladder. It hit the ground with a garish metallic *twang*. Mr. Halls spun around and his young assistant came running from around the house. "What happened?" the lanky boy asked.

Edith narrowed her eyes at Noah; the men did not see him. Noah casually slipped his hands back in his pockets and walked away, headed in the direction of the barn. "You big baby!" she whispered.

"What's that?" Mr. Halls asked.

"Nothing. Sorry. The ladder just tipped over. So weird. Maybe it was on an incline or something?"

Halls frowned. "Guess so. Fix that, will you, Roy?"

The boy righted it, double-checking the placement. Edith waited for the sounds of another crashing ladder, but nothing happened. Hopeful that Noah had just been throwing one of his tantrums, she turned to her painter. "I'm heading into town for coffee. Can I get you anything?"

The man smiled. "Thank you. I'd love just a black coffee and fancy pants Roy likes cappuccinos."

"With four sugars, please," Roy yelled out, grinning.

Edith laughed, gave him a wave. "I'll be back soon." She went to her car, praying that the painters would still be there when she returned.

Noah faced the old tractor like a matador in the ring with a snorting bull. In his head, he heard the chug of its engine. It had once been shiny and red but was now mostly dust and rust. He'd spent so many hours in the seat and under the hood. He'd been using it the day he died.

Edith's revelation annoyed him more than anything else she'd said or done so far. Why hadn't he been taking care of things over the years? Why had he just wandered and moaned his fate? That wasn't like him. In life he had gotten things done. He'd worked relentlessly. And had loved it. He loved nothing more than filling a day with worthwhile tasks so that each night when his head hit the pillow he felt useful and productive. Why had he abandoned that as a dead man?

"Because the dead aren't supposed to fix tractors," he grumbled.

But the dead weren't supposed to haunt houses either. Who was to say what was right and wrong in this situation? Noah went to the old worktable and dug Martin Cuthbert's big toolbox out from under it. Luckily, Kate had not bothered with the things in the barn. He slid open the big doors to let in the light and brushed the cobwebs off the tractor hood.

He was surprised to find himself smiling.

"Fine. I'll fix the tractor, but I'll never forgive her for the blue paint."

Edith stood outside Cori's coffee shop grinning like a giddy child. She couldn't stop a little clap of excitement. This section of downtown was a short row of tiny Victorian cottages, originally built for the families of fishing crews who worked between the islands. Now refurbished as shops and businesses, each was painted in a glorious array of bright colors. One was a law office, one a clothing boutique, one the bookshop, and the end unit Coriander's Coffee. The body of Cori's shop was painted brilliant white with lime green and purple trim. A bright orange sign with the name of the shop hung above the green door. The big front window winked in the morning sun and the air smelled of coffee.

Edith went inside, greeted by the tinkle of a small set of chimes hung at the top of the door. Her smile grew. Cozy armchairs and wooden coffee tables were arranged in small groupings all around the floor. No wobbly tables and stiff wooden chairs here. Several colored crystals hung in the windows, playing tricks with the light. A low bookshelf divided the sitting area from the ordering line. A sign on the shelf read, *Books and beverages are best friends. Feel free to take one, leave one.* The wall along the ordering line side was painted in chalkboard paint, and instructions stenciled at the top in white paint read: *While you wait, leave your favorite words.* Edith stepped up to read poetry, inspirational quotes, and notes between friends.

She wanted to cheer out loud. If she had ever dreamed up her perfect coffee shop, this would be it.

"Edith! Hi!" Cori waved from behind the silver bulk of a large espresso machine. She wore a ruffled red apron and her hair was piled on top of her head. "Give me one second. Pick a chair, I'll bring mocha."

Edith waved back. She chose two empty chairs turned toward each other and sat. While she waited, she pulled out her phone. Last night, she and Milo had had a long talk about what happened at and after dinner. There was a text waiting, sent early this morning.

Milo: How you feeling this morning?

Edith: I'm okay. Had another fight with Noah, but I think I'm making progress. And the house is being painted as we speak . . . I mean, text.

Milo didn't answer, which didn't surprise her. Practice kept him away from his phone most of the day. She gripped her phone. *Ugh. I miss him so much.* It was strange to suddenly not have her brother around all the time. Though they'd both been busy with their lives the last four years, they still saw each other every day. Not having that contact made Edith feel disconnected, wobbly.

"Missing your brother?" Cori said, interrupting Edith's thoughts.

Edith blinked at her intuitive question. "Yeah, a lot." She took a big mug painted to look like a VW Bus from Cori who had one of her own which was shaped like an octopus.

With a groan, Cori sank into her chair. "Feels good to sit," she declared.

"Is it always this busy?"

"Yep, most mornings. Worse during the warm months when the tourists wander onto the island. But I don't mind it—I love it. Talking to people, making drinks. Owning something that's all mine."

"What did you do before this?"

Cori smiled over her mug, took a sip. "I was a big shot marketing director in Seattle. Pant suits and all."

"What?" Edith almost choked on her mocha.

Cori laughed. "Yep. I know. Twenty years of bowing to the man. One day, I was coming out of the office building after a *very* long day and one of my Louboutin heels snapped off. Got caught in a grate and just *snapped,* like a twig." She cranked her fist down as if breaking the heel. "I stood on that wet street holding that black and red heel. I wasn't sure whether to laugh, or cry, or scream. I had one of those moments of clarity. You know, those moments when you're finally forced to see the things you've been ignoring." She nodded slowly. "So right then I made the decision to never go back into that office building." She shrugged. "And I didn't. Haven't worn heels since either."

Edith shook her head. "That's . . . amazing!"

"I know!" Cori saluted her with her mug.

"Any family?"

"My parents have been gone for a few years. I got married once and then quickly divorced. He had a wandering eye, as they say." She shook her head. "So not really. Just Daniel."

Edith smiled, thinking of her father standing next to Cori, his hand on her shoulder. "Again, I'm sorry about—"

Cori lifted her palm. "Nope. Not allowed. It worked out beautifully. I'm so proud of you both." She smiled, sipped. "I know David hasn't, but did *you* ever hear from your mom?"

"Nope. Nothing." Edith shook her head.

"So weird."

"I know. And I've never really decided if that's good or bad. I don't know if I want to know where she is or what she's doing. It's been too long now anyway."

Cori nodded. "That's tough. I hope she found what she was looking for."

"That's generous of you. I'm not sure I feel that way."

"I think you will one day, but she hurt you, she changed your life. Forgiveness that big takes time."

Edith frowned. She doubted she'd ever forgive her mother. She doubted her mother deserved it. She sipped, sullen.

After a moment, Cori said, "Forgiveness isn't about other people, it's about cleaning out your soul. It's too messy hanging on to stuff year after year."

Edith looked up quickly. "How do you do that? You keep reading my thoughts."

Cori smiled over her mug. "Just the wisdom of age." Her eyes lifted at the same moment Edith sensed someone standing behind her.

"I thought that was you—hi, Edith!"

Edith turned. "Oh, wow. Hi, Janae! How are you?" Janae Grant was the daughter of Paula Grant who owned Better Blooms, the only florist shop on Autumn Island. The shop that had done the arrangements for Simone's funeral. Janae was a year older than Edith, but they had been casual friends in school. Janae's cheeks were cherry-red from the cold air outside, her eyes bright, and her belly protruding a foot in front of her. She put a hand on it as Edith took it in. "And you're pregnant!" Edith added, trying hard not to think of Simone's funeral and those horrible arrangements.

Janae smiled. "Yeah, our second. A boy. Due any day now, as you can tell by how far out I go."

"You look gorgeous," Edith complimented. She'd always admired Janae's lush brown hair, smooth skin, and curvy silhouette. "You still working at your mom's shop?"

"Of course. Mom's eyes are giving her problems, so I help out most days."

"Sorry about that."

"Oh, no worries. She's still there every day, too, telling me what to do." Janae rolled her eyes. "How about you? Are you here visiting your dad?"

"Actually, I bought Simone's house. I live here now. I'm starting a flower farm."

There was a brief flit of confusion on her face. "A flower farm? Really. Are you wholesaling?"

"No. I'm doing the farmer florist thing."

Janae blinked, paused a little too long. "That's great."

Edith felt the tension in her tone. Edith hadn't thought about how she'd be in direct competition with Better Blooms, with Janae and her family. And by the look on her face, Edith could tell that Janae wasn't happy about the news.

"Well, I uh . . . got to get back," Janae rushed to say. "Good luck with the farm."

"Thanks." Edith wanted to say more, but Janae hurried out of the shop. Edith turned to Cori.

"She'll get over it," Cori said casually.

"Did you see her face? I didn't even think about Better Blooms when I got the farm idea."

"Janae and Paula won't like losing their flower monopoly, but don't worry about it. If they're smart, they'll buy your flowers instead of the sad things they ship in."

Edith blinked down into her mug, fighting a rush of embarrassed shame. *What right do I have to waltz in and sell flowers? Better Blooms has been here for forever.*

Cori leaned forward and touched Edith's knee. "There is always room for more in this world. More flowers, more coffee, more creativity, more businesses. Edith, don't feel bad about this."

"Right. Sure." She looked around the room; the clock caught her eye. "Oh, I better go. I promised the painters some coffee. That is, if Noah hasn't scared them off."

"Why would he scare them off?"

"He hates the color I picked. Wants the house to stay white. But it should be blue. I love the blue."

"Good for you. So, you've talked to him?"

"A few times, yeah. He's . . . stubborn and volatile. But also, insightful. It's weird."

"Sounds interesting." Cori turned her mug in her hands, her expression thoughtful. "What's his voice sound like? I've always wondered."

Edith laughed. "Really?"

"Of course! A handsome man *must* have a voice to match. If he doesn't, it ruins the whole effect. I imagine his is deep and raspy, in a sexy way. Is it?"

Edith thought about Noah's voice, already so familiar to her, and decided it fit him perfectly. "Yeah, it's deep, but not really raspy. It has a growl to it, low and intimidating, like distant thunder." Her cheeks went hot. She laughed, embarrassed by her romantic description. *Why didn't I just say it was deep and leave it at that?*

"Well said." Cori studied her face. "He's like an approaching storm. Sounds sexy, indeed."

Edith fiddled with her mug, uneasy to be talking about a dead man in such familiar tones. *He's a ghost! Remember?*

Cori smiled, stood. "Come on. Let's get your painters some caffeine."

Noah had grease in every line of his hands. Black, gritty grease. He held his hands open; a satisfied thrill spun in his gut. He stood next to the tractor, the engine in pieces, neatly laid out on a drop cloth. He'd cleaned everything and started a list of what needed to be replaced. He picked up a semi-clean rag, rubbed at his hands, and went over everything in his mind.

He didn't hear Edith approach.

"You've been at it all day."

He flinched a little and turned to find her standing in the open doorway. Her hair was tied in a messy knot on top of her head, pieces spilling out, and she was wrapped in a thick emerald sweater. His breath caught. He had the urge to open his arms, pull her into his chest, and hold her close. She smiled, eyes moving to the puzzle of engine on the ground.

"Wow. This looks serious. Is it beyond repair?" She stepped closer.

Noah gripped the rag tightly. He realized that for the better part of the day, while his hands had been busy, he'd forgotten he wasn't actually alive. He frowned deeply, the reality sitting down heavily on his shoulders.

"Are you okay?" Edith whispered.

Noah met her gaze. "The tractor will work just fine. There's the list of parts."

Her eyes narrowed at him, and he wondered what she was thinking. "I'll get what you need," she said. A tense moment of silence passed. She took another step closer. "The sun is setting. Do you want to come inside? It's getting cold." She wrapped her arms around her torso.

"I don't get cold." He hadn't meant for it to sound so sharp and accusatory.

Edith stepped back, face tight. "Right. Sorry." She turned quickly and walked away.

Noah rolled his eyes at himself. He threw the rag to the floor and hurried after her, despite his better judgment. She startled as he came up beside her. He wanted to say something but wasn't sure what. So, he walked beside her in silence. She glanced at him a couple times. Finally, she said, "Have you seen it yet?"

"Seen what?" he asked, hyperaware of her body beside him.

She smiled, a little mischief in her expression. She let her eyes direct him. He followed her gaze to the house. He stopped. The house—his house—was blue. While he'd been working, he'd forgotten about this. His first instinct was to frown, but then he stopped. In the fading peach-flesh light of sunset the blue looked rich and luxurious, like the sky as it clears after a midday rain. The white trim winked bright and brilliant.

He had to be honest: it looked incredible. The house stood fresh and awake, alive once more. It hadn't looked that way in a long time. Something tight in Noah's chest unwound.

Noah turned to Edith who'd been watching him with

eager eyes. She grinned. "Told ya so," she said with a satisfied laugh.

He felt himself smile back. "Looks ridiculous."

She laughed harder. "No, it doesn't, and you know it."

"I'll admit nothing."

"Of course, you won't. Big jerk."

He laughed, surprised at the unfamiliar sound and sensation. "Crazy woman," he teased back.

Edith's cheeks glowed pink in the failing light. "I'm going to make some tea and watch *Star Trek*. The TV arrived about an hour ago, and it's sort of a Simone tradition."

"Oh, I know it is."

She looked at him expectantly; he wasn't sure why. Quietly, she added, "So, do you want to join me or are you gonna putter in the barn all night?"

His eyes went wide. "Join you?"

"Yeah." She shrugged. "If you want. No big deal if you don't."

But possibly a big deal if I do.

Noah looked back toward the barn. He told himself he should go there and stay there as much as possible. He should cut off this growing relationship between them. It would only cause them both pain. His words betrayed him. "You got the episodes with that Q guy?"

Edith beamed. "I got them all. It's called Netflix."

Noah nodded. He gestured to the path to the back door. "After you."

Ten

FOR THE THIRD night in a row, Edith sat on the couch with Noah, watching *Star Trek*. He sat on one end and she on the other. She sipped tea and he sat very still. She glanced over at him, unsure what to think about this budding ritual. *It's better than fighting with him, I guess.* He felt so real sitting there, arm draped on the back of the couch. The only thing that reminded her of his ghostly state was the way his form went slightly blurry around the edges when she wasn't looking directly at him.

A quiet knock came at the front door. Edith popped up and went into the foyer. She adjusted her old hoodie and opened the door. "Hey, Dad."

David held a large box. "I got those parts for the tractor. I can install them on Saturday, if you like."

Edith looked back over her shoulder; Noah was gone. She hadn't told her dad about the ghost or Noah's work on the machine.

David added, "I know you're not much for cars and such—not sure how you knew which parts to get—but I can look it over. If you . . . want me to. I'd like to help."

She didn't want to take the work away from Noah, but there was a desperate edge to her father's request. He was still trying to find his way back into her life. One successful moment over broccoli cheese soup couldn't erase all the years of awkward distance. "Uh, yeah, Dad, that'd be great. Thanks."

Relief washed over his face. "Okay. I'll just leave these on the porch then."

"Okay." Edith wasn't sure what else to say, but it didn't look like her dad was ready to leave. "Did you see Milo's interview on ESPN yesterday?" she asked.

"Yeah, yeah, I did. He's good at that, ain't he?" David lowered the box. Straightening, he put his hands in his pockets and shrugged a little deeper in his coat. "I mean, talking to reporters and stuff."

"Milo can talk to anybody. He's really comfortable around people."

David smiled. "Not like you and me."

Edith smiled back. Her mom had been vivacious and outgoing; Milo got that from her. Edith had her father to thank for her timid shyness. "It's freezing. Do you want to come in?" Edith stepped back.

"No, no." David shook his head. "Thanks, though." He half turned. "See you Saturday."

Edith nodded and slowly closed the door. She turned to find Noah standing directly behind her, eyes hard. "He doesn't know," he said flatly.

"Know what?"

"About me."

"I don't know. Maybe Cori told him."

"Why didn't *you* tell him? And why did you give him the tractor?"

Edith blanched. "He really wants to help. He's trying to be a good dad. I didn't want to tell him no. I didn't think . . ."

"You didn't think it would matter to me?"

"That's not—I thought you'd understand."

"I'd help him. Two sets of hands are better than one."

"I—" Edith closed her mouth. She had no idea what to say. Should she have told her dad about her ghost? It was easy to talk to Cori about Noah. She'd even managed to discuss it with Milo. But her dad, or anyone else? The man standing in front of her was dead—a spirit, a ghost. That wasn't something you dropped into casual conversation. He wasn't someone you introduced to everyone who came to your door. "You're angry?"

"It's my tractor."

Edith pressed her teeth together and took a breath. "It's also my tractor, and I'm not going to keep fighting like toddlers over things."

Noah folded his arms. "I started the job and need to finish it."

Her attention caught on the word need, the desperate way he'd said it. Her defensiveness drained away. "I'm sorry. I honestly didn't mean to hurt you."

"Of course not. I'm just the resident spook." He folded his arms, petulant.

Edith scoffed, defensiveness back. "One minute you're nice, the next a *complete* nightmare. I'm trying to do what you told me and give my dad a chance. It was a nice gesture to him, not a purposeful slight to you. What is your problem?"

Noah flinched, his expression souring. Edith held her breath. He stepped close, his face inches from hers. He whispered, "My problem is that *I'm dead.*" He held her eyes for a tense moment and then disappeared. Edith jerked away from the empty space in front of her, the heat of Noah's body lingering in the air.

Flustered, she turned slowly to look at the TV hung above the fireplace. The *Star Trek* episode was still playing; the sounds of dialogue muffled by the pound of breath in her ears.

Walking stiffly, she went back to the couch and sat heavily. She berated herself for not considering Noah's emotional tie to the tractor. He'd been out there all day for three days, occupied and . . . happy. As happy as Noah seemed to get, anyway.

And I just pulled it away from him. Stupid!

Edith tried to imagine what it must be like for Noah. The long days of nothing, watching his things taken away, taken over. A fractured existence of feeling so much but having so little. The loneliness, the confusion. The anger. Edith imagined that she'd be incredibly angry to find herself stuck in the purgatory of life after death. To be left alone, left behind. She knew exactly what that felt like.

Tears filled her eyes. "I'm sorry, Noah," she whispered.

He appeared next to her, sitting on the couch, elbows propped on knees. "Me too. I apologize, Edith," he said in a hushed voice, without looking at her.

Edith wanted to reach out and take his hand. "I'll tell my dad. You can fix the tractor together."

After a long pause, he answered, "No. You're right. You can't tell everyone about me. I don't want the whole island knowing. I don't want me, you, or this house to become some kind of supernatural showcase." Finally, he turned to her and she felt the full weight of his pain. "You have to keep me a secret."

"I agree," she repeated. "I'm really sorry. I wish it were different."

He looked stricken by her tenderness. "Give me something else to do."

Edith nodded. "I'd love to fix up the old chicken coop. Make it nice, put chickens in it again."

He nodded in return. "I'll start first thing."

Edith gave him a soft smile. His eyes searched her face for

a moment before looking away. She picked up the remote. "Do you want to finish this?"

"Sure. Do you want another cup of tea?"

"Yeah, that'd be great."

"I'll get it."

"Really?"

Noah stood and held out his hand for her mug. She placed it there, grateful for the gesture. Noah walked around the couch and to the kitchen, his footsteps silent. From down the hall, she heard him call out, "Tea. Earl Grey. Hot!" Loud, and exactly like Simone used to do it.

Edith collapsed to the couch, laughing.

Noah sat listening to Edith breathe. She'd fallen asleep halfway through their second episode, head resting on her folded arms, which were wedged onto the arm of the couch. She looked small, and child-like. She looked peaceful.

He regretted his outburst about the tractor. Of course her father should help with the farm. David needed to be a part of Edith's new life. But then, it seemed, so did he. Working on the tractor had brought him a contentment he thought he'd never find again. It gave him purpose and somewhere to focus his energy. It gave him a distraction from torturous memories of Maggie and growing emotions for Edith.

I've got to learn to control my anger. She doesn't deserve it.

Neither do I.

That thought gave him pause. *I'm hurting myself with all this rage as much as I'm hurting Edith.*

A ripple in the air made Noah look up. Toby appeared by

the windows. Noah frowned, "What are you doing out of your tree?" he whispered.

Toby grinned. "I missed you. And I wanted to see the new lady." Toby tugged at his brown suit coat and then walked forward. He stopped by Edith's side and peered down at her with wide eyes. "She looks like Sleeping Beauty. I remember my mother reading me that story." His young, ghostly face turned sad for a moment. "Is she someone's mother?"

"No, Toby. She's not married and doesn't have children."

"She should, one day."

"Yes, one day." Noah's chest hurt. *For that she'd need a man who isn't a ghost.*

"Is this where you've been, Noah, with her?"

"Yes."

"Why?"

"Why what?"

"Why have you been with her?"

"Because I'm helping Edith with the farm."

Toby lifted his eyes to Noah's face, scrutinizing. "You look different."

"No, I don't. Ghosts don't change. We are always the same." He gestured to Toby's eternal child's body.

"You are changing." Toby looked back at Edith. "She is changing you."

Noah frowned. "Stop being dramatic."

Toby smiled and brought a small hand to Edith's soft cheek. "Do you think she's beautiful? I do. I think she's the most beautiful woman I've ever seen."

Edith shifted in her sleep. Noah, avoiding the boy's question, said, "You should go back to your tree now."

"I can hear her heart beating. It's so strong and loud." Toby put his hand on his own chest, a flicker of grief moving over his face.

"I know," Noah whispered. He watched the ghost boy and Edith. A thrash of guilt hit him. Edith deserved to get married and have children. She deserved a life without a cranky old miser haunting her house and yelling at her for stupid reasons. He knew she felt the same connection he did. He knew she was growing attached to him too quickly, as he was to her. He was allowing it to happen and he shouldn't. "I should leave her alone," he said more to himself than Toby.

Toby pulled his hand back from her face. "I think she needs you."

"Don't be ridiculous."

"I think you need her too."

Edith shifted again but didn't wake. "That's enough of that," he told Toby. Noah clicked off the TV and moved to Edith's side. Gently, he lifted her into his arms. "Goodnight, Toby."

"Goodnight, Noah," the boy whispered and disappeared. With Edith tucked close to his chest, Noah went up the stairs and into her room. He laid her carefully on the bed and pulled the quilt over her. As he settled it onto her shoulders her eyes half opened to look at him. "Thank you, Noah."

Her sultry whisper broke his heart—his silent, not beating heart.

The next morning, Edith went out to the chicken coop to find Noah. He wasn't there. A scattering of tools lay in the dirt, the only sign of him. She called his name and walked the property. He didn't answer. He wasn't anywhere. *Where are you?* His absence unsettled her more than she liked to admit. Disappointed, she went to her car. She had a million errands to run, and she'd slept later than she should have. She wanted to thank him for putting her in bed. She wanted to prove to herself she wouldn't be awkward when she did it. She felt self-conscious about the intimacy of it. She'd been so tired she only vaguely remembered the feeling of being in his arms, the effortless way he had carried her and laid her down. And had she imagined the wounded look on his face when she whispered his name?

She needed to look him in the eyes and reassure herself that they still had a casual, banter-heavy, dead guy and living girl relationship. Not more.

Not more than that.

But all that would have to wait since Noah had decided to disappear. *Is he hiding from me?* As she got into her car, she had the thought that maybe he was gone forever. That somehow he'd passed over, moved on, and would never come back. The thought made her stomach ache. She pushed it aside.

He's been here for years; he's not going anywhere.

Noah will be here when I get back, ready to yell at me for something stupid.

While she drove, she debated on whether to stop at Cori's first or last. Finally, she decided to get work stuff done first and look forward to a reward beverage after. At the hardware store, she ordered seed starter trays, landscape cloth, the good flower snips, and asked Mr. Lions to keep his ears open for a deal on a greenhouse. She loaded her trunk with groceries and essentials for the house. She was still using her travel-size shampoo. Then she drove across town to the stationery store, owned by Sissy Moyels.

Edith hurried inside For the Love of Paper. The small store had a few rows of shelves with notebooks, cardstock, cards, and envelopes. It smelled of new paper and gladiola candles. Sissy sat at the checkout desk, her reading glasses low on her nose. "Hello, Sissy."

The older woman startled, hurrying to pull her glasses down to hang on a beaded lanyard around her neck. "Edith! I heard you were back in town. Hello." There was a slight hesitancy in Sissy's enthusiasm. Her eyes shifted around the room.

"How are you?" Edith rested her hands on the desk, glad to be in the warm space and out of the cold day.

"Oh, fine. Fine." Sissy avoided her eyes, shuffling a few things on the desk.

Edith remembered Sissy being much friendlier. Edith held back a confused frown. "I'd like to have some stuff made for my new farm. Stickers for the bouquet paper, business cards, stationery—stuff like that." Sissy squinted. Edith frowned at the expression. "Do you still do the custom stuff?"

Sissy pushed one paper under another. "Well, we do, but I can't. Sorry, Edith."

Edith blinked. "Umm . . . okay."

Sissy looked up to meet Edith's eyes. "I'm really sorry, honey. I'd love to do it, but . . ." She looked past Edith's shoulder to survey the room. Edith's pulse quickened. Sissy leaned forward and lowered her voice even though there was no one else in the store. "My daughter married Paula's oldest boy. So . . ."

"So . . . I don't understand. Paula, from Better Blooms? What does that have to do with me placing an order with you?"

"Paula's all flustered about your new farm. She's worried you'll take all her business. Actually, she's furious. And I don't like to stir the pot. I don't want to make trouble for my Luanne. Paula is already not the easiest mother-in-law, and if she heard I did work for your new business . . . well, you know."

Edith opened her mouth, but no words came out. Her whole body flushed with balmy heat.

No, I don't know. What is happening?

"I'm *so* sorry, honey. Really." Sissy shrugged.

Edith blinked again, her stomach turning. "Okay. That's all right. Thanks," she managed to force out. She didn't know what else to say so she turned and hurried out. Once in her car, she tried to stop the rush of embarrassed anger heating her neck. *What just happened?* She pressed her cold hands to her hot cheeks.

Don't cry. It's fine. It's fine. No big deal.

Automatically, she reached for her phone and dialed Milo. "Please answer," she whispered. She turned on the car and rolled down the windows for some cool, fresh air. "Answer!" she hissed the same moment Milo picked up.

"Whoa! Easy, girl."

"Milo, I—" Her throat closed.

"Uh oh. What's wrong? Edith? Edie . . ."

Finally, she managed. "I'm being ostracized."

"You read too much. Simple words, please. I'm just a lowly football peasant."

Edith spilled out what had happened with Sissy. Repeating it only made it worse.

"Are you serious? I'll punch her. I don't even care if she's a frail old woman. I have no qualms about bringing down the hurt." Milo scoffed and Edith smiled a little. "I mean, *seriously*?" he added, voice tense. "Also, please note I used the word *qualms*. Maybe not so peasant, after all."

Edith laughed, the medicine she needed. "Yes, well done. Now, what do I do? I don't even know what to think. What if other business owners do this? What if no one wants my flowers? What if I go to all this effort only to be run out of town? Milo, I'm gonna be run out of town!"

"Whoa. Easy, girl. This isn't the Wild West. And the world is bigger than Autumn Island. Plenty of people will want your flowers. And screw that old paper store. Order everything you need on Etsy; that's what people do now. Modern world conveniences . . . meet Edith Daniels."

Edith let out a breath. "I feel like Hester."

"Who's that? Is she the crazy lady who owns that crystal shop?"

"No. You're back to being a peasant, and illiterate. *The Scarlet Letter.* Ring any bells?"

"Vaguely." He paused. "Edith, I'm so sorry. That really sucks. You don't deserve it at all."

"It really does suck. I was going to go to Cori's, but I just want to hide from the world."

"Hey, don't let those old gossips ruin your life. You do what you want to do. Let it go. Shall I sing it for you? It'd be my unending pleasure. Ready?" Milo drew in a loud inhale.

"Oh, no. Please don't."

"But it feels so good." Milo took another dramatic deep breath.

"Stop! Resist the urge."

Milo laughed. "Hey, starting something like this is a big deal. It's not going to go smoothly all the time."

"I know, but this felt so . . . personal. It makes me feel so . . . weird."

"The old adage that 'it's not personal, it's business' is total crap. Everything feels personal. That's normal."

"Totally does. I never imagined *this.*"

"Rise above. Fight for the flowers. You get to decide how you react."

Edith smiled. Realizing her body temperature had

returned to normal, she rolled up the windows. She sighed. "Sorry I keep calling you in a panic. I promise I'm not constantly freaking out."

"No apology necessary. Call anytime. You know that."

"Yeah. Thanks. So, how are you?"

"Got a hot date tonight."

"Faye?"

"You know it. I'm taking her to this little Indian restaurant. The guys keep telling me it's amazing and romantic and all that."

"Good for you. Is it going well?"

"Yeah. You might even say—prepare yourself, this is *big*—that I have a girlfriend."

Edith gasped theatrically. "Should I giggle like a teenager?"

"Please do. I do it all the time."

Edith laughed normally. "I'm glad, Milo. Really glad."

"And how are things with Mr. Ghost?"

"It's . . . going." Edith didn't have the strength to get into details. "We're figuring it out."

"Good. I can't believe I just asked that question. I have to keep reminding myself that he's real."

"I know." Although, Edith thought she had the opposite problem. She needed to remember that he wasn't alive, wasn't real like her and Milo. "Well, go get all pretty for your date."

"Hey, I'm already pretty."

"And humble."

Milo laughed. "You got this, Edith. The beginning is always the hardest. You'll settle in. And in a few months, you'll have fields full of flowers and be too busy to even notice all the losers in the background."

"Yes, Coach."

"Go team!"

"Talk to you later?"

"Yep, I'll call you and we can giggle over the details of my date."

"Can't wait. Bye."

"Bye, sis."

Edith looked down at her phone. Some of her nerves came back now that she wasn't talking to Milo. She wanted that mocha and to talk to Cori for a minute. But what if Paula was there or someone else who'd decided Edith was the enemy invader? She wondered what Noah would say about this.

Edith froze.

I want to tell Noah about my day and ask for advice. Like a friend.

Oh dear.

She brought herself back to Milo's advice instead of wondering about what Noah would say. "I get to decide. And I decide to go to Cori's."

Edith backed out and headed toward the shoreline.

Noah pounded a little harder on the nail than was necessary. His efforts to avoid Edith this morning had worked but left him with a foul taste in his mouth. His mind told him it was right, but his instincts told him something different. Listening to her call his name so hopefully and not answering had driven him mad. And now this innocent nail was paying the price.

It pleased him that Edith wanted chickens. The yard felt empty without them. He missed their silly antics and the fresh eggs. Their manure would be good for the soil too. She had good instincts for farm life. Noah gave the nail one more slam.

He wiped his brow out of habit—there was no sweat.

At the sound of a car crunching on the drive, Noah jerked around. *Should I hide again? No, I don't want to.* Edith came around the house, coffee cup in hand, and his smile came automatically. He suppressed it and forced himself to turn back to his work. He felt her come up behind him.

"Were you hiding from me this morning?"

"I went for a walk."

Edith hummed a doubtful acknowledgment. "Can I ask your advice about something?"

Noah stopped hammering and straightened up. He looked at her, seeing hurt in her expression. He felt immediately protective of her. "What happened?"

"The woman who owns the florist shop in town is kind of . . . sabotaging me. She's angry I dare to bring in competition."

Noah gave a snort of derision. "All work has critics. Only fools listen to what they say."

Edith frowned.

Noah took a step closer to her. "I'm not saying *you're* a fool." He smiled when she did. "There were many people who didn't like my books. If I had listened to them, it would have paralyzed my work. The most important thing to learn is that other people's opinions of you have *nothing* to do with you. You're not responsible for what they think or how they react. That belongs to them. Just like your thoughts and actions belong to you."

She furrowed her brow thoughtfully. "That's very wise. Though hard to internalize. It's hard not to feel hurt."

"I know. But trust yourself. You have something to give. Don't hold back."

Her face softened. "You sound like Milo."

"Then he must be a smart, handsome man."

Edith laughed, shook her head. "I got to get to work. I have Etsy shops to peruse."

Noah nodded, furrowed his brow. "What's Etsy?"

Edith grinned. "See you for *Star Trek?*"

"I'll make the tea. I'm better at it than you."

Edith scoffed. "It's tea! It's not like it's hard: hot water, bag of tea."

"I stand by my previous statement."

Edith shrugged, smiling. "If you want to serve me, I'll allow it. See you later, Noah."

Noah watched her walk away, dropping his head to the side to admire her form. He begged the hours to fly by so he could sit on that green couch beside her.

Eleven

December

EDITH STOOD AT the living room windows watching the rain beat down on the front yard. The whole world felt drenched, drowned; it'd been raining for three days. Mixed with the sound of the rain was the determined pounding of Noah's hammer. He'd been on the roof for the last hour trying to patch a few rotten areas that had given way under all the water. Edith had spent all morning toweling up the mess.

Watching the gray landscape, she had to admit she was glad Noah was up there and not her. Having a handy ghost around had its advantages. She turned away from the window and back to the Christmas tree. She'd finished with the lights, but still needed to put up the antique mercury glass ornaments she'd bought last week. Checking her watch, she decided she had just enough time to get it done before Milo arrived.

Edith picked up the box of ornaments nestled in tissue paper. She paused to look around the room. The fire crackled in the hearth, the books slept on the bookshelves, the walls had photos and paintings. She'd draped a garland of pine boughs and winterberries across the mantel and thrown red plaid pillows in the corners of the green couch. The windows had curtains, the floor a rug. Edith smiled at the cozy scene, still amazed this was her house, her life.

She couldn't wait for Milo to see it.

As she carefully placed the last bauble, she heard the back door open and *slam* shut. She sighed. "Can't he ever just *close* the door normally? Aren't ghosts supposed to be quiet?" She set the box aside and headed for the kitchen. Noah stood on the rug in front of the back door, tugging off his boots. His hair was plastered to his head, his clothes soaked flat against his body.

"What's the damage?" she asked as she grabbed the waiting towel from the back of a chair. He grunted as she handed it to him. "That bad, huh?" she added.

He threw the towel over his head and rubbed at his hair. "We need a new roof."

Edith didn't miss his use of the word we. They'd both been allowing it to creep into their vocabulary lately. She sighed again. "Yeah, I know. But the roofers can't come until mid-January."

He pulled the towel away, his dark hair an attractive mess all over his head. "Well, the patches I put on should hold until then. Blasted rain needs to stop."

"We'll need to watch for mold. A lot of water got in. Poor old house. You sure about those patches?"

"Yes, and I'll check everything again in the morning."

Edith pursed her lips, worried. Noah rubbed the towel across his eyes. She wanted to press her hands to his head and slick back his hair. Folding her arms, she said, "Better give me your clothes. I'll wash and dry them."

Noah dropped the towel and tugged off his heavy flannel and then his Henley. Edith pressed her teeth together at the sight of his bare chest. It was hard to see him as a ghost when he looked like that. Noah paused to return her stare, something meaningful passing between them before he said, "I guess I'll need other clothes."

Edith laughed. "Do you have any other clothes?"

Noah frowned, looked down at his naked torso. "Uh . . . no."

"You've been wearing these clothes since the '70s?"

Noah shrugged, the muscles in his shoulders moving. "It's never really been a problem. I don't make a habit of being out in the rain, and they don't ever seem dirty."

Edith pursed her lips. "Well, I don't think you'll fit in my clothes, and you can't walk around here naked. My brother will be here any moment, and also . . . eww."

Noah shot her a wicked grin. "I just fixed your roof, woman, and now you insult me?" He took a step toward her.

Edith grinned back. Noah shook his head and she noticed he had a thick smudge of mud on his neck. "You've got some mud . . ." She matched his step forward and picked up the towel.

"Where?" he said, bringing his hand to his face.

"No, on your neck. I got it." She brought a gather of towel to his neck and rubbed away the dirt. He smelled like rain and wind. Her pulse tripped over itself. Feeling his eyes on her, she lifted her chin to meet his gaze. His stone blue eyes clouded as he studied her. Beads of water were caught in his beard. Without thinking, she brought the towel to his face and gently wiped them away. His hand came to her hip, the slight pressure bringing her body nearly against his. She let her forearms rest on his warm chest.

"Edith . . ." he whispered in a gravelly voice.

She felt dizzy, her breath quickening. A small voice in her head asked: *What the heck are you doing?* But she ignored it and let the sensations of Noah's skin take center stage. Something about having this much contact with his ghostly body made her feel slightly off balance. Like teetering on an unsteady rock, solid but likely to tip and send her falling. Her senses twanged with heightened awareness. Noah's body was warm despite the thin layer of icy rain. She could feel her own heart rushing in her chest, but his remained silent except for the steady rise and fall of breathless breathing. Unable to look away from him, she drank in his eyes, more gray than blue in the rainwater light. The unrelenting storm pounded on the house, echoing all around the room.

The only other time she'd felt this slippery sense of reality accompanied by such potent awareness was in vivid dreams. Touching Noah pulled her into another world.

"Noah . . ."

"Well, this is pretty dang awkward."

At the sound of Milo's voice, Edith jerked away from Noah as if she'd been shocked by a live wire. She spun to find her brother filling the doorway, hair flat with rain. His teasing expression made her flush with hot embarrassment. He smiled and raised his eyebrows expectantly. "I didn't hear you knock," she blurted out stupidly. She felt suddenly light-headed and filled with cold.

"Oh, I did knock. The rain must have drowned it out. Or, you were too distracted to hear it." He smirked. "If I'd known you were otherwise engaged . . ." His eyes went to Noah. "Hi. I'm Milo, Edith's brother."

Noah stood rooted in place, blinking quickly. He looked to Edith and she briefly met his eyes. *He looks as disoriented as me. Does he feel this too?* She looked away first. "Noah Winters," he mumbled to Milo.

Milo's eyes went fully wide, all the humor washed away. His gaze snapped back to Edith. She just shook her head again. "I'll help you with your stuff," she said and hurried to push past her brother into the hall, without looking back at Noah. Milo followed silently. It wasn't until they were safely in the guest room with the door closed that he pressed her. "You wanna tell me why I caught you making out with *a ghost?* He is the ghost, right? Noah Winters—that's him? I mean, is it possible to kiss a ghost?" He scoffed. "I could see him," he mumbled, more to himself than Edith. "He looked so real."

"We weren't making out." Edith sat down on the twin bed; her legs felt numb.

Milo stood at the door, feet planted wide apart, a barricade. He folded his large arms. "At first, I was thrilled to see you with someone. I've hated the thought of you here alone. But if that's Noah . . ." He frowned, shook his head. "I know you've been hanging out and stuff, but . . ." Milo shook his head again. "Help me out here, Edie. Did we fall into some *Twilight Zone* dating show?"

Edith didn't smile. Her whole body felt shaky. *Did I almost kiss Noah Winters? Did he almost kiss me? And why did it feel so . . . extraordinary?* She looked down at her trembling hands. Milo crossed the room and sat beside her. "Edie?"

"I don't know what that was. There was mud on his neck and then . . ."

Milo didn't answer right away. They sat in silence, Edith's mind grappling for a hold of understanding. Finally, he asked, "So you guys have been getting pretty close then? The fighting has turned . . . into something else?" he asked.

"I guess so. It started a few weeks ago. We watched *Star Trek* one night and then it turned into *every* night. Noah wanted to watch the whole series in order. He's a Netflix newbie and is fully embracing the idea of binging." Edith pressed her lips together to stop the rush of words. She took a slow breath. "Every night he sits closer to me. Just a little. Or maybe I sit closer to him. I'm not sure." She forced herself to look up at Milo to read his expression. He looked as confused as she felt.

131

"So, you're falling for a dead guy . . . over Captain Picard and the starship *Enterprise*?" He scoffed. "Am I the only one who finds that—oh, I don't know—super weird?"

"Milo!"

"But, Edith, *he's a ghost.*"

"That is so not helpful. I know that!"

"Sorry, I'm still trying to grasp his existence. Kind of hard to go from that to romantic issues."

"There are no romantic issues."

"Uh . . . yes, there most certainly are. That's what we are talking about. Let's not go right into denial mode."

Edith scrunched up her face at him. "Okay, fine. Well, it won't happen again. We've just been spending a lot of time together. Maybe we both forgot."

"Forgot?" Milo lifted his eyebrows and pointed at the door. "That guy is dead, sis. Dead and ghostly. That's not something you should forget."

Edith flinched, turned away, her eyes suddenly hot with tears. "He seems so alive," she whispered. "And when I touched him . . ." The words wouldn't come.

"Maybe you should have come to New York for Christmas," Milo offered tenderly. "Maybe it wasn't a good idea to stay here with him, after all."

Edith balked at the idea. "No!" Then softer, "No, really. I just . . ." She shook her head. "How was your flight?"

Milo furrowed his brow. "Wow. The Queen of Avoidance, ladies and gents, Edith Daniels!" He mocked her with a round of applause.

She grabbed at his hands. "I'm not avoiding."

"He's *not real*, Edith." Milo's gaze was loving and anxious. "And the look on your face right after—I can't explain it. I think this might be dangerous."

"You're wrong. That's the problem. He's so very real."

Edith looked at her brother, hating the expression on his face. "He's not dangerous. He's just . . ."

"Dead."

"Could you stop saying that?"

"It's an important point. Kind of the main one here. What I just saw seems like a mega-mess waiting to happen. You can't fall for a ghost, my friend. There're like three billion men in the world, take your pick. But not this one. No matter how nice he looks without a shirt."

Edith clenched her hands together and dropped her chin to her chest. "I know," she whispered, close to tears. She felt Milo's disbelief without looking at him. "But I . . . I've never felt like this with anyone before."

Milo sighed, his expression full of worry, maybe even pity. "That is not a good thing, sis. Don't you see that? You can't compare this to real life, this is not real."

Edith nodded, looked away. They listened to the quiet house, and Edith wondered what Noah was doing downstairs. *Am I really falling for him? Is that possible?* The twist in her stomach told her it was all too possible and that she'd allowed it to happen over the last few weeks. She'd seen it, felt it, and chosen to pretend it wasn't a problem. Just friends, she'd told herself.

Just friends. That's all it can be. So, stop it.

After a long-weighted moment, Milo said, "You need to ask him to leave."

Edith's body stiffened in revolt. "He can't leave. He's not here by choice."

"But he could stay away from you. Go somewhere else. Leave you alone. He needs to leave you alone."

Tears fell in her lap. "I know." Logically, yes, she knew, but the full strength of her attachment to Noah cried out in livid protest. It felt like an addiction, a twisted new habit she absolutely had to kick. *But I don't want to.*

Milo sighed, "This might sound harsh, but I could find an exorcist."

Edith scoffed and pulled back from him. "Milo, come on!"

He lifted his hands, palms forward. "Hey, this is new to me. I'm just following the pattern. Unwanted ghost— exorcism." He sliced his hand through the air to emphasize each word. "I actually looked into it after you first told me about him. There's a church in Seattle that has a guy." He lowered his hands, gaze employing. "I'll admit it: I'm scared for you, sis."

Edith opened her mouth, but her protest died away as she looked at her younger brother. All her life she'd been protecting him. Did she need him to protect her now? "I can't do that to him, Milo. He doesn't deserve it. I'll talk to him. Okay?"

"All right. But this is not one of those things you avoid for a long time. Have you considered that he might *want* to be exorcised? A little help moving on after all these decades of being stuck here?"

Edith felt another stab of repulsion. "But it always seems so . . . violent."

"Too many movies. The priest would just help him pass on. I think, anyway. I'll find out more."

"If that was an option why didn't Simone do it for him?"

Milo shrugged. "I have no answers here. Only questions. Sorry."

Edith took a long inhale and slowly blew the air out. "I'll talk to Noah."

"Okay, Good."

They lapsed into silence. The sound of rain filled the

room. Edith realized her head was pounding. *Ugh. What do I do? How do I ask Noah to leave his house?*

Milo looked over at her. "The house looks amazing, by the way."

Edith gave him a small smile. "It does, doesn't it? Do you like the blue?"

"It's fabulous. Blue Farmhouse Flowers—it's really awesome. And it feels so chic and cozy, like something out of those *Country Living* magazines you hoard, which I, of course, never casually perused while eating cereal. I am far too manly for that."

She shook her head. "Sure, you didn't. But, yeah, that was the idea."

"How's everything else?" Milo prompted, trying to pull her out of her head.

"The farm stuff is really coming together. I just got a screaming deal on an old greenhouse someone is getting rid of. That goes in after Christmas. Dad fixed the old tractor and Noah taught me how to drive it. I cleared the back fields last week." Edith felt a little pang of shame mentioning Noah's name.

Milo smiled knowingly. "And bitter, old Paula? Any more problems?"

Edith rolled her eyes. "She's bad-mouthing me to anyone who will listen. Every time I go into town, I hear about it. She told Cori that I already poached an important client. Not true! I have no clients. I haven't run into her yet, and I haven't seen Janae again either. But I'm sure it will happen one of these days. I have no idea what I'll say to her. Maybe I shouldn't say anything."

"Tell her to step off or you'll challenge her to a break-dance fight. And I think you'll win. Well, maybe. Paula might have skills, who knows?"

Edith rolled her eyes. "You are so weird."

Milo grinned, pleased with himself. "Well, how about you show me everything?"

"I'll give you the house tour. We'll have to wait for the apocalyptic flood to end before I can show you the outside stuff."

Milo stood. "And is there food? I expect nothing less than awesome food for the next three days." He patted his stomach. "Gotta keep up my energy for that big Christmas Day game, you know."

"Yes, of course there is food. I made cinnamon rolls this morning."

"Excellent!" Milo opened the door. Softer, he said, "Don't wait to talk to him."

Edith nodded, emotions welling in her throat. "I won't."

"Maybe we can all figure it out together."

She gave her brother a smile. "Oh, and we're having dinner with Dad and Cori tonight."

"What? You didn't tell me that!"

"Surprise!"

"Oh, man. You can't just spring that on a guy. Why do you hate me so much?"

Edith rolled her eyes and hurried down the stairs.

Noah sat on the back-porch steps, allowing the rain to beat down on his bare back. His whole body felt scalded and he welcomed the icy water. *How can my spirit feel this much? How can I feel this way without being alive?* He put his head in his hands. *Edith in my arms—that felt like being reborn.*

His desire to kiss Edith had not ebbed with her exit. In fact, it had only swelled and roared louder. He looked down at his fingers, still tingling at the spots where he'd connected with her hip.

And now her hulk of a brother was here. He'd seen the look of horrified disgust when Milo realized who Noah was—no, *what* he was.

Noah let the shame fill him, and overflow.

He'd indulged this relationship far too long. He should have hidden himself away the moment Edith arrived. *What compelled me to be so involved with her?* He and Simone had only occasionally conversed over the decades. He rarely showed himself or intruded. But with Edith . . . everything was different.

Noah lifted his head and let the water drag down his face. "It has to stop." Maybe he'd go sit in the old tree with Toby or squirrel away in the barn and never show himself. But he knew if he stayed close enough, he'd give into seeing and speaking with Edith. He didn't seem to have any willpower around her.

"Where do I go?"

His afterlife had chained him to the house. He could go only a few miles away and then for only a short time before the pull overpowered him. He always ended up right back here, snapped into place like a rubber band. His options were limited. He glanced back over his shoulder. "Which was never a problem until now."

Turning away, he rubbed a hand over his wet face. Would he be here now, like this, if Maggie had lived? He'd asked himself this question a thousand times over the years but suddenly it held so much more weight. If they had lived a long, normal life would his soul still be clinging to this house? Would it still be grappling for connection? Perhaps it wasn't her death so much as his reaction to it. What had he advised Edith recently? *You own your thoughts and actions.* After Maggie's death, he'd made all the wrong decisions. Reacted in all the wrong ways. That was what forged his path to this state and to this moment.

I created my own purgatory.

He heard Edith and Milo returning to the kitchen.

And I won't drag Edith down here with me.

Edith went to the sink to put water in the kettle for tea to accompany the cinnamon rolls. Out the misty window, she saw Noah sitting in the rain, his shoulders and head collapsed forward. Her whole body filled with an urgent ache. The way he hung his head broke her heart. She lifted a hand to knock on the window, to call him inside.

Come meet Milo. Sit at the table with us.

But, no.

That wasn't right.

That wasn't how it was supposed to be, as Milo had so bluntly pointed out. Noah wasn't supposed to be a part of her life. The thought brought angry tears to her eyes.

"Edith, you all right?" Milo asked from behind her. She startled and looked down at the water overflowing the pot.

"Yeah," she hurried to say while keeping her head turned away from him. "Just looking at this crazy rain." She fiddled with the water, needing a moment to remove the hurt from her face. She peered back out the window, fighting the urge to call out to Noah.

With strained effort, she forced herself to drop her eyes. The ache roared in protest. *Who cares if he's a ghost? Invite him in. Make it work.* She pressed her teeth together and stepped away from the sink. After a difficult breath, she said to Milo, "Do you want one or two rolls?"

Milo clicked his tongue. "Amateur. Just put the whole platter in front of me, please."

Edith dutifully shook her head. "Good thing you have all those muscles to burn calories."

"Where's Noah?" Milo looked around the room and back into the hall.

Edith stiffened, turned away again to go to the plate cupboard. "He probably went out to the barn. Don't worry—I'll talk to him later. But let's eat and catch up."

"Sounds good to me. We need a strategy for this ambush dinner. There's something I need to tell you and Dad."

"What?" Edith looked at him as he shifted uncomfortably in his chair. She felt a pulse of instinct. "Don't tell me you proposed to Faye already?"

Milo snorted. "No! No way."

Edith waited a beat for him to expound. "Well, what then? Tell me now."

Milo shook his head, serious. "No, I think it'll be better if we wait."

"Really?" A sense of unease crept into her heart.

"Yeah. Sorry." Milo's expression had her stomach twisting into a knot.

It's something serious. What is it?

This day is not going as I planned.

"Are you okay?" she asked.

"Of course, yeah. It's not me."

"I don't like this."

"Please, just trust me," Milo said, reaching for a roll. "It'll be better to tell you when we are with Dad.

She let out an abrupt sigh. "Fine."

Edith turned away from Milo and grabbed the plates. On her way back to the table, she paused at the sink, leaned forward, and looked out the window.

The porch stood empty; Edith shivered.

Twelve

NOAH SAT HUNCHED in the attic of David Daniels's garage. It was the only place he could think of to get away from Edith and out of the rain. She wouldn't think to look for him here, and he couldn't take the rain beating down on him for one more second. So, he sat on the dusty floor between several moldy, forgotten boxes. Leaning against the rough wall, feet planted on the floor in front of him, he let his wrists hang over his knees and closed his eyes.

He counted his breaths. Those fake breaths he didn't actually need but his spirit still performed out of habit. He missed actual air moving in and out of real lungs. He missed the beating of his heart. He missed Edith. And it'd only been an hour.

Good grief, how am I going to do this?

The idea of sitting here avoiding her and not helping on the farm felt worse than being dead. It felt suffocating, like being buried alive.

Stop it! How can that be right? You're fine without her. Have been for decades.

Noah froze at the sound of footsteps on the stairs. He allowed himself to fade out of view. Cori's wild hair popped up above the floor. She looked around. "I know you're here, so you can give up the disappearing act."

Noah sighed and allowed her to see him. He greeted her with a deep, disapproving frown.

"What the heck are *you* doing in here?" she asked. "And why is this wave of sorrow pulsing off of you so loud I heard it in the kitchen of the house across the yard?"

"None of your business," he growled. When she smiled, his anger only sparked. "What are you grinning at like an idiot?"

Cori laughed as she finished coming up into the small space under the eaves. "She was right about your voice *and* your temper. Learn some manners, Noah Winters! You're the one squatting in *my* attic."

"It's David's attic."

"What happened?" Cori asked, ignoring that detail.

Noah kept his mouth shut and looked away. Cori advanced across the floor and sat on an old, up-turned five-gallon bucket. She didn't say anything for so long that Noah started to feel uncomfortable. "What are you doing?" he snapped.

"Listening to your pain. It's so loud, like it's screaming, man." She passed him an empathetic smile. "I'm Cori, by the way."

"I know."

"Yeah, but we've never been properly introduced. Nice to meet you, Noah Winters. I'm Coriander Keddington." She dipped her head.

"That's a mouthful."

She shrugged. "My mom was a vegan chef and a bit of a mystic. She taught me a few things about ghosts. So," she folded her hands, "how did you die, Noah Winters?"

He pressed his teeth together, debating whether to just disappear. But the idea of going back out in the rain disgusted him more than listening to Cori. "Why should I tell you?"

"I'm curious. Come on, indulge me. Looks like you got nothing better to do."

He shook his head. He hadn't thought about the actual moment of his death in a long time. It startled him how quickly and vividly the details came back. "It was an accident," he started, voice low. "I was plowing the backfields in the early spring. The weather had been bad for weeks, and I was behind on my work. One morning the rain held back, so I went out. It was too muddy, but I did it anyway. The tractor got stuck, mud more than halfway up the wheels. The moldboard was only just sticking out of the ground."

"Moldboard?" Cori interrupted.

"The plow attachment." Noah furrowed his brow, seeing the scene before him. "I went to try to unhitch the moldboard. I slipped in the mud." His hand came automatically to his forehead. "I hit one of the blades. Right here. I can still feel how it sliced into my head." He closed his eyes, a shiver moving up his spine. When he opened his eyes again, he added, "Next thing I knew, I was standing over my own body. Same clothes, same body, only *not* the same. I watched myself bleed out. I sat there with my body for three days before someone came. I missed too many calls from my editor, and he sent the police to the house."

Cori blinked, her eyes misty. "I'm sorry."

"No need to be sorry. It was an accident."

"You died alone."

He flinched. "Everyone dies alone."

"Cynical, aren't you?"

"Can you leave me alone now?"

"Not yet." She leaned forward a little. "Why do you think you're still here?"

Noah shook his head. "Cruel twist of fate? I don't know."

"I do."

Noah leveled his dubious gaze on Cori. "What are you talking about?"

"You're still here because your soul is unfulfilled. It didn't get what it needed when you were alive, so here it is—still trying."

"That's ridiculous."

"No, it's not and you know it." Cori lowered her voice. "And now there is Edith."

Noah gave her another hard look. "And now there is Edith," he echoed, knowing Cori was right. Too right.

Cori nodded sagely. "I gotta go make dinner." She stood, brushed away the dust from her pants. Noah watched with narrowed eyes as she walked to the steps. She turned back. "Just remember that Edith has a soul that's seeking things too. Be careful that your broken soul doesn't destroy hers." She took the steps, her footfalls quiet.

Noah stared, unblinking and utterly wasted, at the empty space she left behind.

"This is too weird. This can't be real. Pinch me, Edie." Milo held out his arm, shoving into Edith's face. She pushed it away.

"Stop being so dramatic, Milo. It's just dinner."

"With Dad and his *girlfriend.* Did you hear that? Our dad has a *girlfriend.*" He dragged out the word in a teasing tone.

"I know! It's not new to me."

"But you got to admit it's still weird."

Edith looked up at their boring family house. "Yeah, it's still weird. But Cori is awesome. Let's go." Edith moved forward but paused when she noticed Milo hadn't followed.

"What is it?" His face was solemn, gaze looking at the driveway.

"Do you remember the night Mom left?"

Edith briefly closed her eyes. "Yes, of course." She stepped back to him and folded her arms.

"I haven't thought about that in a long time. But lately . . . and now, standing here . . . do you ever picture her walking out to the car? You know, getting in and *actually* driving away? We always talk about the bigness of her leaving, but what about all the little steps that got her there? Or rather, that pulled her away."

Edith closed her eyes. "I know what you mean. I try to imagine what she was thinking and feeling, but it never makes sense. I imagine her stopping at the car, looking back over her shoulder. Reconsidering. I imagine her driving away and needing to stop for gas or food. What did she think then? Sitting in some café eating a hamburger. Did she think about how you love hamburgers? Or how I don't like ketchup on mine, only mustard? Or did she remember that time Dad had a five-minute debate with the waitress at Babe's about how Dr. Pepper and Mr. Pibb are *not* the same thing? Edith shook her head, pressing her teeth together to stop the painful words. Then, quietly, "How did she unravel her life from ours?"

Milo took a breath, nodded. "She brought home *Trouble*, the game, that night. I was so excited because Tim Gerard had *Trouble* and we played it all the time at his house. I think we played it until we broke the popper thing." He smiled, folded his arms. "We played with Mom and ate Twizzlers. She kept saying, 'It's *Trouble* and Twizzler night.'" Milo's jaw flexed as he swallowed. "Like it was the coolest thing in the world."

"We played past bedtime." Edith allowed his sadness and her own to pulse through her.

He nodded. "We felt so cool and so"—Milo huffed out a breath, shifted his weight—"loved. How could she do that one minute and abandon us the next?"

"I've given up trying to understand it."

"No, you haven't. None of us have. We will always wonder. Keep that in mind, Edith."

Edith fought the knot in her throat. "Why? What's going on, Milo?"

Milo shook his head. "After we eat. I promise I'll tell you everything."

Edith let out a frustrated breath. "Fine. We better go in."

Milo sighed. "Yeah, yeah." His expression cleared. "Let's step into this alternate reality."

Edith knocked on the door. "Prepare yourself."

"What—" Milo began to ask, but the door flew open. Cori stood there grinning from ear to ear, in hot pink jeans and a turquoise blue sweater with little white pom-poms. "Holy cow! You're huge!" she exclaimed, eyeing Milo. Then she rushed at him and threw her arms around his neck. Edith brought her hand to her mouth to stop a laugh. Milo gave her a look of pure confusion. He'd probably been less scared with three-hundred-pound linebackers running at him.

Cori pulled back. "Look at these football muscles." She kneaded his biceps. "Normal people just don't have muscles like this. Milo, you are not normal."

Milo smiled awkwardly, "Uh . . . thanks?"

Cori laughed, playfully smacking his arm. "Nice to meet you."

Milo nodded, still smiling like an idiot.

Edith resisted another laugh. "Hey, Cori," Edith said.

"Hey, girl. You guys come in." Cori shut the door behind them. "Throw your coats on the couch and grab a mug. There's coffee. David went to get some more beer—Milo, he

146

thought you guys could watch the game together after dinner—but he's not back yet."

"Which game?" Milo asked.

Cori shrugged. "Who knows? I just know he made a big deal of getting the right beer."

Edith watched Milo's face as he took in the room. She knew exactly what he was thinking and feeling as his gaze moved over the corner fireplace and olive carpet. It'd been just as long for him since being back home. She let her eyes rest on the coffee table, the sound of the *Trouble* bubble echoing in her head. Milo caught her eyes, and she was certain he heard the same echo.

"Have a seat, Milo," Cori directed. "Edith, come help me with this."

Edith followed Cori. The kitchen smelled of beef stew and fresh bread. "Smells amazing. What can I help with?"

Cori tugged Edith's arm and brought her face close to hers. "What happened with Noah?"

Edith blinked. "What?"

"I talked to Noah. He was extra cranky."

Edith winced. "You saw him? Where?"

Cori released her arm. "I think he's hiding out. Did you guys fight or something?"

"Something. Definitely something."

Cori searched Edith's face with her knowing gaze. "I see. Interesting."

"No, *not* interesting. Confusing. So dang confusing I think my head is going to explode."

"Tell me more."

Edith looked back over her shoulder at Milo. "Later, okay?"

"Okay. I get it." Cori moved to stir the stew. "Oh, before I forget—will you make me some cute little centerpieces for the shop tables for the day of the Bell Festival? Is it too late to ask that?"

"No, of course not. I'd love to!"

"Just simple and festive. I usually buy a bunch of daises and split them between the tables, but Christmas Eve calls for something special. And since you are the expert . . ."

"I'm all over it. That'll be fun."

Both women turned at the sound of the front door. "Found it!" David announced as he hurried into the house. Cori gave Edith a *we'll continue this later* look. David stopped at the table. "Hey, Milo. How are you?"

The women watched carefully as the men said their hellos. Edith noticed the stiffness in Milo's shoulders and the tense way David shifted the beers to his other hand. "Hey, Dad," Milo answered plainly.

"I got that fancy beer you like." He lifted the two six packs like trophies. Milo's eyes moved quickly to Edith. She gave him an admonishing look.

"That's awesome. Thanks," he said.

"I've got the Trail Blazers game recording. We can watch it, if you want?"

"Yeah, sure. That'd be great."

David nodded. He adjusted the beers again. "I know it's not football but—"

"I like basketball too."

Cori leaned close to Edith's ear. "Well, aren't they adorable?"

Edith laughed and the men turned. "What?" Milo asked. He looked between them and frowned. " *What?*"

"Oh, nothing," Cori chimed. "Let's eat!"

It took the conversation a while to get going. Milo and David chugged along, trying to break down the barriers of the years. Finally, they sat around empty bowls and bread crumbs.

Milo had made them all laugh, telling stories of his teammates' bizarre pre-game rituals.

"I kid you not, this guy, this *massive*, tough guy, has like ten crystals hanging in his locker. For good luck." They all laughed, and Milo added, "He carefully wipes them off once a week so the energy doesn't get blocked." He rolled his eyes and joined the group laughing.

"I've heard of guys wearing the same underwear," David said, "but never crystals." He laughed freely; something Edith couldn't remember seeing him do in a long time.

"Well, Chris is his own man," Milo concluded.

Edith took a sip of her water, looking between her father and brother. *This is good. This is nice.* She smiled to herself. *Also, weird. So weird, sitting here laughing.*

Cori put her napkin next to her plate. "Who's ready for dessert? I got hot apple pie."

Edith set down her cup. "I can help."

"No, no. Sit. I got it."

Edith turned to Milo. "Okay, I can't wait anymore. What did you want to tell us?"

Milo's face went flat. "Oh, yeah. I uh . . . yeah, I guess I better. Sad to ruin this nice mood though."

Edith's stomach twisted. "Is it that bad?"

"Is something wrong?" David asked, leaning his forearms onto the table.

"Not really wrong . . ." Milo sat back in his chair and folded his arms.

Edith did not like the seriousness on his face. Cori came back to the table. "Uh oh. What's wrong?"

"Milo's going to tell us something," David said, voice anxious.

Cori looked at Milo. After a moment, her eyebrows lifted. "Out with it then," she directed quietly.

Milo took a deep breath. "About a week after Edie left New York I got a letter at the stadium. Had my name on it, but it was addressed to the stadium. A little weird, but I just figured it was a fan letter or something." He adjusted his arms, still avoiding everyone's apprehensive gazes. "But it wasn't. The letter was from a man who claimed he was married to . . . Phoebe Kendrick, also known as Phoebe Daniels."

Milo's eyes shifted to Edith. Her whole body went stiff as stone. She blinked at her brother and then looked at her father whose face was pale as paper. Cori reached for David's hand.

"She went back to her maiden name," David said absently.

"Wait—married?" Edith asked. "Dad, are you and Mom still officially married?"

David shook his head, eyes on the table. "No. I finally took care of that about three years ago. I thought . . ." He shook his head again.

Milo hurried on. "Well, this guy didn't say much in the letter except that his wife"—Milo's jaw tightened—"was very sick, and he was contacting me without her knowledge. He left a phone number to call, in case I was the right Milo Daniels and wanted to talk."

"Did you call?" Cori asked. Edith was grateful she did; it was what she wanted to ask but couldn't find her voice.

Milo nodded. "Took me about a week to talk myself into it. His name is Don and he's been married to Phoebe—to Mom—for four years. They met in New Mexico, Santa Fe. Mom had a small boutique in the main plaza there. He wandered in one day."

"She left us to open a *shop*?" Edith spat out before she could stop herself.

"Let him finish, Edith," Cori said gently.

Edith closed her eyes and took a slow breath. *A shop? I expected . . . what did I expect? What's a good enough reason to leave your family?* She looked over at Milo and read the same questions in his eyes.

"They live there still, in Santa Fe," Milo continued. "And about a year ago Mom got sick. It's cancer. A brain tumor. Don said that a couple of months ago, while she was deep into chemo and pain meds, she started talking about her family. Her children." Milo took a breath. "She'd never told him about us. He didn't know."

Edith slumped in her chair. She wanted to leave, to run out and find Noah. She shook the impulse away. "Milo, why didn't you tell me sooner?"

"You've been dealing with all this stuff here, and, at first, I didn't even know if it was legit, if it really was *our* Phoebe. But Don found a picture hidden in her things and emailed it to me. It's the one of me and you that Halloween we went as Dorothy and the Scarecrow. Remember?"

Edith nodded slowly. Of course she did. Mom had taught her to sew while making the costumes. Her gaze moved to her father. He'd barely moved. "Dad, you okay?"

He swallowed hard, blinked a few times, and then cleared his throat. "Is she going to survive?"

Milo's shoulders sunk. "No, it's terminal. Maybe six months."

The room went silent. Cori stroked David's arm. Edith stared at her empty bowl, feeling numb. Unsure what to think or say or do. Finally, her anger pushed through. "Are we supposed to flock to her death bed and offer our forgiveness?"

"Edith—" Cori tried.

"Is that what she expects us to do?" Edith pushed on.

"I don't think she expects anything," Milo answered, the

same bitterness in his tone. "It's all coming from Don. I'm not sure she's even able to remember a lot anymore. But yes, he asked if we'd come see her before she dies."

"I'm not going. I can't do that." Edith felt the tears coming and hated them.

"You don't have to," David said firmly. Everyone turned to him. He looked ten years older, his face suddenly sallow. "But there's something you should know before you decide." He took a long breath. "Phoebe didn't just leave on a whim. I asked her to go."

"What?" Edith and Milo said together.

"Edith, do you remember when Mom had that surgery right after Milo was born?"

"Yeah, a little." Edith had a memory of her mother lying in bed, a cold cloth over her eyes.

"She had her gallbladder removed and they gave her some strong pain meds. She was hurting and tired and trying to deal with a newborn. She relied on those pills and then when she tried to go off them, she couldn't. She tried for years, back and forth. Doing well and then relapsing. Each relapse made it a little worse. She hid it pretty well from you kids and everyone on the island, but the night she left . . ." David rubbed a hand over his face.

"The *Trouble* and Twizzler night?" Milo asked, voice thin.

David nodded. "After you guys went to bed, she took a pill. A few, I think. I found her around three a.m. standing over Milo's bed." David swallowed hard, his face filled with pain. "She had . . . a pillow in her hands." He lifted his hands to demonstrate, his fingers trembling. "I asked her what she was doing, and she said she had to save you"— David's gaze went to his son—"from the world. From being sad and lonely and broken."

Edith reached out for Milo, fumbling to take his hand in hers. She wanted to throw up. "She was going to . . ."

David sighed, shook his head. "I don't think so, but it looked like it. It was the *idea* that that was my first thought that scared me the most. That she'd gotten so bad that I worried my wife would hurt our kids." A shaky breath. "So . . . I told her to leave. I told her that she could not be around you kids until she got clean."

"Did she go into rehab?" Milo asked.

"I don't know. I sent her with the address of a good one I'd been saving for the right moment. She said she would go, but when I called a few days later they had never heard of her. I waited for her to call to tell me where she was and what she was doing, but she never did. I actually thought . . ." He closed his eyes, shook his head. "I thought she probably overdosed and died or committed suicide."

"Why didn't you tell us?" Edith asked, her emotions warring in all directions. She felt unsteady, her whole body quaking.

"How do you explain that to a kid?" He shook his head again.

"I wasn't a kid, Dad. I was eighteen!"

David flinched. "I'm sorry. I didn't know what to do. It seemed simpler to let you think she'd just decided to go."

Edith scoffed. "It would have been better to know she was sick and *couldn't* be our mom than to spend all these years thinking that she didn't want us." She looked to Milo, who nodded his agreement.

"But would it, really?" Cori asked. "Either she left to pursue something else or she left because of her addiction. The reason she left doesn't really change the outcome or the hurt. She still never came back."

Edith opened her mouth to protest but realized Cori was

right. Milo said, "But knowing it was addiction does help soften my anger, my judgment. That kind of thing screws with everything in your life."

"But why didn't she get help and come back to us?" Edith asked.

David shook his head. "It broke my heart," he mumbled. "I was so angry at her for not being stronger, not doing better. I waited so long for her to come home. So long . . . I really thought she must be dead." He took a long breath. "That's why I've always been so proud of you both: for your strength." He looked between Edith and Milo. "I think I will go see her, but you don't need to." He turned to Cori and she nodded, supportive.

Edith turned to Milo. "Do you . . ."

He shook his head. "I don't know. I can't decide." He squeezed her hand, which was still locked in his.

Edith felt the dam of her chest might burst open and spill out the confused contents of her heart. Her mother was alive but dying. Her mother had been an addict and could have come back but didn't. Her mother had never told her new husband about her first family.

But she kept our picture.

What for? Out of love or guilt?

The words from that hasty note pinned to the fridge echoed in her head. *You'll be better off without me.*

The mantel clock struck nine. The time Edith usually cuddled up on the couch with Noah and *Star Trek.* She craved the simplicity of that right now. She wanted the normalcy of how it'd been until today, just her and her ghost enjoying each other's company. What would Noah advise her to do? She desperately wanted his advice.

"I need to go." She tossed her napkin on the table.

"Don't run away, Edie," Milo begged tenderly.

"I'm not. I just have to think. This is . . . so much." She stood. "Thanks for dinner, Cori. I'll see you tomorrow, okay?"

"Yeah, sweetie. Good night."

"Milo, stay as long as you want," Edith offered. "I'll see you at home."

Milo nodded. "We'll talk later."

Edith grabbed her coat and hurried outside. She took a big gulp of the cold air and blinked back tears. She jogged back through the yards and burst into her house. "Noah? Where are you?" She went into the living room and stared at the empty couch. "Noah? Come on, *please!* Don't hide. Not now. Noah?"

Her eyes moved over the glowing Christmas tree. She sank to the couch, her coat and scarf still on. "Noah? *Please!* I need . . ." Edith's throat grew tight, her jaw clenched. Her head throbbed. She collapsed onto her side and let the sobs escape.

Thirteen

NOAH STOOD AT the living room window looking in at Edith as she cried. It felt so wrong to see her lying there suffering surrounded by all her Christmas cheer. He'd listened to the family's conversation and felt Edith's pain deep in his own chest. He hadn't known about Phoebe's addiction. David shouldn't have waited so long to tell Milo and Edith, but Noah couldn't really fault him. What an impossible situation.

It took everything inside Noah not to go to Edith when she had called out to him, when she had begged him. The plea in her voice ruined him, but he worried that going to her now would ruin them both even more. He couldn't be the one to further damage Edith's gentle soul; it'd been through enough. And the craving she'd ignited in him earlier had yet to fully fade. He worried he couldn't trust himself around her.

Not yet. Maybe not ever again.

He still wasn't sure what to do but knew he needed some distance in order to figure it out. He shouldn't even be here now, peering in her window. He touched the glass. "Forgive me, Edith."

Edith fell asleep, tucked onto her side on the couch, her face wet with tears. She startled awake when the front door opened and shut. She pushed herself up, desperately hoping to see Noah there. Instead, it was Milo, his head hung low. Edith glanced back at the mantel clock. "You stayed a long time," she mumbled.

He sat down next to her and released a long sigh. "We watched the game and drank that weird beer. Why did Dad think that was my beer?" Milo shrugged. "Anyway, we had a good talk while we watched. He opened up more about Mom's struggle and how hard it was for him." Milo shook his head. "It's not fair; she was just taking medicine to get better and then . . ."

"I know," she managed.

He turned to her, eyes sincere. "I think I'm going to go and . . . I think you should too. I want us to go together."

She started to shake her head. "I don't—"

"Please think about it. I think it would help bring us closer together—you, me, Dad. It wouldn't really be for her. It'd be for us. You started bringing us back together when you moved here, and this feels like another big step. I realized tonight that I miss my dad."

Edith closed her eyes. She rubbed at her forehead, a throbbing headache deep behind her skull. "I don't like it when you're deep and serious and right. I like it when you act like an idiot." She opened her eyes.

Milo smiled. "Plenty of time for that, sis. Want me to sing to you now? 'Santa Claus is Coming to Town' or 'Please Daddy Don't Get Drunk This Christmas'? That one kind of fits the mood. Good old John Denver, dragging everyone into a depression with a Christmas song."

Edith half-laughed. She could still see the question in Milo's eyes; he was waiting for a real answer. Normally, she did anything and everything for him but this . . . "I need some time to think about it. Okay?"

"Absolutely. But remember: She's dying."

"Nice, Milo."

"Just stating a fact."

Edith shook her head. "It's so weird."

"I know."

"I'm sorry you carried that on your own for so long. Sorry I was so wrapped up in all this"—she gestured loosely to the room—"that you didn't feel like you could talk to me about it."

"It's okay. I am an adult. Do I really have to keep reminding you of that?"

"Adults still need people to talk to." She thought of Noah and her pathetic calls to him earlier. She took a breath. *Maybe it's for the best if he stays away.*

Milo matched her slow breath. "So, Netflix time? What show can we escape into?"

"I have *While You Were Sleeping* in my list."

Milo rolled his eyes. "Okay, fine. But only because Sandra Bullock is hot."

"Don't pretend to be all tough and manly. Everyone loves that movie."

"You're so deluded, my friend."

Edith gave him a playful shove and then reached for the remote.

Fourteen

EDITH WOKE BEFORE dawn Christmas Eve morning. She blinked at the gray darkness and rolled over to her back. Staring at the ceiling, she listened to the early silence.

For the first time, she was completely alone in the house.

She'd dropped Milo at the airport last night; he had to get back to New York for his Christmas Day game. She missed him already. She missed the familiarity of having him in the house, the comfort of his goofiness, and the space he filled that Noah had left empty.

Noah had been gone for four days.

Edith didn't understand it, and the speculation was killing her.

Is it my fault? That moment in the kitchen—did it ruin everything?

Is he hiding from me?

Did he cross over? Is he gone forever?

I didn't get to say good-bye.

Lost in the carousel-spin of questions, she didn't notice the first birdsong or the sun filling the room. The buzz of her phone finally brought her focus back. She rolled over to answer it. "Cori, hey."

"Hey, girl. Sorry to bug you so early. One of my baristas just called—her kid has strep throat. I told her to stay home, but we have the Bell Festival today. And since you're already coming with the centerpieces I thought—"

"I'll help. Give me ten minutes to get dressed."

"Thank you! You're the best."

Edith jumped out of bed. "Don't thank me yet. I'm not a barista."

"You can bus tables or restock pastries. I just need hands!"

Edith laughed. "I'll be right there."

Twenty minutes later, Edith accepted an apron from Cori. "What's first?" she asked. They stood in the back of the shop, next to the one long stainless-steel table stacked with boxes of pastries and bags of espresso beans. Everything was meticulously organized and clean. Edith could see the corporate side of Cori coming out in this space.

"We open in a half hour. People will be pouring in for hot drinks before they head over to the town square for the bell ringing. Wait—you grew up here. You know this!"

Edith laughed. "I've always loved the Bell Festival. Best Autumn Island event."

"I agree; this one really is magical." Cori gave her a dreamy smile. "Okay! So . . . I haven't finished the bell display in the front window. You're creative—can you handle that?"

"I'd love to!"

"Great. Put out these fabulous centerpieces you made—love them, by the way. Rosemary and cinnamon. So brilliant and so perfect."

"Thanks."

"And finish that window."

"Got it!"

"Go forth!" Cori smiled and pointed to the door through to the main shop area.

Edith lifted the box of centerpieces and serpentined her

way through the regular employees, busy behind the counter doing prep work. She smiled to herself, soaking in the energy of the morning. She hadn't been to a Bell Festival in years. The Daniels family had always gone to the festival, even after Phoebe left. Each festival was a solid point in her timeline of memories. Every year on Christmas Eve, they walked down to the town square, which was decorated with several live Christmas trees and packed with people. At exactly eight in the morning the whole town rang small silver bells. A tradition that heralded back to the earliest days of the island when the sailors would ring bells as they pulled into the harbor, signaling their safe return. The sound of the bells meant coming home.

After the bell ringing, there were booths of homemade items for last-minute gifts, breakfast foods, and kid crafts. A band played while people danced to keep warm. And then around lunchtime everyone went home to be with family.

Edith set the box on the nearest table. She really wished Milo could have stayed to go with her, Cori, and David.

She looked down into the box of centerpieces and realized with a jolt that this was her first real flower job. It had felt like a favor to Cori, but really it was a job. Cori had ordered and paid for sweet little centerpieces for all the tables in her shop. Edith let out a little laugh. "My first job!" Another thrill moved through her.

Edith lifted the first one out and took it to sit next to the register. "Cute!" one of the busy baristas said in passing. Edith had taken live sprigs of rosemary from her yard—*thank you, Simone*—and cinnamon sticks, tied them together with twine and a small silver jingle bell. Each bundle sat in a small eight-ounce quilted Mason jar. Simple and perfect.

She hurried around the room, placing them all, smiling

the whole time. The little touch of nature made all the difference in the space.

This is what I love: adding life to things.

She turned her attention to the window.

Cori had started to hang tiny silver bells, dozens of them, from the top of the window. Each bell hung from an emerald green satin ribbon, all different lengths. Only half the window was finished. Edith set to work stringing and hanging.

She finished in ten minutes. The morning sun reflected off the bells, sending flashes of light around the room, and the breeze from the heater had them swaying just enough to give off a tiny tinkling. "Gorgeous!" she whispered.

Cori came rushing out. "Okay, people. Here we go! Let's caffeinate the masses and then go ring some bells."

Noah paced the cramped space of the garage attic. He resisted the urge to pick up a box and heave it at the wall. A fiery irritation itched under his skin. He'd spent the last four days holed up in this wretched place and was ready to explode. He wanted to walk the fields, work on the chicken coop, and stand under the stars. But mostly, he wanted to sit next to Edith on the green couch.

I want to spend Christmas with her.

He groaned. "Stop it, stop it, *stop it.*"

His willpower failed. He picked up the bucket Cori had sat on a few days ago and hurled it against the wall. It made a half-satisfying twang and *thunked* to the floor. He didn't feel better.

"Maybe going cold turkey isn't a good idea." Noah knew that the Bell Festival would start soon. He'd been to every single one since he was born. He'd gone every year after his death too, hiding and observing. It was the only social event he enjoyed. He admired how it honored the island's past and captured the spirit of the season. He wasn't so ornery that he didn't appreciate holidays.

This year Edith would be there.

"Don't go, don't go, *don't go.*"

He stopped pacing.

"Forget this. I'm going."

Noah promised himself he'd stay unseen and far away from Edith. But he had to get out of this stale attic. He went down the ladder and out the side door, which David always left unlocked. Walking in the fresh, cold air eased his irritation. He relaxed his shoulders and turned his face to the sun.

The sound of the happy commotion hit him first, then the smell of pine and baked goods. He went down Main Street, following the crowd. He passed the bookshop, a once favorite place, and Cori's colorful coffee shop. A line snaked out the door. He entered the town square. Children ran and chased each other, ringing their bells.

The Christmas before their wedding, Maggie had had special bells made, engraved with their names. Those bells had sat on his mantel for ages, a constant reminder of what should have been. As he ducked behind a large Christmas tree, he thought of them now tucked under a floorboard in the master bedroom. Those bells were the only things he'd saved before they cleared out his house. That and his last, unfinished manuscript. It sat under the bells, wrapped in twine.

His eyes swept the immaculately decorated square. There were at least a dozen trees, ornamented to the max by different organizations on the island. Garlands of pine boughs, ribbon, and bells framed the air, strung from the tall black lampposts. He drank in the festive energy.

His gaze snagged on Edith, standing on the opposite side with Cori and David; they each had their hands wrapped around a coffee cup. His chest constricted with a deep pulse of pleasure at the sight of Edith standing in the sun in her red coat, a green scarf, and her cheeks flushed pink from the cold. Her elegance stood out in the crowd, the beauty all around paling in his eyes.

Does she miss me?

His selfish soul wanted her to miss him, but his practical brain prayed that she didn't. He hoped she was better at letting go than him.

The square was now bursting at the seams with coat-clad townspeople. The mayor, a classy woman in her early sixties, stepped to a small stage fitted with a single microphone and welcomed the crowd. She started a speech about tradition and all the things the bells represented for the island. But Noah couldn't focus on her words; Edith pulled at all his attention.

He wanted to move closer, but forced himself to stay on the opposite side of the square.

The mayor cued everyone to get the bells ready.

On her count, the bells rang out, filling the air.

Edith's eyes cut through the maze of people and halted on Noah.

No, no, she can't see me.

But she did, and immediately charged forward, pushing through the crowd toward him. He froze. Bells rang all around them, deafening. Noah kept his eyes on Edith. Her mouth moved, calling his name, but he couldn't separate her voice from the din. Though he couldn't hear her, he *felt* her call, a deep prick in his heart.

His body shook with the need to go to her, to meet her in

the center of the square. To pull her into his arms and apologize for leaving. To kiss her as the bells rang.

She was only about six feet away now, her expression so desperate. The bells stopped ringing and loud cheers took their place. She plowed through a rowdy family, her gaze moving off his for a moment while she avoided a toddler at her feet.

Noah slipped away, breaking her heart and his own.

Edith burst through the crowd into the open space where she'd seen Noah standing. But he wasn't there. Breathless, she snapped her head from side to side, searching. She circled the tree, twice.

Did I imagine him? Have I missed him so much that now I'm hallucinating?

She turned and looked again. Her heart pounded.

"Edith! What the heck are you doing?" Cori emerged from the sea of people, stumbling into place next to Edith.

"I saw him!"

"Who? Noah?" Cori looked around too. "I don't see him."

"He was here. I saw him. He was right here and now . . ."

Cori reached for Edith's arm. "Oh, honey."

Edith turned to her, something in Cori's tone pulling on her full attention. "What is it?"

She sighed. "Noah asked me not to say anything, but I can't watch you worry like this."

"You talked to him?"

"Yeah. He's staying away. He's worried you guys have gotten too close. He's trying not to hurt you."

Edith dropped her gaze to her gloved hands. She fingered her empty coffee cup in one, her bell in the other. She hadn't rung it; she'd just been lifting it when she saw Noah across the square. "He's staying away on purpose," she said slowly, allowing the words to sink in. "But then why was he here?"

"I don't know. Are you sure you saw him?"

"Yes . . ."

Cori frowned. "He's staying away because he cares for you."

"It doesn't feel that way."

"I know. I'm sorry. But don't you think it's best?" Cori gave her arm a little squeeze.

Edith fought with her emotions. It didn't feel right, not at all. But she knew it was. "I know. I know."

Cori nodded, her expression sweet with empathy. "You need to let him go, for both your sakes."

"I . . . miss him. Is that weird?"

"No, of course not." Cori rubbed her arm. "Come on, let's get one of those giant donuts. A little sugar to feed the emotions—sound good?"

Edith nodded automatically. As Cori turned away to lead them through the chaos, Edith took one last look around. Her heart dropped when Noah still wasn't there.

Fine. Stay away.

But don't let me see you.

Stay far, far away, Noah Winters.

Edith felt Cori stiffen beside her but was only half aware. "Paula, now is *not* the time," Cori said, her voice flat and hard. So unlike Cori. That got Edith's attention; she stopped scanning the crowd and turned. Paula Grant, owner of Better Blooms, stood with her fists dug into her ample hips, elbows out in defensive angles. Her round face was twisted into a scowl, and her pale pink puffy coat did nothing to flatter her figure.

"Paula?" Edith asked, still a little dazed.

Paula didn't look at Edith. She spoke to Cori. "Should I cancel your daisy order? I saw that *someone else* provided your centerpieces this morning."

Cori scoffed. "Edith is David's daughter. So *yes*, of course, I'm going to get my flowers from her now. Please don't make it a big deal."

Paula's scowl deepened. Edith's heart pounded uncomfortably. "Paula, I—"

Paula lifted a gloved hand, palm out. "I don't want to talk to you."

"Please, don't treat Edith that way, Paula," Cori said sternly. "She's just building her life. It has *nothing* to do with you. There's plenty of business to go around."

Paula shook her head and then turned promptly on her heel and disappeared into the crowd. Edith and Cori stood, rocking in the woman's hateful wake. "I can't believe she did that," Cori finally said. "What a—" She looked at Edith. "Don't listen to her! She's just angry and doesn't know how to act."

Edith felt nauseous. She felt beaten to a pulp. "I'm going home," she mumbled.

"Oh, no! Don't let this ruin the festival for you. Stay. We can spend too much money on homemade lotions and bath bombs."

Edith shook her head. All she wanted was the safety of the green couch. She never imagined Paula would lash out like that. She'd never had someone be so hateful to her. All she wanted to do was hide. Edith pulled away from Cori. "I can't. Sorry."

Pushing her way through the crowd, she ran to her car,

hardly able to catch her breath. She drove home with the awful scene on repeat in her mind. *I don't want to talk to you.* How could Paula hate her so much?

"I'll never be able to go into town again," Edith whispered. She slowed the car to a stop at the entrance of her driveway. A brand new sign had been installed a week ago. A large barn wood plaque with iron letters stained blue around the edges. Blue Farmhouse Flowers. The sign shop had etched her logo of a little blue farmhouse and one white peony in the corner. The sign was amazing, but looking at it now only made Edith feel exhausted.

She continued down the drive.

Once in the house, she flopped onto the couch, face down in one of the red plaid pillows. *I don't want to talk to you.* And that look on Paula's face—the woman looked ready to rip out all of Edith's hair. When Milo told her to fight for her flowers, she never imagined an *actual* fight. Edith squirmed as the moment replayed in her mind. She dreaded confrontation and had worked hard most her life to avoid it. It made her feel small and heavy with shame. She knew she'd done nothing wrong and Paula was one hundred percent out of line.

A noise made her lift her head and push away from the pillow. She looked over the back of the couch. The front door stood ajar, a breeze pushing it open more. Edith froze. *Did I leave it open?* She couldn't remember. It was possible or . . . "Noah? Is that you?" Silence answered. "I saw you in the square and Cori told me you're trying to stay away." Edith got off the couch. "Please don't," she added in a quieter voice. When still no answer came she went to the door and closed it. She let her forehead fall to the wood. "I need you to tell me I'm not pathetic and that Paula Grant is the worse person on the planet. I need you to swear at her and make me feel better.

Because she was so awful to me just now." Edith's stomach turned. "So awful."

She was certain she felt Noah nearby. Maybe she was only imagining, hoping.

"Are you there?"

Stop talking to the ghost.

Another rush of shame punched her in the gut.

You can't want the friendship of a ghost. Stop it.

Edith pushed away from the door. She decided to distract herself with field planning. Grid paper and a calculator sounded good right now. And hot chocolate with a candy cane stirred in. Lots of it.

Noah hovered at the top of the stairs, feeling utterly wasted. He should have gone back to the attic, but when he heard her car on the drive, he had to make sure she was all right. She should still be at the festival. Had he ruined it for her?

Of course I did. I'm sorry, Edith. I'm sorry I'm so weak.

He listened to her talk to him. He breathed a sigh of relief knowing it hadn't been only him that ruined her day. He felt a hot stab of anger toward Paula Grant. *What did you do, you pompous old cow!* Noah frowned. That was exactly the kind of phrase Edith needed to hear right now, the kind she had just begged him for, and he hated that he couldn't give it to her.

"I'm so sorry, Edith."

Noah slipped down the stairs and out the front door without a sound.

PART II – HARVESTING

Early March

EDITH STOOD AT an old folding table in her greenhouse. Simone's seed box was open next to her, and several seed trays loaded with lovely dark soil were lined up, ready for planting. From Simone's box, she took the letter Simone had written her. Edith read through it with a smile, a tug of love at the sentence, *I know it'll be tough, but you'll find a way to use them.*

"I found a way, Simone," she whispered. "Now, let's get these babies growing."

Edith pulled out the packets of sweet peas, Iceland poppies, zinnias, and marigolds. She carefully labeled each tray and then, using the eraser end of a pencil, she quickly made a small hole in each section of the trays. With seeds in her palm, she used a pair of tweezers to pick up and drop the tiny seeds.

She loved the repetitive precision of it. The way her mind stayed rooted in the task and didn't drift off into the rocky territory of her emotions. As she gave the trays a mist of water, she heard thunder roll in the distance. She hurried to clean up and then ran back to the house just as the first raindrops started.

Her phone rang the moment she closed the back door behind her.

"Hey, Milo."

"Time is up, sis. You've put it off for over two months. Don says Mom is in final days. It's now or never."

Edith rubbed at her forehead. She moved to the kitchen sink to look out the window at the beginning of a serious rainstorm. Her first crop could certainly use the water, but if it got much harder she worried there'd be damage to the hoop tunnels or flooding. And now Milo was pushing her about visiting their dying mother. She said, "It makes me feel sick— the whole idea of it. And leaving now is almost impossible. The first snapdragons, daffodils, and sweet peas will be ready to harvest next week."

"Take *one* day. Fly out early, visit her, and fly back. I'll meet you there. It won't take long."

"You don't know when to quit."

"This is important. I really feel it is. Dad already went and she wants to see us."

"But she doesn't *deserve* to see us."

"That's not the point. She made mistakes, but she was your mom for eighteen years, Edie. A good mom, for the most part. That has to count for something."

Edith went to the table and collapsed into a chair. Her throat constricted with coming tears. She looked at her new cabinets, a gray-caramel finish in a Shaker style. The thin brick backsplash and the mason jar pendant lights gave the kitchen that old farmhouse feel. And the stainless-steel appliances and gorgeous white-gray granite that fresh, new feel. Simple and gorgeous. The renovation had taken only a few weeks, and she loved it. "What would I even say to her? I can't stop being mad at her."

"Say that."

"I should tell a dying woman that I'm so mad at her it makes me feel sick?"

"Yep. You need to tell her, and she needs to hear it so she can apologize. I believe the technical term for it is *closure*." He pulled the word into a long admonition.

Edith closed her eyes, rubbing at her forehead again. She'd never been this exhausted. She'd been working non-stop for ten weeks. When she wasn't building hoop tunnels or laying down landscape fabric or planting successions of seeds, she was advertising, building her social media, and accepting clients. She had her first big event—a posh baby shower on Orcas Island—in a month. And just this morning she had booked her first wedding for mid-May. Blue Farmhouse Flowers was alive and kicking; she loved every second of it. Which was why she didn't want to devote any energy to her dying mother.

But Milo was right.

How will I feel if she dies and I don't go?

She sighed. "Okay, what day can you go?"

"We're going tomorrow. I just pushed confirm on our tickets. Check your email."

"Milo!"

"Tomorrow! I don't want you to change your mind."

She heard a little smile in his voice but refused to give into his humor. "Fine! I'm hanging up 'cause I have a million things to do before the morning."

"Flight leaves at eight-thirty."

Edith groaned. "I'll have to get up at like four."

"You can do it! I'm on the red eye tonight. So, mine is worse. See you in New Mexico."

"I hate you."

"Sorry—can't hear you. You're cutting out." Milo made static noises into the phone. "I'm going into a tunnel . . ."

Edith hung up, forcing herself not to smile. She looked at the wall clock; it was a little after six in the evening. She shook her head and tossed her phone onto the table.

I wish Noah were here to help.

The weeks without him hadn't dulled her connection to him or her desire to see him. If anything, it'd grown brighter and harder to ignore. *Darn it, Noah Winters.* Her phone had landed near a copy of one of his books, the front cover curled back from reading. She'd been reading it while eating pasta for lunch. She couldn't stop reading his books. They were strewn throughout the house, one nearby at all times. She'd even bought a whole pile of new books as a distraction. But it didn't work. They sat by her bed, spines unbroken, pages unread, while Noah's paperbacks grew ragged from her obsessive reading.

Edith forcefully exhaled as she got up from the table. An entire day off the farm. She groaned. She had work to do and words to her dying mother to rehearse.

What are you doing, woman?

Noah lingered at the edge of the fields watching Edith struggle with the end of a hoop tunnel that had blown loose in the wind. Noah had learned his lesson at the Bell Festival and made sure to watch her from a spot she could not see him. He wouldn't torture them both with any more accidental sightings.

He'd watched her closely over the weeks despite knowing

that he should stay away. He couldn't help it. *You're haunting her,* he told himself over and over, but it didn't stop him from coming out of the garage attic to check on her at least once a day. Her skill with the farm amazed him. She was careful and smart, organizing her fields and greenhouse for maximum production. She'd finished work on the chicken coop herself and painted it a fresh sage green, a nice compliment to the blue. She'd planted hundreds of flowers, mostly by herself, with only the occasional help from Cori and David. And at the same time, she'd had the roof replaced, the kitchen and master bathroom remodeled, and watched every episode of *Star Trek: The Next Generation.*

Without him.

"Get inside," he hissed at her now as she struggled in the rain. "I'll fix it. Get inside before you freeze." She was upset about something; he could tell even from this distance. Something more significant than dealing with the hoop in this weather. He waited for her head to turn away and then slipped closer. Her rain boots sunk deep in the mud between the beds, and the hood of her raincoat had long been abandoned. Her hair was soaked and her cheeks were red with cold. He wanted to scoop her into his arms, carry her back to the house, and put her into a hot bath.

Noah ground his teeth together at the image.

When the wind pulled the slick plastic from her hands, Edith let out a string of words that made Noah smile. But his smile fell when he realized she was crying. His whole body clenched. Edith latched onto the plastic and finally got it to do what she wanted. She sniffed loudly and mumbled words he couldn't hear over the rush of the wind.

She snatched her tools from the mud and trudged back to the barn. He followed her, aching to help. She hurled the tools onto the workbench, swearing again as other tools crashed to the tabletop.

What's wrong, Edith?

She ran back through the yard and into the house. Noah went around the front and slipped in from the porch. He heard her muttering to herself. "You left us, and I had to change my whole life. Ugh, no."

What? Is she talking about me?

Edith threw off her rain gear. "I needed my mom. You weren't there. I had to be the mom to Milo. Dad could barely function."

She's talking about Phoebe.

Edith shook her head. She moved from the kitchen, headed to the stairs. Noah tucked himself behind the wall in the living room. He heard her foot hit the bottom step and then silence. "Noah? Are you there?"

Noah closed his eyes. *No. I'm sorry.*

"Noah?"

He clenched his teeth so hard. *Why did I come into the house?*

"If it is you"—her voice was so quiet, so desperate—"I'm leaving in the morning to go see Phoebe before she dies. Watch the fields, please." She waited a beat and then continued up the stairs.

When he heard the shower running, Noah stepped out of the living room to stand at the bottom of the steps. "My pleasure, Edith," he whispered.

The flight was delayed.

Edith rolled her eyes. *Of course it is. This is a sign I should have stayed home.*

She texted Milo: Flight delayed. Snowstorm in the Rockies.

Milo: Okay. It's not a sign.

She frowned. Why did he have to know her so well?

Edith: It so totally is a sign.

Milo: It'll be fine. Go find the airport bookstore and buy a bunch of books. That will make you feel better.

Edith: No, it won't.

But she went anyway, browsing to pass the time. She bought two novels and a cute notebook even though she had two blank ones at home. There was some comfort in holding the small stack of books. *Why is Milo always right?*

She didn't have a carry-on since it was a day trip, so she shoved the books in her already full purse and headed back to the gate. To her surprise, the delay had shortened by fifteen minutes and they were about to start boarding. Her stomach dropped.

No, this is good. Let's get this over with.

The storm made for a turbulent flight. Edith stumbled off the plane in Santa Fe worried she'd have to run straight to the bathroom.

Breathe. Deep breaths.

And French fries. Where are the closest fries?

Her phone beeped. Milo: I'm outside in a rental car.

Edith: Okay. Currently trying not to puke.

Milo: Flight or Mom?

Edith: Mostly flight but also Mom.

Milo: Me too. We can do this, I promise.

Edith had been so entrenched in her own misery she hadn't really stopped to think about how Milo must be feeling as dejected as herself. Maybe more. He'd only had Phoebe for ten years. He'd been cheated out of more than Edith.

Edith: We will do this together. See you in a minute.

Edith felt better after a few salty fries; it always did the trick after a bad flight. She carried the greasy bag in one hand and ate with the other as she made her way out to the arrivals pick-up area. She easily found Milo and dropped into the passenger side of the black SUV, hyperaware of the silence in the car. Without a word, she held the bag out to him. He took a few fries and ate them, making no move to drive away.

"I feel like an FBI agent," Milo said over his mouth full of fries.

"Or like we're in a presidential motorcade."

"Why do all government agencies like black SUVs?"

"They look cool."

Milo nodded and they went silent, the attempt at humor falling flat.

After several minutes, Edith whispered, "Are we really gonna do this?"

Milo ran a hand over his face. He had bags under his eyes. "Don said she's pretty lucid today. It's a good day to go."

Edith nodded. "Okay. Then let's do it." She offered him the last fries, which he chewed thoughtfully.

"What is she going to look like?" he asked quietly. Edith heard the little boy behind his voice. "Will we even recognize her? I'm not a fan of sick people or hospitals. You know?"

"Me either, but I think we'll recognize her." Edith looked out the windshield at the sunny New Mexico day. "I wonder if she'll recognize us." The car was so warm. She turned on the A/C. Her mother had been beautiful, with her big brown eyes and long, earthy-brown hair. Phoebe had loved headbands; she had a big collection she pinned to hangers with clothes-pins. Edith scoffed quietly. She hadn't thought of that in years. Headbands of every color and design, hung in the closets next to the sweaters. Phoebe had even made some of them. But that wouldn't be the woman Edith and Milo saw today.

Edith tried to think back to decode the signs of her mother's addiction. *How did I miss it? Can you really hide something like that?* There'd been headaches and late mornings. Edith had often made her and Milo's school lunches, but she hadn't thought much of it. She'd been blissfully oblivious of her mother's real life.

And that made her deeply sad.

"What are you thinking?" Milo asked.

"I'm wondering if I could have helped her. If I'd known . . . could I have done *something*? More chores, more meals . . ."

Milo smiled sweetly. "Good old Edith. You can't fix every problem. You were a kid!"

"I took care of you! And I was a teenager, not a kid. Why does everyone keep calling me a kid?"

"Eighteen is still a kid, admit it. And it wasn't your job to fix Mom. That was her job."

"I know." Edith sighed. "It's weird to realize your parents were and are human. Struggling, unsure, broken human beings. When you're little you think they know everything, that they don't make mistakes. But then you become an adult and realize you don't have anything figured out, so, of course, they didn't either."

"I know. Very weird. And then you learn about all the things you missed as a kid, the stuff that went right over your head. Like your mother was addicted to pain meds." He shook his head, eyes focused on the windshield. "The bliss of childhood."

They were quiet for a moment, the A/C fan buzzing. Finally, Edith said, "Okay. Let's go. We can't keep sitting here."

"I guess not." Milo put the car in drive. "Wish I had some

cool pilot sunglasses and a machine gun to match my intimidating black SUV."

Edith smiled.

Edith and Milo stood outside the automatic doors of Morning Mesa Care Center. A few people walked around them and went inside. A rush of sanitized air came out each time. Edith sensed the heaviness of the place, the weight of so much death.

"People come here to die," she whispered. "This is a place for dying."

"I really don't want to go in there," Milo answered, voice thin with fear and void of humor. A middle-aged couple came out the door, the man holding the woman around her shoulders as she sobbed into a Kleenex. Edith and Milo looked at each other, eyes wide. Milo said, "We've come this far. Tally ho."

"Right." Edith took a breath and then led the way inside. A pleasant woman at a polished mahogany desk smiled. "Hello. Who are you here for?" she asked.

"Phoebe Kendrick, please."

"Of course." The thin woman in a gray pantsuit nodded and then pushed a clipboard at them. "Sign in, please. Are you family or friends?"

Milo's eyes drew wide again. Edith answered, "We're her children."

"Really? I didn't know Phoebe had children. Glad you're here."

Edith frowned. "We live out of state," was all the explanation she offered.

Once they had their visitor badges, the receptionist pointed to the right. "Last one on the left, end of the hall. Enjoy your visit."

When they were a few steps away, Milo leaned close to Edith. "Why do they even bother saying stuff like that? *Enjoy your visit*—umm, I don't think so. This is Death Central Station. No one enjoys themselves here." He scoffed and rolled his eyes.

Edith smiled, feeling her tension ease for a brief second. "They should just hand you a box of tissues and a Xanax."

Milo smiled back. "Now *that* would be customer service." They stopped at the closed door. A small whiteboard on the door gave Phoebe's name and a list of times. "I think I need a whole bottle of Xanax," Milo whispered.

Edith's stomach twisted into a knot. She couldn't catch her breath. *Oh my gosh. My mom is in there. I haven't seen her in twelve years.* Milo reached out and took her hand. She nodded, and then stretched out a shaky hand to knock on the door.

A moment later an older man, bald and wearing round glasses, opened the door. His face broke into a smile. "Edith, Milo? I'm Don." Don wore khakis and a periwinkle golf shirt. He was short and thin, his face friendly and deeply wrinkled.

Edith could only nod.

"Glad you came. She just woke up, so perfect timing. Come on in." Don stepped aside to let them in. Edith wasn't aware of her legs moving, but she found herself in the room. It looked like an expensive modern hotel room expect for the large hospital bed in the center. And Phoebe in the bed, a withered shadow of a woman with a bright teal scarf tied around her head.

Edith tightened her grip on Milo's hand; she worried she might faint.

Phoebe's head rolled to the side. Her eyes were sunken, her skin parchment thin and yellow, but there was a spark in her expression that Edith remembered. Phoebe started to smile but then sobered. Tears slipped from her red-rimmed eyes. Don instantly came to her aid, dabbing away the tears and taking her hand.

Edith looked at Milo who was blinking too quickly and gripping her hand too tightly. He gave her a desperate expression. Edith swallowed hard and turned back. "Hello, Mom." It felt much too simple, too little, but those were the only words she could find.

"Oh, Edith," Phoebe sobbed. She took a ragged breath. "And my little Milo. You both look so . . . amazing. And not so little anymore."

Don gestured to two waiting chairs near the foot of the bed. Edith and Milo released hands and sat stiffly.

"Thank you for coming," Phoebe said. Her voice was ragged, so different from the smooth melodic sound Edith remembered. "I know . . . I know this is hard."

"How are you feeling?" Milo asked tentatively.

"Like I'm dying of cancer." Phoebe gave a small smile. Milo smiled back. "It was good to see your father," she went on. "I'm so glad he found Cori. She sounds wonderful." Phoebe coughed and Don handed her a water mug with a straw.

"Yes, she is," Edith answered. "She owns a coffee shop in town."

Phoebe nodded. "I heard all about it. And all about Milo's football career and your flowers, Edith. You've both done so well." She smiled, but soon the corners of her mouth turned down. "I'm very sorry, my sweet kids. You'll never know *how* sorry. There just aren't words."

Edith took the opening. "Why didn't you get help and come back?"

"I did get help, eventually, but not for years. After I left, I really spiraled into some dark places. I was so angry at myself, so lonely. I turned to the pills, even more than before. There were crappy waitressing jobs and nasty apartments. Then there was living in my car." She pulled in a shaky breath. "One night, about five years ago, I walked out in front of traffic on a busy road. Didn't even know I was doing it. Ended up in the hospital and then rehab." She coughed again, drank some water. "Honestly, when I finally cleared my head, I was so ashamed and so embarrassed I didn't have the strength to come back. And you were mostly grown by then; I felt I'd disturb your lives more than help. Going back felt . . . selfish."

"We've—I've been so angry for so long," Edith's voice cut off, the tears coming hard. "I was so confused. We didn't know why you left. We never knew. I gave up college, I gave up . . . a lot."

Phoebe closed her eyes. "I know." She seemed to sink deeper into the bed. Don wiped at more tears. "And I'm not asking you to *not* be angry or to forgive me. I'm not asking anything. I deserve that anger; I earned it. All I want is the chance to say I'm sorry."

"Were you ever happy?" Milo asked. Such a simple, yet profound question. Edith looked at him. *Generous, sweet Milo.*

Phoebe half smiled. "I loved my little shop and the friends I made here. Don helped a lot. I had some happiness, but there was always the regret and shame. Always. Even now—maybe *the most* now. I'm so sad I didn't do better. I hate that I didn't get help soon enough to make my way back to you. I'm ashamed I was too weak to face you all once I did get my life in order. Mostly, I'm so sorry I wasn't there. I'm sorry I missed your lives." Phoebe, tears rolling down her face, turned to Edith again. "Thank you for taking care of Milo, Edith. You're incredible and you deserve everything you want. I hope you get it all."

Edith buried her hands in her face and sobbed. Something in her chest snapped free, and she felt like she could breathe again. She thought of Noah, of how his anger and grief broke him. She realized she'd set herself on the same path. She didn't want to live like that. It was time to forgive her mother. "I'm glad we came," she managed though her emotion-thick throat. Phoebe smiled sweetly, a wash of relief moving over her cancer-pale face.

Milo's hand came to Edith's back to rub gentle circles.

"Why don't you show Mom pictures of the farm, sis?" Milo encouraged quietly.

Edith wiped at her face, nodding. She took a steadying breath.

Phoebe said tenderly, "I would love that."

Sixteen

THE WHOLE THING lasted only two hours.

That was all Phoebe had strength for and all the time Edith and Milo had. But it had felt like days—in a good way. Once the initial tension fell away, Edith found herself enjoying talking to her mother and Don. She loved watching Milo make Phoebe laugh. She savored the sense of freedom humming in her soul.

Don walked them to the front doors. "I can't thank you enough. Really. I know that wasn't easy. But she's been holding on for this; you've made a real difference. I think she can go in peace now."

"Is there really nothing they can do?" Milo asked soberly.

"They've done it all and more. She's ready. I'm not, but she is." He smiled sadly and then held out his hand. "Again, thank you. I'll keep in touch."

"Thank you, Don," Edith said as she shook his hand. She and Milo stepped out into the hot New Mexico afternoon, pausing in the same spot they'd stood two hours ago.

"Sooo . . ." Milo started.

"That was intense."

"Understatement."

Edith turned to him. "Thank you—"

He lifted a hand. "Say no more." He put his arm around her shoulders and squeezed. "Come on. We got planes to catch."

The drive back to the airport gave them ample time to discuss every moment and every emotion. Milo pulled into the rental car area. "I think you were right about the closure thing," she told him as they got out of the car.

"Duh. I'm always right."

She gave him a doubtful look. "I wish we could hang out some more. But things to do, people to see."

"Football records to break! Flowers to harvest! Naps to take on the plane! High ho silver!" Milo thrust his fist in the air.

Several people turned their direction. Edith only laughed. "Go back to New York, weirdo."

Milo stopped her with a hand on her arm. "Hey, one more thing. Any sign of Noah?"

Edith's jaw clenched. "No. I swear sometimes I feel him there, but I think I'm just imagining it."

"Do you really think he's just hiding from you or did he pass over? Or . . . whatever."

"For his sake, I hope he's passed on, but I don't know."

Milo nodded. "Well, at least it's over."

The words made her feel profoundly sad. She tried to keep the emotion out of her expression. "Right. Things are good."

Milo raised one eyebrow but didn't push it. Instead, he said, "We will probably be back here soon for the funeral."

Edith immediately thought of Simone's funeral. She nodded. "I want to do the flowers."

"Good. I'll let Don know." Milo checked his watch. "I gotta fly." He flapped his long arms.

Edith scoffed. "Just go already. Stop embarrassing me."

"But I live to embarrass you!" Milo gathered her into a big hug. "Bye, Edie."

"Bye, Milo."

Noah paced up and down between Edith's neat rows of hoop tunnels protecting all the flowers. He drank in the smell of wet earth and the energy of growing things. He picked up some stray twigs stuck against the tunnels and tossed them away. The sky was deep black and studded with stars. A thin waxing crescent moon hung in the west.

Noah put his hands in his pockets and smiled.

A sound made him turn.

What is that?

It didn't sound like Edith's car. It sounded like . . . laughter? A twinge of instinct had Noah running before he even realized it. He raced through the fields, looped around the house, and stopped on the driveway. He listened again. Yes, definitely laughter, and it was coming from the road end of the driveway. He ran fast, that instinct yelling at him that something was wrong.

Noah skidded to a stop behind one of the old big leaf maples at the end of the driveway. A group of three young men were gathered around Edith's new sign. Two of them held large red jugs. One held a burning lighter.

NO!

The sign caught flame, roaring to life in a bright yellow swoosh. The men stumbled back, laughing, tripping over each other. Noah's anger burned hotter than the wood. He rushed forward, waiting until he was standing in front of the burning wood to appear. All three men yelled and jerked further away, two of them falling hard to the ground.

Noah launched himself at them, throwing the remaining one to the ground to meet his friends. All three scrambled back toward an old beater truck, swearing and staring wide eyed at Noah. Noah herded them against the truck. He disappeared and reappeared closer, just to scare them a little more. He grinned at their frightened gasps.

"Don't move," he growled. The men huddled together. Noah could smell the alcohol oozing off them. He kicked the gas cans aside. He glanced over his shoulder at the sign, which fell from its post to the ground, a total loss.

I'm so sorry, Edith!

He snapped his head back to the idiots whimpering on the ground. "What do you think you're doing?" No one spoke. Noah swore under his breath and then, "Answer me!" he yelled. It was taking all his control not to kick the life out of each one of them.

"We just . . . we just . . ." one of them sputtered. He was a big guy but blubbering like a child. "My mom was pissed about the Starling wedding. We just . . ."

"You just got drunk and decided to destroy private property." Noah shook his head, mumbling a few choice insults under his breath. The sound of a car on the road made them all turn. Noah stood and held out his hand. "Don't move! Understood?" The men sniveled confirmation. Noah wanted to disappear—too many people had seen him already—but he needed someone to call the police. He stared at the oncoming headlights unable to make out the car behind them. It came to a jerking halt. Edith jumped out.

"My sign!" She ran toward the burning heap. "What—" She turned to find Noah and the men. In the flickering firelight, Noah watched her face drain of color. "Noah?" she breathed.

"Edith, call the police."

"But—"

"Right now!"

Edith shuddered and then reached into her coat pocket. She dialed the number and relayed the information to the island police. "They said five minutes." She came closer, blinked at him. "What happened?"

Noah's whole body shook with his desire to touch her. *It's been so long.* He cleared his throat. "This one is Paula's son." He pointed. "She's mad about some wedding, and these morons took it upon themselves to burn your sign."

Edith lowered her gaze to the man who withered under her scrutiny. "The Starling wedding? What? *Why?*"

Paula's son looked at Noah and then back to Edith. "They promised it to my mom, but changed their minds when they heard about you and your farm. She's really mad. She—"

"That's enough!" Noah barked.

Edith scoffed, shook her head. She looked over at the smoking sign. She brought her hands to the sides of her head. "You found them?" she asked after a moment, turning to face him.

"Yes," he answered quietly. "But not soon enough."

Police sirens echoed from down the road. Edith dropped her hands and glared at the men sitting in the dirt. "I'm pressing charges."

The men shrugged deep into their coats. Noah held back his smile. Edith's gaze found his face. He tensed his hands into fists. "Thank you," she said. She took a few steps toward him but stopped when the police car arrived. Noah wanted to reach out to her.

He took one step closer. "I have to go, Edith."

She nodded. "I know."

Noah lifted his hand but then pulled it back. He disappeared, running as fast as he could back to the attic.

Edith stood looking down at the charred remains of her beautiful sign. The crippling embarrassment and shame she'd felt at the Bell Festival came crawling back. She wrapped her arms around her middle, shivering in the cold dawn air.

Cori stepped up beside her and held out a large coffee cup. Edith took it without a word. After a few minutes, Cori said, "I never liked that Roy Grant. No good, waste of space, spoiled youngest child. But this . . ."

"Was I wrong to press charges? Should I have been more forgiving . . . or something?" Edith asked. She felt as if her whole body had been hollowed out. She'd only slept about three hours in the last forty-eight. And too much had happened in those two days.

"No way. They need to know the consequences for their actions." Cori sighed. "So does Paula."

"What do I do? Should I go talk to her?" Edith shrank away from the idea. "Do I *have* to go talk to her? I can't run a business in fear of this kind of backlash."

"No, you can't, and you shouldn't have to. Let's think about it and give everyone a cooling off period." Cori kicked a smoking hunk of sign. "No pun intended. And maybe this will put things in perspective for Paula and *she'll* come apologize."

Edith looked over at Cori who was smirking incredulously, and then they both started laughing. Edith didn't really know why she was laughing, but it felt good. Cori put her arm around Edith's shoulders. "You've had a day, haven't you? How was the visit with Phoebe?"

"It was . . . important. It was good." They started to walk back to the house. "You were totally right about forgiveness being about cleaning out your soul. I thought about Noah and how he ruined his soul. I don't want to be that person. I'd become so attached to my anger that I didn't even know how much it was hurting me. Seeing Mom and hearing her apologize showed me that it's time to move forward. And who knows . . . if she hadn't left and changed my life maybe I wouldn't be here now."

"Oh, I love that. I'm glad it went well. Your father needed that closure as well. He's been better since he got back."

"I noticed that. I actually heard him humming while working on the greenhouse fan the other day." Edith smiled.

Cori laughed. "I'm so happy for all of you. I hope Phoebe can move on with some peace."

"Me too." Edith stopped at the porch steps. She did a quick scan of the yard.

"What is it?" Cori asked.

"Noah was here."

"What? When?"

"He was the one who found those guys. He held them until the police came." Edith shook her head, smiling. "He scared the life out of them."

Cori let out a huge laugh, tossing back her head. "They *so* deserved that. But that's really unlike Noah—to let outsiders see him."

"I know. He left before the police arrived. And those guys were pretty drunk, so I'm guessing the police will dismiss anything they say about a ghost pushing them around. I kept Noah out of the story and said I drove up on them."

Cori nodded, thoughtful. "You okay?"

Edith turned her hot cup between her palms. "I miss him. I know that sounds insane, but I do. I look for him everywhere. I keep reading his books. I even swear he's in the room sometimes."

"It doesn't sound insane." She sighed. "He misses you too."

"Do you see him, Cori? Have you talked to him at all?"

"No, not since around Christmas. I've looked for him, but he's got this hiding thing down."

Edith took a drink of her coffee. "It's weird knowing he's around. Do you think . . ." Edith bit her bottom lip.

"What?"

"Milo mentioned bringing in a priest to help Noah pass over, move on—whatever it is. Do you think we should try that?"

Cori folded her arms, her gaze shifting away. "No, I do not."

Edith had never heard Cori's voice so serious. "Why not?"

"Because he's not ready. Sending a restless soul away will only make him more restless. What he needs is here."

"What do you mean? What does he need?"

Cori shrugged. "Maybe he needs to let go of his wife and her death. Maybe he needs to forgive her or himself. Maybe he needs to *want* to move on. He acts angry about being here, but I actually think he's *afraid* to leave."

Edith hadn't considered any of that. She'd never imagined that it might be Noah himself keeping his spirit trapped here, but it made sense. "I never thought of it that way. So, you think it's up to him?"

"I do, but just like someone who's alive it's hard to let go of those deeply rooted habits. You know that. Noah hasn't had his Phoebe-cancer-bed-moment, like you just did. Noah is *very* accustomed to being sad and angry."

"He needs that moment."

Cori narrowed her eyes at Edith. "Yes, he does. Maybe what he needs is *you* to help him get it."

Edith's stomach leaped. "What? But . . . we all agreed it was wrong to get so close to him. I'm alive, he's dead."

"I know but maybe..." Cori shook her head. "No, you're right. That's so messy. You can't fall in love with a ghost just to save his soul. What happens to you after he leaves?"

Edith gasped, tightening her grip on her cup. She felt suddenly sick. *Fall in love with him? Is that what was happening? What is happening? And will he leave completely one day? He should, but still . . .*

"Oh, sorry, honey." Cori rubbed Edith's upper arm. "Sorry. Nope. Looks like staying apart is the right way to go."

Edith inhaled a shaky breath, trying to banish the idea of Noah passing over out of her mind. "How do you know this stuff, Cori?"

Cori tugged her red beanie down further on her head and clicked her tongue. "Well, my mother was a bit of a mystic. She saw ghosts, even talked to them. Everyone, including me, thought she was losing her mind. I'd find her in the kitchen of our Chicago apartment, cooking up a storm, and having a conversation with an empty room." She lifted her eyebrows. "As soon as I was eighteen, I got as far away from her and her chef/ghost whisperer lifestyle as I could. It took me all the way to that soul-sucking job in Seattle." She let out a breath. "And that's where I saw my first ghost. On my thirtieth birthday actually. At some posh restaurant with my posh boyfriend and a big group of stupidly posh friends." She sighed. "I was *terrified* but pretended to be fine for the party. When I got home that night, I called my mom for the first time in five years."

Edith stepped closer to put her hand on Cori's arm. Cori went on.

"That theory about souls not being ready to leave—that's my mom's theory. She'd talk about these ghosts as if they were her therapy clients. I guess they kind of were." A small smile. "She had a gift and passed some of that gift on to me. I don't see as many ghosts as she did. My gift is more about sensing things about people—about emotions and such—but there has been an occasional ghost." She shrugged again.

Edith smiled. "That's amazing, Cori."

Cori laughed quietly. "Some days it is and some it isn't, but I'm much happier embracing it than suppressing it. And it helps me make people just the right kind of coffee, the drink that fits their needs. And they come back and buy more and more and *more* . . ."

Edith laughed, raising her cup in salute. "You have me under that spell."

"There's a lot of magic in life that people ignore."

"I agree. I'm trying to see it. I see it in this place."

Cori gestured to the house. "You're doing a good job. Building a whole farm—that's pretty magical."

"Thanks. But Noah . . ."

Cori searched her face for a moment. "I'm not sure, honey. I wish my mom were still around. I have some of her journals; I'll look through them to see if there's anything helpful. But you need to do what feels right to *you*. Not me, not Noah, not Milo. *You.*"

Edith nodded, trying to decide what did feel right. *I have no idea.* "Thanks." She gave Cori a hug. "I better get to work. Farmers don't get emotional recovery days."

Cori laughed. "That's what the coffee is for. Come for dinner tonight?"

"Love to."

Cori waved goodbye as she headed back to her car.

Seventeen

EDITH HURRIED INTO the warm house. She unwound her white scarf as she moved down the hall to the kitchen. She needed a quick breakfast before she hit the fields. She stepped into the kitchen and froze. The empty coffee cup slipped from her hands.

"Noah?" she breathed.

He sat at the table, hands folded on top, disconcertingly still and serious. Despite the tension in the set of his shoulders and jaw, he looked so at home there, so right sitting at her antique, round, farmhouse-style kitchen table. His blue-gray eyes locked on hers. "I don't want to do this anymore."

"Do what?" she asked automatically, her voice shaking.

"Hide from you. Sit in that horrible attic."

"Attic?"

"It's not important." He stood abruptly and she flinched. He lowered his voice. "It's driving me mad and it feels . . ."

"Wrong," she finished.

"Yes. So wrong." They stared at each other for a long, tense moment. "I don't know what will happen if I stay," he whispered, stepping closer. "I don't want to hurt you; I don't want to be selfish. But I want to . . ." He sighed in frustration, shook his head.

She nodded her head, ignoring the possible consequences. "Stay," she whispered back. It was all the invitation Noah needed. In two swift steps he had her in his arms. She gasped at the burst of relief, at the rush of pleasure. *This feels right.* She tightened her arms around him, and he did the same. Like before, all those weeks ago, she felt a heightened sense of the sounds and smells around her tempered by an odd slipping sensation. She savored it, accepted it. It was much better than not being held by Noah.

He pulled back and took her face in his warm hands. "Are you sure?"

"Yes." She smiled. "Plus, I'm really sick of making my own tea. You were right: you're better at it."

Noah laughed, the quiet sound sending ripples of warmth through her. He rubbed his thumbs across her cheeks. "How could you watch all those *Star Trek* episodes without me?"

"We'll start over."

"Good idea."

Noah's eyes dropped to her lips and Edith felt a twinge of panic. What would happen if he kissed her? She saw the same question move across his face. Noah cleared his throat and lowered his hands to her upper arms. "What can I help with on the farm today?"

Edith smiled, savoring the idea of working side by side in the fields. "Oh, I will put you to work."

Noah laughed again. She could get used to that sound. "We need to tie sweet peas to the trellises and clean up the sign mess and weed and order baby chicks—that adorable coop needs chickens—and maybe fifty other things."

Noah stepped back and gestured to the back door. "Then we better get started."

Noah set Edith's steaming mug of tea on the side table. She smiled up at him from the couch. She'd changed into a pair of apple red cotton pajamas and had a gray fleece blanket on her lap. Noah sat in the middle of the couch and kicked off his boots. She moved closer and instinctively he lifted his arm to guide her into his side. He closed his eyes at the sensation of her body pressed against his. He turned his lips to her silky hair, recalling the moment he'd seen her in the church at Simone's funeral, the sun illuminating her rose gold hair. He'd been drawn to her from that moment, even before he knew her.

Edith leaned into his kiss as she turned on the TV. "Thank you for your help today," she said.

"Thank you for giving me so much work."

She laughed.

"No, I mean it. That is what I need—to use my hands."

She nodded against his shoulder. The *Star Trek: The Next Generation* theme music played. Noah smiled, so content to be back on his green couch with Edith. A few minutes into the show, Edith said timidly, "Tell me about your wife." Noah stiffened, a practiced reaction to anything involving Maggie. He frowned. Edith lifted her head and sat back to look at him. "I'm sorry. I shouldn't have asked."

"No, no. It's okay. I just . . . it's not easy to talk about her."

Edith nodded. "What was her name?"

"Maggie." He swallowed. Edith brought her hand to his temple and ran her fingers back through his hair. Bolts of sensation moved through his entire body. He took a breath. "Maggie Point. She moved here from Vancouver our junior year of high school and that was it for me. Of course, it took me almost six months to work up the nerve to talk to her."

Edith smiled. "What did she look like?"

"She was a tiny thing, maybe five two, with long, golden blonde hair and these big, bright eyes. She loved to wear sundresses, even in the winter. She'd pull off her big coat and stand there in a watermelon print sundress with snow boots." He shook his head. "We were going to get married right after high school, but the war started."

"World War II? You fought in the war?"

"I flew bombers. My brothers, Aiden and Roger, fought on the ground in France. We lost them both."

"I'm so sorry. Did you have any other siblings?"

"No, just us three boys. My parents almost lost all of us. My plane was shot down in the Pacific. I spent a few days on a raft, waiting for rescue."

Edith shook her head and moved her fingers over his beard. "I can't even imagine that."

Noah took a long breath. "I still don't know how I survived that crash. We took Japanese fire to both engines. My whole crew was lost that day, but there I was with only a broken ankle and a few cuts and bruises." He shook his head. "It never seemed right or fair."

"You were *alone* on the raft?"

"Yeah."

"That's awful. I'm so sorry."

"It *was* awful. It's hard to explain what your mind does in a situation like that. It . . ." Noah shook his head. "I still can't describe it. I thought about nearly everything I had ever done, seen, heard, thought. It was like the rock of the raft shook everything loose and there it was, laid out in front of me. I never expected to be rescued."

"I'm so glad you were." Edith lowered her hand to his chest. "What happened when you got home?"

"Maggie and I got married a few months later. I bought

this land with some of my GI Bill money. We were about to start building the house when she . . . had her accident."

"What happened?"

Noah sighed. "Maggie loved horses. Her father owned a whole herd, and she helped run the family ranch. It was on the south side of the island, huge property. Donald Point bred and sold beautiful jumping horses. Maggie was a gifted jumper, and a good trainer and teacher. She was fearless." Noah saw the image bright in his mind: Maggie on a horse, leaping over tall gates, smiling like it was the greatest thing in the world. "She had a wall of blue ribbons. But her fearlessness had a dark side. One day while training a new horse . . . she fell. Just the right—or really, the *wrong*—way." He pressed his teeth together and then finished, "She broke her neck. Died instantly."

Edith took his hand in hers. She didn't say anything, and Noah appreciated her silence. He was amazed at how easy it was to tell her these things. How cathartic. "And I didn't handle it well," he admitted. "I was never very social, but after that I got worse. I closed myself off from everyone and everything but this farm and my novels."

"I can understand that. I kind of did the same thing after my mom left. I closed off to everything but helping Milo. And then I hid behind him from my own wants and desires. I used my trauma as an excuse."

Noah met her gaze. "Exactly." Edith smiled and then settled her head back to his shoulder.

"Did you start writing before or after Maggie's death?"

"After," he said, pulling Edith close. "It started as a way to distract myself, to fill the silent hours. About a year after Maggie's death, right after I moved in here, we had this massive storm. It rained for days without stopping, and I was going mad with boredom and the torture of my own thoughts.

I saw an Agatha Christie novel sitting on the shelf and thought: Could I do that? Could I write a whole book? I gave it a try and found out that I could."

"Just like that? It was easy?"

Noah laughed. "No, it was *not* easy. But that's what I liked about it, what I needed. The challenge, the work of figuring out a story. I got addicted to that."

"Were you a reader? A book person?"

"Yes, of course. Aren't all the best people?" Noah smiled, his cheek moving against Edith's head. "You could even say a book saved my life. I had one with me on that raft. I read it six times while I waited. It was the only break I had from all those thoughts."

"What book?"

Noah laughed. "*Rebecca* by Daphne du Maurier."

Edith laughed too. "Really? I *love* that book. Why did you have *that* one?"

"I'd picked it up from a street vendor near Pearl Harbor. I thought my mom might like it. It was just a ragged little paperback, and I'd tucked it into my jacket pocket. Forgotten all about it. But I was so grateful to have it on that raft. Rebecca and Manderley saved my life. Or, at least, saved my sanity while I waited for that rescue ship."

Edith laughed. "That's amazing. I love stories like that. Do you still have it, or did you give it to your mom?"

"I did give it to her. She cried over it, and also anytime anyone mentioned *Rebecca*. I died before my parents, so I don't know what became of that book. Too bad." Edith tensed slightly at the mention of his death. Noah rubbed her arm to remind them both that he was solid and real, even if he was dead.

"Do you have anything from your life? Besides this couch and the house?"

Noah looked toward the stairs. "I have a few things. Stay here. I'll be right back."

Edith gave him a curious look as he pulled his arm away. Noah hurried up the stairs and into Edith's room. His eyes moved over her bed, unmade and inviting. His gut pulled and he forced himself to focus on the floorboards. It took a minute, but he found the right one, near the windows in the turret. An odd sensation moved through him as he unearthed the dusty box of bells and the twine-bound stack of paper. They had been silently waiting for over forty-six years.

He went back downstairs and set the dusty items on the coffee table. Edith leaned forward. "Is that a manuscript?"

"Yep, my last. And unfinished."

Edith set the bell box aside. "*Storms in the Desert*," Edith read the title from the top page. "Is it an Anson Lake mystery?"

"Of course. Set in Southern Utah about a string of murders in Arches National Park." He sat next to her.

"Can I read it?"

"It's not done."

"So, finish it and then I'll read it."

Noah blinked at her. "Finish it?"

"Why not?" She gave him an entreating look. "If you can do farm work, you can write. Right?" She grinned at her word play.

Noah furrowed his brow, looking from her to the stack of yellowed papers. "I don't know . . ."

"Think about it. Maybe something to fill the nights?" Her encouraging smile grew as she placed a hand on his thigh. "I'll get you a typewriter. I saw a gorgeous Remington Rand last time I was at the antique warehouse. I was itching for a reason to buy it. I'll go get it."

"But . . . should I?"

"Why not?" She pressed her hand into his thigh, a gentle nudge. "Would you rather leave it unfinished?"

"That's always bothered me. I like to finish things."

"There ya go. I can't wait to read it." Edith looked back at the table. "And the little box—what's that?"

"Open it," he urged, gesturing to the box.

Edith slipped down from the couch to kneel in front of the coffee table. She carefully lifted the lid of the square red box. She gasped. "Bells! They're gorgeous." She turned to him. "Are these Festival bells?"

"Of course. Maggie had them made for our first Christmas together."

Edith lifted one, the bell tinkling lightly. "She had them engraved with your names."

Noah nodded. "They are pure silver. The sound is perfect."

Edith wiggled her hand to make it ring. "Wow," she whispered. "Beautiful. I'm so glad you saved these." She moved to replace the bell but paused to gasp again. She set the bell on the table and lifted a yellowed photograph from the bottom of the box. "She *was* beautiful." Her eyes moved over the black and white wedding photo, and then she tipped it towards him. "You look so different without a beard. So young!"

Noah laughed as he looked at his young self and his young bride in their wedding attire. He was surprised to find it didn't hurt to look at the picture. "We *were* young," he mused.

"I love her dress. So classic. And your dress uniform— very sharp." Edith looked it over once more and then returned it to the box. "Where were these hidden?"

"Under the floor in your room." He smiled.

She laughed. "Got anything else secreted away?"

"No, that's it. That's all I wanted." He moved to help her

back to the couch. She settled against him, reaching for his hand.

"I'm glad you came back from the attic. Whatever attic that might be."

Noah laughed. "Your dad's garage."

Edith laughed loudly. "Oh no! That *is* horrible. I was terrified of that place as a kid. I was certain there were unnatural things living up there, just waiting to pounce. Although I don't think it was ever really haunted . . . until recently."

Noah heard the tease in her voice, and reached down to tickle her ribs. She squealed, wiggling away from him. He pulled her back. He wanted to kiss her. He wanted to lift her into his arms and carry her up to her bed. But he contented himself with her head on his shoulder. "I'm glad I came back too," he whispered to her.

Around midnight, Edith finally pulled herself away from Noah to get some sleep. She left him looking at his last manuscript. She did a rush job of getting ready for bed and then snuggled under the covers. She reached for her phone and found a text from Milo. There was a cute selfie of him and Faye at a Dierks Bentley concert. Apparently, Faye loved country music. Country, football, and flowers. Edith shook her head at the funny combination. In the photo, Faye had on a stylish pink cowboy hat, and Milo was grinning like an idiot. Edith laughed.

Milo's accompanying text read: I think I'm a cowboy at heart. Why have I never listened to country music?? This concert rocked so hard. And I'm digging Faye in that hat. How was your night?

Edith rolled onto her back to reply. Her thumbs hesitated over the keypad. *Do I tell him about Noah?* She frowned. The night had been one of the best of her life, but she wasn't sure she wanted to endure the backlash of Milo's practicality. She didn't want to hear about how Noah was a ghost and that she shouldn't get close to him. She wanted to savor the time they'd shared because it felt so right. It felt so comfortable.

And wasn't she supposed to be living her own life now? She didn't need Milo's approval or blessing. When she felt ready to broach the subject with him again, she would but not tonight.

Edith: Just a chill night of watching TV. Glad you had fun at the concert. You're gonna buy a cowboy hat now, aren't you?

It was after three in the morning in New York, so Edith silenced her phone, plugged it in to charge, and rolled over to sleep. She drifted off to sleep thinking of Noah's lips pressed to her hair.

Eighteen

Early April

EDITH STOOD AT the end of the sweet pea rows with a massive harvest of flowers in her arms. Behind her the vine-like flowers climbed trellises nearly eight feet high. She lifted the blooms to her face and inhaled deeply. "Bliss," she whispered into the petals, "pure bliss." The simply sweet flowers in deep red, lavender, soft pink, white, and gorgeous salmon were growing incredibly well. They loved the moist air and cool spring temperatures of Autumn Island. And the rich, fertile soil Edith had given them.

"Stop smelling the flowers and get back to work."

Edith looked over the flowers at Noah who came toward her with a haul of sunshine yellow snapdragons. "Hey, I'm working plenty," she said. "But you gotta stop and smell the roses . . . I mean, sweet peas."

He smiled at her and her heart melted. "Is this enough for the grocery store bouquets?" he asked, referring to the snapdragons.

"Yeah, that'll work."

Noah placed them in a bucket. "Okay, I'm going to check on those chicks." He brushed a hand along her hip as he passed. Pleasure sparked along her skin. "See if they are warm enough," he added.

"Okay," she managed to respond. He smiled back over his shoulder, and a tendril of heat moved through her chest. She carefully put the bunch of sweet peas into a clean bucket of water and went back to harvest more. She moved quickly down the row with her flower snips, making expert cuts. It was early in the morning, the best time to harvest flowers. Edith reveled in the solitude, and the soundtrack of birdsong and beat of her snips filling the air.

The classy baby shower on Orcas Island, a neighbor island, was tomorrow. The woman organizing the event, the pregnant woman's cousin, wanted to fill her house with sweet peas. She'd told Edith how the mother-to-be, Scarlet, had grown up with the nickname Sweet Pea. Her grandmother had loved the flower and loved her granddaughter, giving Scarlet the nickname shortly after her birth. So, it was sweet peas everywhere for Scarlet's first baby. And ninety-year-old Grandma would be there to see it all.

Edith adored how flowers were so connected to people and life. Everyone she talked to could tell a story about a flower that had been important in her life. Flowers were a powerful ordinary joy, a little bit of everyday magic. And she loved the chance to work with that magic.

She dropped another bunch into a bucket. Her right hand cramped from all the snipping, but she needed two more buckets. She hurried down the second row of trellised sweet peas.

"Hello? Anyone out there?"

Edith stepped back to look down the row. A man holding a clipboard stood squinting into the sun. "Right here!" she called out and hurried toward him. "You here with my sign?"

"Yep. That's me. What happened to the other one?" He pumped a thumb back toward the road.

Edith pulled off her gloves as she stopped in front of him. She recognized him from the first sign installation. "Uh . . . some drunks decided to set it on fire."

The man's eyes went wide. "Seriously? That's terrible."

"Yep. I actually don't want to put this new one on the road. I'm thinking we hang it from my front porch instead. Will that work?"

"Sure. No problem. Just show me where."

Edith led him back to the house. The men who'd torched her sign had been charged with trespassing and destruction of private property. They had a court date for sentencing in a couple weeks. Edith didn't really care how the judge decided to punish them; she just wanted the conflict to be over. Paula had made no effort to reach out. Edith had written a dozen letters to her and thrown them all away. She'd picked up the phone to call her at least twenty times. And she'd avoided going into town as much as possible.

But today she had to deliver Cori's weekly order of centerpieces.

Edith and the sign guy spent a few minutes figuring out the details. Once he had set to work, she hurried back to the fields. She hauled the sweet pea buckets on a garden cart back to the big fridge she'd had installed in the barn. "I'll see you guys later," she told the flowers. From a shelf, she pulled a box with the centerpieces for Cori's coffee shop—champagne bubble orange poppies in baby blue ceramic coffee mugs.

"Headed to Cori's?" Noah said, coming from the back where the chick brooder was set up.

"Yeah, and if I don't hurry, I'll be late." She shut the fridge. "Oh! The sign guy is out front."

"Okay, I'll stay in here until he's gone." Noah came

closer. "And don't worry about running into Paula. But if you do, punch hard."

Edith laughed loudly. "Come on! I can't *punch* her. It's much more complicated than that."

"I know. All you can really do is be honest with her, talk to her. But it's not your job to change her or make her listen. I think you should take her some flowers and go to her shop. Get it over with."

"Really?" Edith's stomach knotted at the idea.

"It's festered long enough. Make the move. Walk in there with a peace offering of flowers and hopefully she'll be reasonable. If not," he shrugged, "you did all you could."

"Yeah, you're right. It's just . . . terrifying." Edith laughed. She opened the fridge again to scan the flowers. "Okay, I'm gonna do it. I'm thinking . . . snapdragons. Will you grab me a blue Mason jar from the shelves, please?" Noah went to get the jar, while she gathered a bunch of the fresh snapdragons. Her pulse quickened.

Am I really going to do this?

How will Paula react?

Noah came back with the jar, half-filled with water. Edith gently arranged the flowers. "Okay," she sighed, "here goes nothing."

"Good luck."

Edith nodded. "See you later." She lifted to her toes and kissed his cheek.

"I'll be here." Noah briefly squeezed her arm.

Edith parked in the back of the coffee chop and hurried through the back door into the kitchen area. "Cori? You here?"

Cori came in through the swinging door. "Hey, girl."

"I'm sorry I'm late. The sign guy showed up."

"You're not late." Cori smiled. "I'll help you put these out, but first . . ."

Edith didn't like the look on Cori's face. "What's wrong?"

Cori sighed. "Sissy Moyels was in here yesterday. You know, the stationery lady?"

"Yeah, I know." Edith's stomach dropped.

"She told me that Paula called the Starling family yesterday, and went off on some crazy rant."

"What? About me?"

Cori nodded. "And about how they'd promised her the wedding. Apparently, she and Rachel Starling had a twenty-minute yelling match."

Edith groaned, dropped her face into her hand. "Unbelievable."

"Did Rachel call you or anything?"

"No. Why would she?"

"I was worried Rachel might fire you just because of Paula's freak out."

"What is *wrong* with her?"

"You know . . . Jud left her last year."

"He did?" Edith felt a pulse of empathy despite her anger. "I didn't know that. Why did he leave? They've been married forever."

"He met some girl online." Cori rolled her eyes. "It was a big thing. He moved to Portland to be with her. What any woman sees in Jud Grant is *beyond me* but . . . Paula's had a hard time. I wonder if she sees that flower shop as all she has left."

"And she thinks I'm going to take it away from her."

"That's what I'm guessing. Not an excuse, of course. But I think that's where her head might be. People do strange things when they are sad and angry."

Edith nodded. "I know that all too well." She blew out a long breath. "Should I give up the Starling wedding?"

"Of course not! That's business you earned. But something needs to be done."

Edith leaned her hip against a table and rubbed at her forehead. "Which is why I'm going over there. Right now."

Cori's eyes widened. "Really? It's not like she can be reasoned with. She's not thinking clearly."

"I brought a peace offering." She pointed to the snapdragons. "It's not much, but it's way past time we worked this out. I'd rather jump off a bridge, but . . ."

Cori nodded. "I'll go with you. Provide some backup."

Edith smiled, suddenly weary. She laughed nervously. "What the heck do I say to her?"

"Be kind and understanding. That's all you can do." Cori shrugged. "Maybe some empathy will break the ice."

Edith drove the three blocks to Better Blooms. She and Cori went to the door together, Edith gripping the blue jar of yellow snapdragons. "It's early," Edith said. "Do you think she's here?" Part of her hoped she wasn't. But she saw Paula through the big front window, behind a table of sample bouquets.

"She's here," Cori whispered. "Unto the breech, my friend."

A doorbell chimed as they went in and Edith felt like she might throw up. Paula straightened from behind the flowers. She looked up with a smile that immediately vanished. She narrowed her eyes severely. "What are you doing here?"

Edith looked at Cori with wide, desperate eyes. Cori gave her an encouraging expression. To Paula, Cori said, "Edith just wants to talk, Paula. You know, like grownups."

Paula grimaced, pulling her lips back over her teeth.

Edith swallowed hard. She set the flowers down in front

of Paula who sneered at them as if it were a jar of worms. *What do I say? What do I say?* Noah's words came to her: *Just be honest.* Edith took a steadying breath. "I love flowers. I always have. Simone taught me everything I know. Which helped me deal with the aftermath of my mother leaving. I just want to bring life and beauty to people's days the way Simone did for me. Did you know her?"

Paula's face softened slightly. "I did, of course. We talked about flowers several times. I didn't realize you two were so close."

"Oh, yeah. Simone was basically my mother after my mom left. Now, living in her house, growing flowers on her land, it's a dream come true. I don't want to hurt you or your business, Paula. I'm sorry about the Starling wedding. I didn't know. But I swear to you I'm not trying to take your business. I want us *both* to be successful." Edith paused to gauge the older woman's reaction. It was hard to tell what she was thinking, her face still hard.

Paula's eyes went to the snapdragons. She fingered a petal, silent for a long time. Edith looked at Cori who gave her a subtle shrug. Edith was ready to try something else when Paula said, "Did you know that snapdragons mean presumption?"

Edith blinked. "No, I didn't."

"All flowers have a meaning. They have their own language. In Victorian times people would send bouquets like letters, each flower communicating some specific sentiment, like friendship, apology, love."

"That's so beautiful," Edith said. "I love that idea."

Paula nodded, her expression relaxing more. "My mother taught me. She had this little book with all the flowers and their meanings, like a dictionary. I spent hours looking up different flowers and memorizing their meanings. My mother loved snapdragons." She dropped her hand from the flower and sniffed quietly. She wiped at a few tears and then finally met Edith's eyes. "I think I've been incredibly presumptuous."

Edith resisted the urge to let her jaw drop. Instead, she said gently, "I should have talked to you in the beginning. I didn't think."

Paula shook her head. "It's been a rough year for me. I admit that when I heard what Roy and his goons did to your sign, I felt sick. That was so wrong. I never meant for that to happen."

"Thank you."

"And Roy will pay for it."

"Thank you. I appreciate that." Edith nodded, her shoulders relaxing.

"Since my husband left—or because he left—I've presumed the whole world is against me. Your farm was an easy way to justify that pattern. Does that make sense?" Paula gave her a desperate expression. "It doesn't. I must sound crazy."

"No," Edith shook her head. "I know *exactly* what you mean. My mom left us. I know what that feels like and how it affects everything else in your life. I'm sorry that happened to you."

Paula sighed. "Thank you for understanding."

Edith smiled. "I'd love to know more about the meanings of flowers, if you'd like to share."

"That'd be nice. I haven't pulled out that old book in ages. I need to remember *why* I do this. Your story reminded me that it's more than a business." Paula sighed. "I'm so sorry, Edith. All that stuff that happened—that isn't like me. I'm so embarrassed."

"Thanks for saying that. Let's just move forward, okay?"

Paula smiled and gave a little scoff. "You were so brave to come in here."

They all laughed. Edith said, "Simone always told me to remember that we don't know people's stories. We don't know what's really going on unless we ask. I should have come to you sooner to ask, to talk. But I'm not as brave as Simone."

Paula laughed. "I think, maybe, you are. And she taught you well. These snapdragons are gorgeous. Never seen such healthy-looking ones. Would you be interested in supplying me with some flowers? I can't get stuff like this from the wholesalers."

"I'd love to. Let's have coffee next week and talk details."

"Sounds like a plan."

Edith smiled at the older woman, somewhat dazed at the turn of events. "I'll email you. See you next week." She and Cori left the shop and got into the car. They'd driven a block before Cori erupted with laughter. Edith couldn't help but join her.

"I *CAN NOT* believe that just happened," Cori exclaimed. "This proves it: Your flowers are magic! You set those things in front of her and everything changed."

"I'm in total shock! I mean, I know flowers connect people and bring back memories, but that was *amazing*. When we walked in there and she said in that nasty voice, 'What are *you* doing here?' I thought I was going to have to punch her, like Noah joked about. It was his idea to come—"

"Wait—Noah?" Cori's head whipped around to look at Edith.

Edith's stomach dropped. She hadn't told Cori about Noah's return. She grimaced. All the excited energy of the moment vanished, replaced by tension. "Cori, I . . ."

"Oh my gosh! He's back and he's with you. I knew I sensed a change in you, but I kept attributing it to the flowers. To your first harvest. But Noah . . ."

Edith gripped the steering wheel. "It's good, I promise. He's helping me on the farm. We talk. It's good."

"How long has he been back?"

Edith grimaced again. "Since the sign fire," she mumbled.

Cori blinked. "Wow. I'm so sorry you didn't feel like you could tell me."

"Oh, no. It wasn't that. I just . . ." Edith sighed. "I didn't tell Milo either." Edith pulled into a parking spot behind the coffee shop. They sat in anxious silence for a moment, the car idling.

"Were you afraid I'd be angry or judge you?" Cori asked gently.

"I think I was afraid you and Milo would try to talk me out of it again. Try to tell me it's wrong or unnatural or . . ." She exhaled and frowned at her window.

"Because it feels right to you?"

Edith turned to her. "Yes," she answered simply.

"Then it's right." Cori nodded. "And I'm happy for you."

"Really? Or are you just saying that? I know it's . . . unusual."

Cori smiled, "Hey, honey, I'm all about the unusual."

Edith laughed, nodding.

Cori reached over and took her hand. "You can always talk to me about *anything*. Okay?"

"Okay. Thanks." She sighed, but the tension still hovered between them. "Noah told me about his wife, and how he saved his last manuscript. He's been working to finish it."

Something moved over Cori's face but was gone too quickly for Edith to decide what it was. "That sounds nice."

"It was. It is." Edith couldn't dispel the awkwardness. *It will never be normal to talk about Noah like a regular person. Never.* She looked down at the console, avoiding Cori's gaze.

"I better get back in," Cori said. "Evan is running the

front today, and he always forgets to sweep up the espresso residue."

Edith nodded. "Thanks for going with me. Oh! The centerpieces."

"I'll put 'em out. Get back to your flowers." Cori opened the door. "Say hi to Noah for me. And tell him he broke my bucket."

"What?"

"Oh, he'll know. Bye, girl!" Cori waved as she walked past the front of the car.

Noah knelt beside the chick brooder, a large steel feed trough filled with pine shavings and ten multi-colored baby hens. Hung above it were two heating lamps to keep the babies warm. Edith had ordered a variety of breeds. She'd said she wanted a melting pot flock. He'd have preferred all classic yellow Orpingtons since he was having a hard time keeping track of which one was which. Of course, Edith did it effortlessly and had named them all. He reached in and quickly scooped one into his hands, the chick peeping softly as she watched him. He quickly checked each one; glad to find them all healthy.

"My mother hated chickens."

Noah turned to find Toby standing behind him looking over his shoulder. "Hey, Toby. Haven't seen you in a while."

Toby nodded. "You were hiding."

Noah nodded, sighed. "Yeah, well . . ." He frowned and changed the subject. "Why didn't your mother like chickens?"

"They always got in her garden and ate her greens."

"Didn't she have a fence?"

"Yes, but they always found a way in. She never could stop them. But I like chickens; they're funny. Can I hold one?"

"Sure." Noah scooted over and Toby came to the edge of the trough. "Do you remember the right way?"

Toby nodded. "Two hands, like you're holding a mug of hot chocolate."

Noah smiled. "That's right." He watched as Toby deftly reached in and snagged a brown and yellow chick. Toby smiled with pride.

"Are you staying with Edith now, forever?" He asked, eyes on the chick as it peeped at him.

Noah squirmed. *Forever.* Time was an issue. He had eternity, it seemed, frozen just as he was, but Edith didn't. She would age and progress. She'd grow older than him. He'd thought about this problem a lot lately, and no matter what way he approached it he felt that their relationship had to have a time limit. An expiration. It could only last a short while before the differences between them presented too many problems to ignore.

"I wish I could stay with her forever but . . ." He couldn't finish.

"But it wouldn't work because you couldn't get married and have children." Toby nuzzled the bird to his cheek, and she closed her eyes, content with his attention.

Noah felt like Toby had kicked him in the chest. He shook his head. "No, we couldn't. That's a big problem." Noah realized that he'd been thinking about Maggie less and less over the past weeks. His anger and hurt had slipped to the background, offering no competition to the radiance of spending time with Edith. She was helping him, but was he helping her? Besides, the free farm labor, of course.

Toby leaned down, let the chick go and selected another, a yellow one. He adjusted his small ghostly hands around the bird, and she fell instantly asleep. "I like this one," he cooed. He lifted his eyes to Noah. "There's someone new."

Noah felt a chill move through him. "What?"

Toby nodded. "A woman. A ghost. I've seen her from my tree, twice. She likes your house."

Noah looked back toward the house through the open barn doors. The chill only deepened. "Do you know her? Have you talked to her?" he asked.

Toby shook his head. "She's very pretty and wears a yellow dress. Like this color." He lifted the chick.

"But no one has died here or near here recently."

"She feels . . . different. Different than you and me."

"How?"

He shrugged. "Hard to say." He studied Noah's face. "You've changed too."

Noah frowned. "What do you mean?"

He sighed, frustrated. "I don't know. You look more . . . *real.*"

Noah squinted at him, trying to understand. He knew he felt different, but did that have anything to do with how Toby saw him? "We've always looked real."

"But you feel more solid now, like water turning to ice." Toby returned the chick.

Noah, uncomfortable, dismissed the observation. "Will you tell me if you see the lady in the yellow dress again?"

"Sure, Noah."

"Thanks." Noah pushed up to standing. He heard Edith's car out front. "You can stay with the chicks if you want, Toby."

Toby smiled and turned back to the brooder.

Noah made his way toward Edith, wondering about the ghost in the yellow dress and if he really had changed because of Edith. He found her standing in the front yard admiring her new sign. She flashed him a brilliant smile. "Looks good, huh? I think I like it here more than out front anyway."

He nodded. "Looks great."

"I have a story for you."

"Paula?"

"Yes."

Noah's eyes widened. "Did you give her your right hook?"

Edith laughed. "No, but I did make her cry."

Noah's eyebrows lifted.

"Come on, I'll tell you about it while I make the sweet pea arrangements for the shower." She held out her hand and Noah gladly took it.

Nineteen

EDITH WOKE WITH a start, unsure what had pulled her from sleep. She blinked at her dark room and listened, her pulse throbbing in her neck. After a moment, the haze of waking dropped away, and she heard the clacking of typewriter keys from downstairs. *Just Noah writing.* She closed her eyes to go back to sleep but then opened them again.

No, that wasn't it.

The typewriter hadn't startled her awake. She was certain.

But then what?

There was an odd sensation on the back of her neck. She stiffened, her heart rate skyrocketing again. Slowly, she rolled over. Her breath stopped cold in her chest. A woman, her face completely hidden in black shadow, hovered unmoving in the far corner, near the turret. Her dress glowed an unearthly yellow, like strange moonlight. Her hands were clasped calmly in front of her.

Sweat broke out along Edith's spine.

She blinked again and again, trying to make the figure disappear. The woman remained, completely motionless. Edith could feel her evaluating gaze from the shadows.

"Noah," Edith whispered hoarsely. She swallowed. "Noah!" Her voice gained strength. "Noah! NOAH!"

He burst into the room, plowing across the floor. She sat up as he dove onto the bed and pulled her against his chest. "What's wrong?" he breathed into her ear.

"There's someone in the room." Edith pressed her eyes shut and buried her face in his shirt.

Noah tensed. She felt his head moving side to side as he searched. "Where, Edith? What did you see?"

"A woman, by the turret."

"What did she look like?"

"All I could see was her yellow dress."

His body tensed even more. She pulled back to look at him. His face had paled. "You know her?" she asked.

"No, but Toby told me about her just today."

Edith's brow furrowed. "Toby?"

"He's the ghost of a young boy, lives in that big oak tree in the northeast corner of the property."

Edith blinked at him. *Another ghost?* "How many are there—how many ghosts?"

"Just me and Toby, but he said there was someone new. Did you feel threatened by her?"

Edith forced herself to turn and look at the corner, trying to decide exactly what she'd felt. "I didn't feel like she would hurt me physically or anything like that. But I still felt . . . threatened. Like she wanted something from me." She scrunched up her face. "That's not right, but I can't really describe it. She was so still and calm. I couldn't see her face."

Noah started to pull away, and she tightened her grip on his arms. "I'm just going to check out the window," he reassured her gently.

She nodded and reluctantly released him. She watched him move to the window and then around the room. She felt cold and unsteady without him holding her. He checked out in the hall and then made his way back to her. He leaned down, hands on the bed, face near hers. "She's gone."

Edith shook her head. "I don't understand. Who is she? Why would she be in my room?"

Noah sighed. "I don't know. Do you think you can go back to sleep? It's only a little after two."

Edith shivered. "Can you stay for a little bit, please?"

Noah winced. "I'd love to, but . . . is that a good idea?"

Edith smiled softly. "I promise I won't make any moves on you."

Noah laughed, shaking his head. "But I don't know if *I* can make that same promise." His gaze went to her lips, his eyes darkening with desire.

Edith's pulse quickened again but in a whole different way. She reached for his arm, tugging him forward to sit on the bed. His expression was wary but full of longing. *What are we so afraid of?* Maybe it was the haze of the nighttime or the surge of adrenaline in her blood, but suddenly she wasn't worried about anything. She slid her hand up his arm and to his beard. She loved the feel of it under her palm, the tickle of it on her fingertips. She loved the mix of brown and silver-white hair.

Noah closed his eyes.

She trailed her fingertips over his lips. Without thinking, she lowered her hand and pressed her lips to his. Soft and gentle, a hesitant invitation. "I'm breaking my promise," she told him in a sultry whisper. Noah gasped quietly. His arms came around her, pulling her close as he deepened the kiss. Instantly, she felt that slipping sensation, a wave of instability. But the delicious pleasure of the kiss stripped her of any ability to stop. She savored the smooth texture of his lips and the rough pull of his beard. She relished the urgency in him and the equal answer in her own body. She couldn't feel the bed beneath her anymore.

Free falling.

Edith allowed herself to tumble and spin with the delight of Noah's hands tangling in her hair, his lips exploring her lips and face and neck. The desire she'd kept at bay for months poured out, eager and willing. She felt the same release in Noah, the powerful urgency in the way he held her so close. Every sensation felt amplified, enhanced, like nothing she'd ever experienced or even imagined.

The dizziness came over her in one big crash.

Instinctively, she jerked away from Noah to grip the sides of her head. She collapsed to the bed with a groan.

"Edith?" Noah said, panicked. "What's wrong?"

She couldn't answer him or even shake her head. She had to focus on her breathing. Her stomach heaved and she pressed her teeth together to keep from vomiting. Noah reached out his hands but then pulled back without touching her.

"Edith, I'm so sorry. I'm sorry."

Her heart beat irregularly. Her head throbbed. *What is happening? What's wrong with me?* Edith rolled over, away from him, worried about her stomach, and tried to find her balance. She opened her eyes. On her nightstand sat a vase of daffodils from the front yard. She reached out a trembling hand and touched them. The moment her skin contacted the petals she felt a grounding sensation pull her back to center. The dizziness vanished, and her head stopped pounding.

Slowly, she rolled back over to look at Noah whose face was broken with regret. He knelt beside her, head and shoulders slumped forward. "I'm sorry," he repeated in a desolate whisper. Edith wanted to reach out to take his hand but didn't dare.

"What happened? What was that?" she whispered back.

Noah shook his head. "I don't know. It felt like . . ." He shook his head harder.

"What?" she urged.

"It felt like I was pulling on you. From the inside." He growled under his breath. "That doesn't make sense. It started wonderfully, perfectly"—he gave her a desperately sweet look—"but then something changed."

"Yes, me too. I felt like I was blissfully falling through the air, and then I got *so* dizzy. Out of nowhere."

Noah blew out a long exhale. "I'm sorry, Edith."

She smiled. "I believe *I* kissed *you*. If anyone is to blame, it's me."

He laughed quietly. "But I had a feeling it wasn't safe. As much as we both like to ignore it, we are *not* the same. I exist *differently* than you."

Edith managed to push herself up to sit in front of him. "I know." Her heart shattered. "It's not fair."

He lifted a hand, hesitated, and then gently caressed her face. Edith closed her eyes at the warmth of his touch. Noah said, "I wish I'd met you when I was alive. I wish our lives had lined up better than this."

Edith's breath caught. "I wish that so much."

His hand dropped to her knee. "I wish I didn't want to kiss you and"—he smiled, eyes lightening, and Edith's heart melted—"so much more," he whispered. "I don't understand how I can even feel this way. Maybe I should just go back to haunting you." A hint of mischief touched his smile.

Edith laughed. "Let's not. I really don't want to organize Simone's seeds again."

Noah's expression sobered. "What do we do now?"

"Well, I don't think I can go back to sleep. Let's go downstairs. You write and I'll answer emails. Just two . . . friends . . . working . . . in the middle of the night." She shrugged.

"Trying to ignore the sexual tension?"

225

Edith burst into a laugh. "Yeah, exactly. No big deal."

Noah smiled. He took her hand in his. The humor left his face. "But what do we do tomorrow? And the next day and the next?"

Edith ached all over. "I don't know."

Noah sighed. "Okay. And the woman in yellow? Are you still worried?"

Edith had almost forgotten about the reason why Noah was in her room. She shook her head. A chill moved up her spine. "I don't know."

Noah sighed. "Okay. I'll make you some tea."

"Uh . . . it's two a.m. I'm gonna need some *coffee*."

Noah rolled his eyes as he moved off the bed. "Well, lucky for you I'm also better at that than you."

Edith scoffed. "There's no way that is true. You'll have to prove it to me." Edith took his out-stretched hand and got off the bed. She followed him to the door, glancing over her shoulder at the far corner as they left the room.

Noah stared over the top of his sleek black Remington Rand 5 typewriter at Edith asleep on the couch. She'd drifted off, slumped over the arm, her computer still open on the cushion beside her. He propped his elbows on either side of the typewriter, interlaced his fingers, and let his chin rest on his knuckles.

He sat at a small wooden desk with a wooden swivel chair, which Edith had brought home with the typewriter. She'd set it up in front of the windows with a small Tiffany lamp and a stack of blank paper. He loved it. He especially loved writing with her sitting across the room on the couch. It felt familiar and intimate.

But Edith wasn't usually on the couch at four thirty in the morning.

Who is this woman in yellow?

He frowned, anxious and uncomfortable. He hated that this new ghost had appeared to Edith. He hated the intrusion and the mystery of it. Noah lifted his eyes to the ceiling, listening. The ghost wouldn't have appeared without a reason.

Who are you and what do you want?

Edith sighed in her sleep and the sensations of her kiss came back to him in a formidable bolt of awareness. He closed his eyes. He'd never felt anything like it—the pleasure or the strangeness that came with it. Noah knew he'd never be able to kiss her again, but that didn't remove his craving. Now that he knew the bliss of kissing her, he wanted nothing else.

Kissing Maggie never felt that amazing.

Noah's frown deepened and he cringed at a pulse of guilt. He shook it away. He'd been stubbornly, cripplingly loyal to his wife for over half a century. He needed to want another woman; he needed to let go of Maggie. He needed to liberate himself from this self-created purgatory.

It's all right to move on. I've put it off for FAR too long.

Pulling his arms from the table, he looked down at the fresh page in the typewriter. It amazed him how quickly and easily he'd slipped back into his novel. One read through and he knew exactly what to do and where to take it. Now, for the first time since his death, there were newborn words on a page and his mind was eager for more.

He moved his gaze to Edith.

She's changing me. She's helping me find myself again.

"I'm going to miss the ferry!"

"No, you're not."

Edith hurried to pull her hair into a ponytail. Noah leaned against the master bath doorjamb, watching her. She wanted to step up to him, grab the lapels of his flannel to pull him close, and kiss him until she was breathless.

But I can't do that and I really don't have time.

She felt wired and jittery after not enough sleep, too much coffee, and knowing that she'd kissed Noah Winters. She grunted as she rushed out of the bathroom. "I can't be late for my first big gig." She dropped to the bed and pulled on her socks.

"You're not going to be late. I already put the flowers in the van."

She looked at him, amazed. "Really? Thanks. Now I just have to find my phone. Oh, and where I wrote down the address of the house."

"Phone is on the kitchen table and the address is on my desk."

She smiled at him. "You're pretty handy, you know that?"

He grinned back and crossed the room to kneel in front of her. He put his hands on her thighs. "You're going to be on time for the ferry. You're going to find the house with no problems. And everyone is going to swoon over your sweet peas."

Edith laughed, warmth spreading though her chest. She brought her hands to his face. "You know I want to kiss you right now?"

"Not as badly as I want to kiss you."

Edith's smile faltered. *This isn't fair.* "I better go."

Noah nodded, cleared his throat. He stood and moved away. "Wish I could go with you."

"Me, too." She slid off the bed, wishing she could say something to make them both feel better. "See you later."

"I'll be here."

Something in his tone made Edith's heart hurt. *Poor Noah, trapped here all the time.* She gave him one last small, knowing smile and then ran downstairs to get her things.

Edith jumped into her new delivery van and headed to the ferry dock. She hated driving this giant vehicle, but it was the best way to move so many flowers. The boxes of bouquets were snug and secure in the back. At least the whole van smelled like sweet peas.

An hour later, she turned the big van, emblazoned with her adorable blue farmhouse logo, onto a private lane. She eased to a stop at a large iron gate and pressed the call button. When a woman's voice answered, Edith said, "It's Edith with Blue Farmhouse Flowers." Saying it sent a thrill through her, kicking up her heart rate.

The gate swung slowly open.

"Oh, my gosh!" Edith whispered to herself. "Here we go."

The wooded driveway curved down a gentle hill. Soon the trees opened to reveal a stunning modern house of glass and steel perched on the cliff's edge. Edith's eyes went wide. "Whoa!" she whispered, feeling a bit intimidated by the luxurious home and its gorgeous topiary garden, complete with large white stone fountain. She followed a side driveway, as she'd been instructed, and parked near another white van with a catering logo on its side.

Edith looked out the windshield at the breath-taking view of the deep sapphire water, studded by lush green islands. She wondered what it would be like to live in this kind of luxury. She wished she'd worn something other than ripped knee skinny jeans, sneakers, and a gray sweater. She looked down at her clothes. "I've gotten way too farmer," she whispered. "Note to self: Wear nicer clothes to these things." She took a steadying breath, more nervous than she'd expected. Then she hurried out of the van, popped open the back doors, and took out one of the boxes. She followed a rock path to a side door and found it open. An indulgent, high-end kitchen stood just inside. Several people were working at a long, white marble island. The cabinets were a dark espresso with flat fronts and streamlined silver hardware. There was a giant Wolf stove and Subzero fridge with double doors.

No one had noticed Edith. She winced, and then forced herself to say, "Hi. I'm looking for April." One of the caterers looked up, a young woman in a crisp white chef coat and black bandana around her head.

"Oh, hi. Yeah, I think April is out in the dining room. I'm sure you can just go on through." She pointed with her knife.

"Thanks," Edith said. The caterer nodded, already back to work chopping furiously. Edith moved across the kitchen and through an arched doorway, stepping into a massive dining room. Down the center of the room was a glass topped table long enough to sit maybe twenty people; it ran parallel to the wall of windows. Parsons chairs, upholstered in soft cream linen, circled it, and the table was set with crystal and silver. It looked like a page from a Restoration Hardware catalog. Edith drank in all the elegance.

"You must be Edith."

Edith turned to find a beautiful woman in her early-forties dressed in a stunning emerald green shift dress with stone gray heels. She had dark brown hair, which was pinned into a simple chignon, and large diamond stud earrings. "April?" Edith asked.

"Yes. Are these the arrangements?" April crossed the room.

Edith looked to the table and then to either side. There was nowhere convenient to put down her box. So, awkwardly, she set it at her feet and lifted out one of the vases. She'd filled lovely curvy, white porcelain vases with the multi-colored sweet peas. They perfectly matched the elegance of this room, bringing in a refreshing splash of color. Excited for April's reaction, she put this first one in the center of the table. "What do you think?"

April frowned and Edith's smile fell. "I thought they'd be much bigger," April said, eyeing the flowers with no visible pleasure.

Edith tensed. The arrangements were almost two feet tall and nearly as wide as her torso. And there were twenty of them. "Well, it's about the volume of arrangements, right? This is only one. When they are all together it will be amazing."

April pursed her lips. "All right. Please get them in place. I have to check the gift table set up."

The woman hurried out of the room, leaving Edith blinking in disbelief. She turned back to the vase of sweet peas, trying to see what April might have seen. But they looked incredible.

Great. Did I give up picky bosses for picky clients?

This April obviously has good taste—look at this place! Is there something wrong with my arrangements?

Maybe I'm not as good as I think I am.

Feeling her exhaustion and doubting her own abilities, Edith hurried back out to the van and hauled in the other boxes. She put four more arrangements on the table and the rest of the vases in the large living room. Everywhere she looked there were tender, friendly sweet peas. Edith prayed April would be pleased now.

How could she not? Look at this room!

The hostess breezed back into the living room. She took a quick inventory and turned to Edith. "That's fine. I'm sure Scarlet will like them. Your check is in the kitchen, pinned to the message board." April turned on her designer heel and hurried back out. Edith could only stand frozen with shock.

It's okay. It's not me, it's her.

Maybe she's just stressed or not an enthusiastic person.

It's okay.

Edith sighed, hating the lump in her throat, and went to collect the empty boxes. Just as she was ready to leave the room, an older woman came in. She gasped and brought a hand to her heart. "Sweet peas!" she exclaimed. The light brown eyes behind her gold-rimmed glasses found Edith. "Are you the flower girl? Are these your flowers?"

Edith smiled, hands full of stacked boxes. "Yes."

The woman, who had to be the ninety-year-old grandma who'd given Scarlet her nickname, moved to one of the bouquets and buried her face in the blooms. She wore a lavender pantsuit, expertly tailored, and perfectly complimentary to her pale skin and bobbed white hair. Edith's smile grew, her pride returning. She took a step closer to the woman who withdrew from the flowers, wrinkled face alight with happiness. "These are incredible!" she told Edith. "Where did you get them?"

"I grew them on my farm."

"You did? You grow your own flowers?" She shook her head. "Well, you have a gift, my dear. Not even my mother grew such healthy, plump sweet peas." She smiled wistfully. "These are my favorite."

"I can tell."

The grandma laughed. Her eyes moved around the room. "This is just wonderful. Scarlet will love it. I love it! What a perfect day."

"I'm so glad you like them." Edith turned to leave.

"Wait—what's your name, dear?"

"I'm Edith Daniels," she answered, turning back.

"Nice to meet you, Edith. I'm Berta McKinley. Do you have a business card?"

"Oh! Yeah, I do." Edith set down the boxes, relieved she'd thought to shove a few in her back pocket. She handed one to Berta.

"My birthday is in a few months, and I always throw my own party. A big, obnoxious thing because . . . why not?" She smiled, her thin face full of warmth.

Edith laughed. "I love that idea."

"I want you do my flowers"—she looked at the card— "Edith of Blue Farmhouse Flowers. How charming!"

"It'd be my pleasure, Berta."

"Oh, and you're on Autumn Island. I learned to ride a horse there. It's so beautiful."

Edith's eyes widened. "Do you mean the Point Ranch that used to be on the south side of the island?"

"Yes! Do you know it?"

"I know of it. I live in Noah Winters' house; he was married to Maggie Point."

Berta put her hand to her chest. She sighed wistfully. "Yes. Maggie and Noah. I knew them both. Maggie, mostly, because of the ranch. I grew up here on Orcas, but my dad took me over on our boat for my riding lessons. I was actually there the day she died."

A chill moved through Edith. "I'm so sorry."

Berta looked at her more closely. "So, you live in the house—does that mean Simone died?"

"Yes, back in June. I grew up next door; Simone and I were very close."

"Did she teach you about flowers?"

"Yes. Everything I know."

"That explains these." Berta gestured to the sweet peas

with a smile. Her eyes took on a far-off glaze. "I haven't thought about Maggie and Noah in a *long* time."

Edith stepped closer, her curiosity hungry. "I'd love to know more about Noah and Maggie. If you wouldn't mind telling me."

"I'm not sure I can tell you anything useful but . . ." she studied Edith's face. Edith hoped she didn't seem too eager. Berta smiled. "We have a few minutes before the party. Let's go out on the deck. April will be annoyed if we settle anywhere else." She leaned toward Edith and whispered, "She's a little uptight, if you didn't notice."

Edith grinned, holding back a laugh. "I understand."

"Toss those into the kitchen and follow me." Berta pointed to the stack of boxes.

Edith hurried to tuck them inside the kitchen archway and then followed Berta out a set of French doors to an expansive deck that ran the length of the back of the house. The air was frigid but the sun warm and, thankfully, the wind calm. Berta led Edith to a set of cushioned chairs set on either side of a small round table.

"I've read all of Noah's books," Edith started as they sat. "They're so intelligent and loaded with all this keen insight into human nature." It was odd to talk about him as if she didn't know him. "What was he like in real life?"

Berta smiled. "Noah was one of those rare men: intelligent, thoughtful, incredibly handsome, and *completely* oblivious to the fact that every girl on the island was in love with him." She laughed. "Even I had my little moment but then Maggie came along. Fabulous Maggie Point. She had all the confidence and vibrancy in the world. And she set her sights on poor, shy Noah Winters."

Edith couldn't help the quick jab of self-doubt, the cross hook of comparing herself to the legend of Maggie. She was certain no one would ever describe *her* the way Berta had just described Maggie. Edith shifted her position under the discomfort and asked, "What were they like as a couple?"

"Well, to be honest, it was a strange pairing. Of course, they *looked* great together, but they were complete opposites in temperament. Where Noah was quiet and thoughtful, Maggie was loud and flippant. Where he was meticulous and hard-working, she was easy-going and easily distracted. She thrived on the attention of others and he hated a crowd. But Maggie pretty much always got what she wanted, and I think she thought she could draw him out of his shell. She didn't really understand him." Berta furrowed her brow. "I really wonder how their relationship would have survived the years had the accident not happened."

"You think they would have had problems?"

Berta shrugged. "It's hard to say. Over the years I've watched a lot of marriages fall apart over less than how people like to socialize. But sometimes opposites really do attract, and it works. Who knows?"

"But he loved her so deeply?"

"Love doesn't really thrive if you can't get along." Berta smiled. "That's the hard thing about relationships: Attraction isn't the same as love and love doesn't work unless you are mature enough to put in the effort. Maggie was many amazing things, but mature wasn't one of them."

Edith frowned. She'd built up this ideal woman in her mind, this impenetrable goddess, but, of course, Maggie was just a young woman trying to figure out her life.

Edith shifted gears. "You said you were there the day she died. What happened?"

Berta sighed. "Maggie loved to push the limits—of just about everything—but that day she got it in her head to raise the gate to the highest point to challenge a young horse. His name was Running Waters. He had this gorgeous blue-gray coat and he could *run*. So fast! I wonder if he should have been a racehorse and not a jumper. Anyway . . . she'd been training him for about a month, and he showed amazing potential. But . . ." Berta shook her head, eyes heavy with the memory. "She asked too much. Waters balked at the last second and launched Maggie from the saddle." Berta paused to take a breath. She spoke quieter. "I *heard* her neck snap, the kind of awful sound you *feel* more than hear. When I got to her, she was gone. First thing I thought was: How will Noah ever survive it?"

Edith shivered, folded her arms. "Rumor has it he didn't handle it very well."

"You heard about the barn?"

Edith flinched, her stomach dropping at the way Berta said it. "No. What barn?"

Berta sighed, and shook her head. "The night of Maggie's death the Point Barn—that big, beautiful barn with all the horse stalls—burned to the ground."

Edith stilled. "Noah set the barn on fire?"

Berta nodded somberly. "He was so devastated, so broken, that he showed up at the barn in the middle of the night with a shotgun. He was headed to Running Waters' stall." Berta met Edith's shocked gaze with a significant expression.

"He went there to *shoot* the horse?" Edith felt cold all over, which had nothing to do with the ocean breeze picking up strength.

"Oh, yes. We all need someone or something to blame when things go wrong. Especially after a tragedy like that. Noah blamed Running Waters. But"—Berta held up a hand—"he *didn't* shoot the horse. Noah had a deep respect for animals. He had worked on the ranch a bit, helping to rehabilitate injured horses. He just couldn't do it. And when he realized he couldn't shoot Waters he just . . . lost it." She shrugged, the gesture full of sadness. "He threw his gun, he threw feed buckets and tack, and kicked in stall doors. At some point a lantern overturned in a pile of straw." Berta paused to shake her head and take a breath. "Maggie's father found Noah collapsed on the floor of the barn with bloody hands and a broken foot, surrounded by flames. He dragged Noah out and let the horses free just in time. The building was a total loss. Barns burn so fast. I saw the flames from my house here on Orcas."

Edith slumped back in her chair, the shock rippling through her to lift goose flesh on her arms and legs. She put a hand to her stomach. *Oh, Noah.* She fought back tears, knowing Berta wouldn't understand such an emotional reaction to her story. "I can't imagine . . ." She couldn't finish the sentence.

"I know. Breaks my heart all over. Of course, you know that he built her house anyway. I thought about going to visit him but never could get up the nerve. I didn't know what to say and I didn't want to intrude. When I heard he turned away all visitors, I gave up on trying to talk myself into it. But now, looking back, I should have gone." She nodded thoughtfully. "Are you okay, dear? Oh, no! I've upset you."

Edith straightened, trying to wipe the emotions from her face. "No, no. I'm fine. It's just a . . . touching story. I wonder what it would be like to love someone like that." The question made her ache. She realized she could easily love Noah that intensely, but could he ever love her like he'd loved Maggie? Not that it mattered since they could never really be together. Edith looked up to see Berta observing her.

"Here's what I know about love, Edith—and I should know, I was married to my Gavin for sixty-one years—it needs *time.* Lots of time to grow and take root. What Noah and Maggie had together never got to the point of deep love, only that shallow but overwhelming infatuation we feel in the beginning. Their love was incomplete and that's why it hurt Noah so much. And that's why he was a fool to deny himself a second chance. He never got to know what *real* love felt like."

Edith's goose bumps spread. "He's incomplete," she breathed, not intending to say it out loud.

"What was that?" Berta leaned forward.

Edith started to shake her head, but the French doors opened and they turned. "Grandma, what are you doing out here?" April's eyes went to Edith with a disapproving glint. "We're about to start."

"I'll be right there." Berta reached out to pat Edith's arm. "Sorry, Edith, I've got to go. It was a pleasure talking with you. I hope that helped."

Edith stood, helping Berta to her feet. "It did. Thank you very much."

Berta smiled and gave Edith a nod. "I'll give you a call about my party soon."

"I look forward to it." Edith felt a bit dazed as she watched Berta walk into the house.

Once Berta passed April, she said, "The deck circles around to the driveway. Don't forget your check." Then she closed the door with an authoritative snap.

Edith managed to turn and walk. She gathered her boxes, and her check, and got in the van. She reached for the ignition but didn't turn the key. She couldn't stop picturing Noah in that barn. "How can I compete with that?" she asked the windshield. It sounded petty, but it felt important. Noah was a ghost because he couldn't let go of his wife. He'd spent over sixty years trapped in his love for Maggie, even if Berta was right and he shouldn't have been. The full weight of Noah's story hit her for the first time.

"And last night I kissed him."

Edith dropped her forehead to the steering wheel. The tears dripped off her cheeks. Without looking she fumbled for her phone sitting in a cup holder in the console. She dialed the number and put it on speaker. *Please answer. Please answer.*

"Edith, what's wrong?" Milo answered.

His brotherly intuition only made her cry harder. "Milo . . ." was all she could manage.

"Okay, take a few breaths. I'm here."

She listened as he moved from a noisy space to a quiet one.

"Edith? What happened?"

The words came out in a cry-mashed, high-pitched mumble. "I kissed Noah Winters and now I don't know what to do."

Twenty

"I FEEL LIKE this is an impossible situation."

"Come on, Edie, we can figure it out."

"How? He can't leave. I'm not leaving. And we can't just stop feeling what we feel. We are *both* trapped." Edith rubbed her thumbnail along the stitching on the steering wheel. The van was still parked at April's house, and she was starting to feel self-conscious. If April happened to find her . . . Edith started the van, and drove out of the long driveway.

"He should go back into hiding," Milo suggested.

"That didn't work. It was worse because we both knew we were close."

Milo sighed. "And Cori said he'd pass on if he found what his soul needed?" Milo laughed without humor. "That doesn't sound difficult or cheesy at all!"

"It's not funny, Milo."

"I know!" Milo blew out a long exhale. "Okay, so he just needs to find it, find that thing. What is *it*?"

"I don't know. It's not like he can find Maggie. She's dead and not a ghost."

"Are you sure?"

Edith frowned. "What do you mean?"

"Well, she wouldn't be a ghost in your house. She didn't die there."

Edith's hands tensed on the wheel, and she looked at her phone propped in the cup holder. "You think she's at Point Ranch? But that's not there anymore. It's luxury homes now."

"But she could still be there, right?"

Edith shook her head. "Even if she were, Noah can barely leave our property, let alone go to the other side of the island. I bet it'd be the same for Maggie. *If* she's there and that's a big IF."

"But it's a place to start. You should go look."

"Go look for Maggie's ghost?"

"Yep."

"Right now?"

"No time like the present."

"But I need to get back to the farm."

"Excuse! Go look. It won't take long."

"Uh, yes it will. I can't just drive around the streets yelling out her name. That's all private property and gated mansions. I'll get arrested for trespassing. And I *really* don't have time for that."

"Ask Cori. Maybe she knows an easy way to find a ghost since her mom was the expert and all."

Edith chewed on her bottom lip. Could Maggie really be there? Could finding her help Noah move on? Edith's stomach knotted. "I don't know."

"Do you have any other ideas?"

Edith sighed. "No."

"Well . . ."

"Okay. I'll go ask Cori." She turned onto the main road. "But there's still one big problem."

"What?"

"If I reunite Noah and Maggie, if I help heal his soul, and he leaves . . ." Edith's throat tightened. "Milo, that means he'd leave me." Her body went cold, her heart recoiling at the idea.

I'll be left behind again.

Another person I love will leave me.

Milo was quiet for a moment. "I know, Edie. I don't have an answer for that one."

Noah moved to pull a weed from near his foot but stopped when an odd shot of electricity moved down his spine. He froze for a moment, eyes and ears alert. He was at the far end of the fields, near where Edith had planted her dahlia tubers. He'd turned around fully before he saw the flash of yellow at the end of the row.

He took off at a full sprint.

Skidding to a stop in the place he'd seen it, he found nothing. The rows were empty. He moved quickly to the right, looking down each path between the beds. Nothing. Nothing. *Nothing.* Another jolt up his spine. As he spun around a flash of yellow moved just out of the edge of his vision.

He ran faster this time.

When once again he found only soil and hoop tunnels, he stood at the edge of the field and balled his hands into fists. "Who are you?" he yelled. "What do you want?" He waited for an answer, but none came. He growled under his breath. "Stay away from Edith. You hear me? Leave! You don't belong here."

A thick, tar-sticky sense of dread welled up inside him. It was something in the air, or maybe inside of him, but he knew something was wrong. Noah turned in a full circle again, gaze intent on the fields. He hated the feeling of being out of control, of not knowing the problem.

"What's wrong, Noah?"

Noah jerked around, relieved, but also annoyed, to find Toby behind him. "Did you see her?" Noah asked quickly.

"Who?"

"The woman in the yellow dress. I saw . . . or *thought* I saw her."

Toby shook his head. "But the air feels strange. Is that because of her . . . or *you*?"

Noah dropped his gaze to the ghost-boy. "It's not me. Why would it be me?"

Toby tilted his head to the side. "I'm not sure. I think it might be both of you."

Noah pressed his teeth together. He wasn't interested in Toby's vague, mystic observations. The boy narrowed his eyes. He lifted his hand and poked Noah's stomach with a sharp little finger. "Hey! What're you doing?" Noah snapped.

Toby frowned as he withdrew his hand. "You're too solid. Look . . ." The boy turned his pointer finger toward himself, and Noah watched as the boy pushed into his own abdomen. The outline of Toby's stomach gave the slightest amount, denting like soft dough. Noah frowned. Toby came at him again and pushed harder. His outline didn't give at all. "See that?" Toby asked.

Noah laid his hand over the spot where Toby had pushed. The boy stepped back. Noah wasn't sure what to say other than, "I don't understand."

Toby looked back toward the house. "I told you: you're changing."

Noah thought of the kiss on Edith's bed. He thought of that pull of energy, the way his body had reached out to hers and then drawn on . . . *something* . . . hard. Instantly, he felt sick to his stomach. "No, no, no. Could I be . . . ?" He didn't even know what words to use to describe it. "Am I hurting her?"

"Edith gives things life." Toby said quietly.

Noah's head snapped down to the boy. "What?" His mind latched onto the idea and tried to shape it into something he could understand. Was Edith changing him, more than emotionally? He shook his head. "No, that's not possible, Toby. I'm dead. Dead is dead."

Toby shrugged. "How do you know?"

Noah opened his mouth and then shut it tight. *I don't know. I don't know anything.*

"Can I go visit the chicks?"

Noah blinked at the boy, confused by his child-mind shift of attention. "Uh . . . yeah. Go ahead." He waved him off. His thoughts cranked and spun. He remembered what Edith had said about the woman in yellow: *She wanted something from me.* Icy fear vibrated through him. If, *somehow,* Edith was changing him, giving him life, had this other ghost come for the same? Did she want to pull *life* out of Edith? Was that what had happened during the kiss? Was that even possible?

Noah's knees gave out and he dropped to the dirt, head in his hands.

"What am I doing to her? What have I done?"

Edith cranked the wheel of the van to maneuver it into a parking space in front of Coriander's Coffee. She took a big breath and jumped out of the car, determined to ask Cori about finding Maggie's ghost. No matter how crazy and impossible it sounded. She pushed her way into the busy shop, and, seeing all the customers, almost turned around.

Cori is too busy for this right now. Ask her later.

No, ask her now.

Edith by-passed the line and went straight to the counter. She leaned over to look around the espresso machine. "Cori?"

Cori looked up from the cup she was holding under the steamer. Her eyes went wide. "Edith? You okay?"

"I just need to ask you something. Really quick. I know you're busy. Sorry—"

Understanding registered in Cori's eyes. "Just give me a few minutes. Meet me in the back."

Edith nodded as she let out a sigh of relief. She hurried behind the counter and into the quiet of the back room. She paced the length of the long stainless-steel table, ringing her hands, and trying to understand what was going on in her life.

Cori plowed through the door. "Did something go wrong at the shower?"

"No, it was great. Actually, I met this old woman who knew Noah. But that's not what I need to talk to you about."

"Okay," Cori said. "But I want to hear about *that* at some point." She crossed her arms, serious and ready to listen.

Edith nodded. "I need to find Maggie."

Cori narrowed her eyes. "Noah's Maggie? Well, I think she's buried in the cemetery. But—"

"No, I need to find *her.* I think she might be a ghost too."

Cori's eyes pulled wide. "Why do you think that?"

"It's a theory Milo came up with. I kissed Noah last night and—"

Cori threw her arms out. "Wait—WHAT? Why didn't you start with *that?* You kissed him? You *kissed* the ghost of Noah Winters. Is that . . . possible?"

Edith grimaced. "Yes, apparently it is. But it was . . . weird."

Cori pulled back. "Weird? There's no way that man is a bad kisser."

Edith scoffed. "Oh, no, the kiss itself wasn't weird. That

was amazing, but then it changed. It just . . . something made me feel super dizzy and . . . *weird.*"

"Okay. We've established that something was *weird.*" Cori smiled, teasing.

"I can't describe it, Cori. It was this crazy pulling, floating, falling sensation. It scared us both. Really bad."

Cori sobered. "I'm sure it did. A live person kissing a dead person—that can't go right. But what does that have to do with Maggie?"

Edith leaned back into the table, suddenly exhausted. She shook her head. "He burned down a barn for her. He almost shot a horse and went mad and *burned down* the Point's fancy barn."

Cori blinked quickly and then raised her eyebrows. "What?" she whispered.

"The lady at the party, Berta, she was there; she knew Maggie and Noah. She told me all about it. Noah loved Maggie so much that he burned down a barn and then became a ghost because he was so ruined. He needs her." Edith's voice wavered. "He needs *her,* not me."

"Oh, Edie." Cori crossed the space between them and joined her at the table. She put her arm around Edith's shoulders. "I think you are important to him too."

Edith shook her head and pushed on, determined not to fall apart. "If Maggie broke his soul maybe she can fix it." Edith let out a shaky exhale. She hated the sound of the words and the desolation they brought.

"You think reuniting them is the answer to Noah finding peace and moving on? But what if Maggie isn't a ghost? What if she's not here?"

Edith shrugged, resigned. "We can't go on like this, Noah and I. It's so hard and . . . unnatural. I have to do *something.* This is all I've got."

"Okay. So, we need to look for Maggie's ghost?"

"We think she'd be over where her family's ranch was located. But that's acres of space. Do you know if there's a way to find a ghost? To . . . summon it?" Edith scoffed. "I can't believe I'm saying these things."

Cori nodded. "Maybe if we had a personal item. I think I remember something about that in my mom's journals. Did Noah keep anything of hers?"

"The bells. Maggie had custom bells made for their first Christmas. One for him and one for her."

"That's good. Okay. Let's check those journals tonight. You can help me look."

Edith nodded. "Okay. Thanks." She sighed. "I know this is crazy."

Cori hugged Edith's shoulders a little tighter. "It's not crazy. You're doing exactly what you should: trying to figure it out. It's an impossible situation."

"That's what I told Milo." Edith leaned into Cori, her cheek against the older woman's chin. "If this works and . . . he . . . leaves, what will I do when he's gone?"

Cori sighed. "You'll have to mourn Noah as if he'd died. 'Cause to you that's what it will feel like. I'm so sorry, sweetie."

Edith closed her eyes. "How unfair is it that the first man I love is a ghost?"

Cori hugged her tighter. "Would you rather you hadn't met him?"

A tear slipped down Edith's cheek and onto Cori's shoulder. "No," she whispered.

Cori nodded against Edith's head. She was quiet for a long time, just holding Edith against her. Edith kept her eyes closed and savored the support, trying her best not to mourn already. Finally, Cori said, "I think you need a chai latte and a nap. Barista's orders." She gave Edith another squeeze. "Okay?"

"Sounds good. Thanks, Cori."

"Come on, I'll show you how to use my fancy machine out there. It's like taming a dragon."

Edith half smiled as she followed Cori out into the shop.

Noah sat on the green couch, elbows on knees, hands interlaced. He bounced his right leg, fidgety, and kept his ear tuned for the sound of Edith coming back. He glimpsed up at the clock. "Where is she?" he murmured. At the sound of tires on gravel, he froze.

He waited in stillness while the van looped around the back to the barn. He didn't move when the back door opened and Edith's purse hit the floor with a soft sound. And he didn't turn when she walked up behind him. He felt the fatigue coming off her in waves with an undercurrent of anxiety. He felt it without looking, and he had to close his eyes under the weight of it.

"Noah, I—"

He cut her off. "I can't hurt you again."

A pause. "Hurt me? What are you talking about?"

"Our kiss. I think . . ." He shook his head. "I'm hurting you and it's changing me."

"You're not hurting me."

"Yes, I am. When we kissed last night—that pulling, falling sensation—I think I was drawing life out of you." He grimaced, closed his eyes.

She took a step closer. "Why would you think *that*?"

"I'm not the same as I was before you came. My body or spirit or *whatever I am* is different. I think . . ." He pressed his jaw shut for a moment. "I think I'm drawing life from you and it's hurting you."

"How? How could that even be possible?"

Noah hated the rim of fear around Edith's voice. "I don't know," he whispered. Her hand came to his shoulder and he jerked away, exploding up to his feet to finally face her. "Don't touch me!"

She flinched like he'd slapped her. "Noah—"

He opened his hands in a supplicating gesture. "I don't know how to explain it, but I can't bear the thought of hurting you in any way. Don't touch me, don't kiss me, don't even come near me."

Edith reached for the back of the couch. Her face grew pale. "No, but—"

"Edith, please!" It came out with much more force than he'd intended. Edith took a stunned step backwards. He balled his hands into fists. "Edith—"

She lifted a hand to stop him, shaking her head as she turned. Without a word she went up the stairs. He flinched when her bedroom door slammed. Noah picked up the lamp from his desk and hurled it with all his might against the wall. The stained glass splintered and exploded across the room. A huge ugly dent in the wall sneered back at him. Noah sunk to the couch and put his face in his hands.

Edith's door opened. Her feet drummed down the stairs. He felt her behind him again. For a long while, he listened to her rapid breaths. "Get out," she hissed.

Noah flinched, his shoulders collapsing forward. The air in the room chilled. "I'm sorry—"

"I want you out. Go to the barn. If you want to throw things and have a tantrum then do it in there. But not in our"—she made a noise that was part grunt part whimper—"*my* beautiful house." Edith sniffed, her voice broken and uneven. "Please, just go. We need . . . space. I need space. I need you to *go*."

He nodded, unable to look at her. "I'm sorry," he repeated, quieter, softer.

Edith fled back up the stairs. Her door closed quietly.

Noah pulled himself up from the couch and went to spend the night in the barn with the chickens.

Edith flung herself down on the bed. She pushed her face into a pillow and let out a frustrated yell. Then, rolling to her side to breathe, she let the tears slide down her face. She hadn't missed the violent, angry side of Noah.

My poor lamp and poor wall.

What just happened?

Edith brought her fingers to her wet lips. Was Noah right? Had their kiss pulled life out of her? She closed her eyes.

No. No way. That's not possible.

But falling in love with a ghost is also not possible.

Just how much life had he pulled? Was she in danger? Could he seriously harm her? The idea made her sick. She'd come to feel so safe and at ease around Noah. She hated the thought that just being near him might hurt her. But, if she did give him life, what did that mean for Noah? Could it mean that he could be human again?

Can I bring him back to life?

Edith reached out to touch the daffodils on her nightstand.

"No, stop it," she whispered to herself. "That's crazy! You can't bring Noah back to life with a kiss." She scoffed. "You're trying to make it real so he can stay. It's not real, he's not real. He can't stay! The only answer here, the only solution, is that Noah moves on. End of story." She waited to feel convinced, but the feeling didn't come.

All she felt was completely wasted.

She closed her eyes and turned her face into the pillow-case to rub away her tears.

I'm so tired.

Maybe because Noah is right.

No! I stayed up all night and it's been a crazy day.

Just normal tired. Normal.

So . . . tired . . .

Twenty-one

"EDITH? EDITH, SWEETIE, wake up?"

Edith blinked, trying to bring her vision into focus. "Cori?"

"When you didn't show up for dinner, I got worried." Cori sat down on the bed at Edith's feet.

Edith sighed. Curled on her side, she looked at the windows, "What time is it?"

"Almost sunset."

"Oh, no. I didn't mean to sleep that long." She puffed out a frustrated sigh. "I was supposed to transplant some daisies today."

"They will keep until tomorrow." Cori frowned severely. "You want to tell me what happened to that lamp downstairs?"

Edith groaned as she rolled onto her back. "Well, *I* don't throw lamps, especially not real Tiffany Studios lamps from 1928."

Cori rolled her eyes. "What made Noah so mad? Did you tell him about your Maggie plan?"

"No. I didn't get a chance. He thinks he's hurting me, that somehow he's pulling life from me." Edith brought her hand to her face and rubbed at her temple.

"What?" Cori scoffed. "Like a . . . vampire?" She raised a cynical eyebrow.

Edith laughed mirthlessly. "I don't know. He didn't make much sense, but he was *so* upset. I kicked him out after the lamp thing. He's in the barn."

"He thinks what happened during the kiss was actually dangerous for you?"

Edith nodded.

"Do you agree with him?"

"I have no idea. I can't make sense of *any* of this."

"Speaking of . . ." Cori held up a book. "I found the journal."

Edith pushed up to a seated position. She didn't feel rested or refreshed. "What does it say?"

Cori flipped the small brown, leather-bound notebook open to a marked page. "I was right about the personal item. Once you have that it's pretty simple." She pointed to a paragraph and handed the book to Edith.

Edith read aloud, "'Hold the object in your hand, close your eyes, and focus on the owner. Silently ask her to come to you. If the spirit is willing and your spirit is pure, she will appear.'" Edith looked up. "That's it? No Ouija boards or spells or blood sacrifices?"

Cori smiled. "Nope. Easy peasy. Or at least it was for my mom and her gift. I don't know if *we* will be as successful."

Edith frowned doubtfully. She looked back at the page. "What does it mean 'if your spirit is pure'?"

"A ghost won't appear if someone means her harm or has questionable intentions. There has to be a reason, a pure intention. Like helping another ghost find peace." Cori gave her a meaningful look.

"Right. Okay." She set the journal on the bed and went to

her dresser. The bells were tucked into the bottom drawer. She took them out and went back to the bed. She pulled off the lid.

"Those are beautiful," Cori said reverently as she touched the silver surfaces.

"I know." Edith lifted out Maggie's bell. "I take this over to the Point Ranch area, hold it, and ask her to come?" Edith scrunched up her face. "No way that works, Cori."

"It would, but it's not necessary."

Edith and Cori both screamed, jerking away from the woman now standing in the half circle of the turret space. Edith clasped Cori's hand and they pressed back against the headboard. Edith's heart raced uncomfortably as she recognized the woman in the yellow dress. "M-Maggie?"

"Hello, Edith Daniels. Yes, I'm Maggie Winters. Nice to meet you."

Her married name slapped Edith across the face. *This is Noah's wife. She belongs to him, not you.* She felt dread replace her shock. "You're here." It wasn't a question.

"I've come for Noah. You've helped him heal and now it's time he moves on."

Maggie looked angelic and otherworldly standing in the buttery sunset light streaming in the windows. Edith understood what Maggie had just said, but it wasn't sticking in her mind. "You're here to take Noah away?"

"Yes. I want to thank you for helping him."

Edith furrowed her brow. She didn't want Maggie to thank her; she didn't want Maggie to be here at all. She knew she *should* want that. Noah would move on, leave, as he wanted. And she'd be left behind. Alone, on her farm, her heart shattered like petals after frost.

He will leave me. I can't survive someone else I love leaving me.

She started to shake her head. Cori spoke before Edith could protest. "He's in the barn."

Edith snapped her gaze to Cori. "No," she whispered.

"It's time, honey." Cori tightened her grip on Edith's hand. When they turned back to Maggie she was gone, and the room hummed with her absence. Edith started to get off the bed, but Cori pulled her back. "This is what needs to happen. You know that."

"He can't leave," Edith whined pathetically. She tried to pull away again.

"Edith, take a breath and think. You can't stop this. You don't really want to. You were going to find Maggie yourself for just *this* purpose."

Edith shook her head, panic itching under skin. She couldn't catch her breath. She tried to listen to Cori, but everything felt so wrong. "No, no. He's supposed to be here with me."

Cori frowned deeply, her eyes misting. "No, sweetie. He's supposed to be there with her. He always should have been."

Edith thought of that burning barn and of the look in Noah's eyes in those first days she'd known him. *He's supposed to be with her.* She took a long, slow breath. *I have to let him go.* She turned to Cori, "I have to say goodbye."

Noah sat in the dirt, leaning back against the cold metal of the chick brooder. He listened to their tiny noises and stared out the open barn doors at the house. *Our house.* Edith had accidentally said it, but they had both come to think of it as such. Noah frowned. It wasn't Maggie's house anymore. It never really had been, had it? Without realizing it, he'd come to think of the house as Edith's. She embodied it perfectly, she loved it deeply. She didn't just understand the house and land, she understood him. Genuinely and completely, like no one else ever had.

Not even Maggie.

Maggie had loved him but never truly understood him. And he'd loved her but not like this. Things with Edith were so different. Noah took a slow breath. "I love Edith," he whispered, his chest aching fiercely.

He loved her and belonged with her.

Noah and Edith. Us. Together. My house and her house. And she just kicked me out of it.

Noah rubbed his hands over his face.

How can I fix this?

A jab of electricity hit him hard in the back of the neck. He jerked upright, away from the brooder, all senses alert. The woman in yellow stepped into the large open doorway. Her face was lost in the shadows of the setting sun, but something in her walk was shockingly familiar.

Noah leaned forward and waited as she advanced.

Another bolt of power hit him in the chest as he realized who it was. "Maggie?" he hissed, his voice failing.

The woman stepped into the light. "Hello, Noah." She smiled her dazzling smile, her face young and fresh, just as he remembered it. Her golden hair shone even in the dull light inside the barn, and her whole person seemed to glow softly. She gracefully folded her hands. "Miss me?" she added, bright and casual. So very Maggie.

Noah stood frozen, unable to move or speak.

No. This isn't happening.

I'm hallucinating.

No, this isn't real.

"Oh, this is real, my love," Maggie said, stepping closer. Her yellow sundress swished lightly as she moved. "I've come for you."

Noah forced himself to get to his feet. "What?" he breathed. "Maggie? Is that really you?" He moved to within a foot and drank in the details of her.

She smiled, her expression soft and tender. "Hey, cowboy."

Noah shivered. "You're not supposed to be here. What are you doing here?"

"I just told you." She laughed lightly. "I've come to get you. It's time."

Noah shook his head. "Time for what?"

"Time for you to move on. You've let go of your anger and hurt. You've healed. So now you can come with me."

"Where?" he breathed, the single word felt like a noose.

"Our own little heaven. I have everything prepared. We'll have everything we didn't get to enjoy in this life."

The words did not bring the relief he had imagined. All those times he had prayed and begged for this, and now the words made him want to turn and run. He thought of *this* place, this haven that Edith had created with her blue farmhouse and fields of flowers. He thought of the planted seeds he wouldn't see bloom. The chicks behind him he wouldn't see grow. The unfinished manuscript on his desk. And Edith . . . beautiful, quiet Edith with all that latent strength inside her. "I'm not ready," he whispered.

Maggie laughed. "Of course, you are." Noah looked over her shoulder to the house. He could barely see the bottom ledge of Edith's bedroom window. Maggie followed his gaze. "Edith will be fine, Noah."

He pulled his eyes back to her. Slowly, he closed the small space between them and lifted a hesitant hand to Maggie's cheek. "You're actually here?"

"Yes." She put her hand on top of his and pressed his palm to her warm cheek. "I'm here. I've waited for you for *so* long and now it's time to go. Time to be together again."

Noah searched his wife's face. He waited to feel that relief, that powerful love he'd felt for so long. He waited to *want* to go. *What's wrong with me?* "Have I changed, Maggie?"

She furrowed her brow. "Changed? There's this gray in your beard and hair." She touched his cheek. "But I like it." Another bright smile.

"No, not that." Noah looked at his hand on her cheek and saw the slight blur of her surface under his touch. That ghostly shimmer. His hand looked solid, impenetrable.

Maggie noted his observation. "Oh, that?" she asked. "You've been earth bound too long. I had started to worry you wouldn't be able to pass over but there's still time. You're okay."

Noah felt a quick vibration of relief, but then a thought came to him: *Toby has been here much longer than me and he's not solid like this.* Noah let his hand drop from Maggie's face. "Some ghosts get stuck? They stay here forever?"

Maggie shrugged, nonchalant. "I believe so but not you. Come on, let's go." She smiled and reached for his hand.

He pulled away. "What happens if I don't want to go?"

The happiness drained from Maggie's face. "Why would you even say that? Don't you want to be with me?"

Noah's gaze flickered to the house. "Why were you in Edith's bedroom last night?"

"I was looking for you."

"Did you see...?" He frowned, dropped his eyes. "Did you see what happened?"

A pause. "Yes," she breathed.

"What did I do to Edith?"

"You kissed her." Her voice was flat.

He growled in frustration. "No, what *happened?*"

Maggie's eyes narrowed. "Noah Winters, you don't belong here. You're supposed to come with me, your wife."

"Maggie, please. Did I hurt Edith?"

Maggie folded her arms. For a long moment, she said nothing. She studied him, her piercing eyes moving over his face. Finally, she answered, "Her spirit tried to join yours. You were pulling her spirit out of her body."

Noah stumbled back as if Maggie had sucker punched him. "What?" he breathed.

"You're a spirit, Noah. She's alive: a spirit *inside* a body. When you touch or kiss her it thickens your bond to this place, this earth. It doesn't give you *life*, it just prolongs your suffering. And when she kisses you her spirit tries to join yours . . . outside her body."

"But that would . . ." Noah brought a hand to his mouth and pressed his eyes shut against a wave of terror.

I wasn't hurting her. I was killing her.

"Yes, Noah. That's why it's best we leave." She moved back to him and took his hand. She placed it between her own and then tucked his arm against her chest. "Remember this? Remember *us*, Noah? You belong with me. Please, it's time to go."

Noah looked into his wife's gorgeous blue eyes. "I need to say goodbye first."

Edith hurtled down the stairs and sprinted through the kitchen. She didn't notice the cold dirt under her bare feet or the chill air on her arms. She cut through the garden. The barn doors were pulled wide open, and as she approached, Noah came shuffling out, hands in pockets, head hung. At the sound of her running over the dirt, he lifted his head, his gaze locking with hers.

She picked up her speed and ran straight into his arms.

He caught her, stumbling back with her weight but keeping them on their feet. His arms tightened around her back. She buried her face in his neck. "No," she whispered. "I'm not ready."

He held her tighter. "Me either," he whispered back.

Edith pressed her eyes shut. She knew Maggie was there, standing stiffly behind them, but she refused to acknowledge her. Noah kept one arm around her waist while the other hand moved up her neck to tangle in her sleep-messy hair at the base of her head. His body trembled. Or was that hers?

"Edith, I . . ." Noah's voice faltered. His lips came to her temple. "We don't have a choice," he whispered against her skin.

She nodded, her throat too clogged with grief to speak. She locked her arms tighter around his neck. She felt his hold on her release. His hands went to her forearms to gently pry her away. She held his gaze, a million words passing between them. His eyes glazed with tears as he stepped away from her. Edith let her arms drop to her sides, painfully heavy.

Cori was there instantly, taking Edith's hand and letting her lean against her to keep from sagging to the ground. Edith's eyes were still locked with Noah's.

Don't go. Stay with me.

He gently shook his head. Maggie stepped up beside him. She slipped her hand around his arm. Edith felt a curl of fiery resentment lick at her throat. *She's taking him from me.* But Edith knew Noah had never really been free in the first place. *I knew who he was, and I did this to myself.*

Noah looked as if he wanted to say something but then his eyes dropped. Edith gasped at the flash of agony in her chest. He and Maggie turned and walked toward the fields. Edith couldn't watch. She pulled away from Cori and walked slowly back to the house, her body quivering from the pain.

She got as far as the rose garden next to the willow tree before she collapsed to the cold grass. She rolled onto her side; limbs tucked close to her body. She didn't cry; she just pressed her eyes shut and let the hurt throb inside her. Cori came to sit in the grass beside her. She put a hand on Edith's back and said nothing.

Noah brought his hand to his face, surprised to find it wet with tears. He hadn't shed a single tear since his death. Not even in some of the darkest moments of his afterlife. Everything inside him felt sodden and weighed down. The more steps he took away from Edith and his house, the worse it felt.

This can't be right.

If I were meant to move on it should feel good. Feel right.

He glanced over at Maggie.

Nothing about this feels right.

"Maggie, I . . ." Noah stopped walking. Maggie dropped her hand from his arm and turned to face him. "I can't do this," he finished.

Maggie sighed. "Noah, this is the natural order of things. You're not supposed to be here. I understand that after so long it's hard to leave, but I promise we will be incredibly happy. Just like we always planned. This little detour is over."

Noah rubbed at his jaw, thinking of his kiss with Edith. Something about Maggie's explanation didn't sit well. "If I stayed and became an earth-bound spirit, as you said, would I still hurt her?"

"It doesn't matter. You're not staying. Why would you want to live like that?"

Noah looked at his hands, the palms open. "I want to stay," he whispered. He looked up to gauge Maggie's reaction.

A flicker of pain moved through her eyes. "You can't."

"Yes, I can. I can feel it. I know I belong here with her." Noah stepped to Maggie, gripping her upper arms. "Maggie, I loved you once, I loved you so much it nearly destroyed me, but I'm not that man anymore. I belong here with Edith. I've never been more certain of anything."

Maggie shook her head, unwilling to look at him. "You're not hearing me: You *can't* stay. This isn't a choice. Your soul is ready to move on, and no one turns away from that."

"There has to be a way. Please help me."

"You've known her for only a few months, Noah. Our love story started over *sixty years* ago. I know you want to be with me. You're just nervous. You'll forget her once you see."

"See what?" Noah growled.

Maggie turned her head to the side.

Noah followed her gaze. An arched doorway appeared a few feet behind them, subtly flickering and glowing in the center of the field. Noah instantly felt its pull, its call to him. Inside the open doorway he saw an expanse of lush green grass leading down a hill to a farmhouse, white and clean, and exactly like the one he'd just left. Sheep and horses in the pastures. Corn and wheat in the fields. He smelled fresh bread and coffee.

"You see," Maggie said, moving away from him to stand near the doorway, "our own little heaven. And it's waiting."

Maggie held out her hand to Noah.

Twenty-two

"MILO, I'M WORRIED," Cori whispered into the phone. Edith could hear her perfectly. "I could barely get her in the house."

Edith lay on the green couch, the side of her face pressed to the velvet. Cori stood near the windows, Edith's phone pressed to her ear. Edith thought of the first night she'd slept in here and how Noah had tried to scare her away. Her lips twitched, trying to smile, but it didn't happen. She closed her eyes.

He's gone. Noah is gone. Forever.

And I have a farm to run. Things that need me to keep them alive.

I don't abandon things I love.

She pushed herself up. "Give me the phone, Cori." Cori spun around, surprised. Edith held out her hand.

Cori hesitated and then said into the phone, "Milo, Edith wants to talk. Here she is."

Edith nodded her thanks to Cori and put the phone to her ear. "I'm fine."

"No way you're fine. I knew I should have booked a flight when we talked earlier."

Edith felt comforted at the sound of Milo's voice. "I'm fine. I promise. I'll be fine."

"I can come out. I'll fly out tomorrow."

"No, Milo, really. I'm sad, I'm hurt, but I have the farm to focus on. I'll heal."

"But Edie . . . you loved him. It's impossible but it happened."

"I know. I'm not going to let that ruin my life like Noah let it ruin his."

A pause. "That's my big sis."

"We knew it would happen," she told Milo.

"Still, I'm so sorry. Does it feel like when Mom left?" he asked.

Edith thought briefly of their mother. She realized that if Noah had left a few months ago Edith would have blamed her mom. She would have seen it as a pattern in her life, just another person she loved who'd left her. But that wound had healed. Noah leaving had nothing to do with anything but his own path.

"I thought it would," she answered, "but no. Mom didn't leave because of me and Noah didn't either. They both needed to go for their own reasons. I can handle that."

"Yeah, so true. Sure you don't want me to come? I will."

"Thanks, but really, I'm okay. I wouldn't want your feet to get slow 'cause you have to come visit me."

Milo laughed. "No one can slow down these feet."

She smiled. "Good. I need to check on the chicks and then get some sleep. Call you tomorrow?"

"Yes. Anytime. I'll keep my phone close." Milo sighed. "I love you, flower girl."

"Love you, too, football boy. Say hi to Faye for me."

"I will. Goodnight."

"Night." Edith lowered her phone to her lap.

"I can check on the chickies," Cori offered.

"I want to do it. I need to do something." She looked at Cori who nodded her understanding. "Go home and get some sleep, Cori. I'll see you at the café bright and early. I'm gonna need a really big mocha tomorrow."

Cori laughed quietly. "Yes, you will."

Edith stood and walked over to pull Cori into a big hug. "Thank you. I couldn't do this without you."

Cori sniffled. "You're my girl. I'm here for you, anything you need. Okay?"

"Okay."

Cori pulled back, eyes swimming in unshed tears. She patted Edith's cheek. "Get some sleep."

"You too." Edith walked her to the front door and watched her go down the porch stairs and across the lawn. She closed the door and wanted to sink to the floor and start crying again but didn't. She went to the kitchen and pulled on her work boots and coat.

The night sky spread clear overhead, thick with glittered stars. Edith put her hands in her pockets and inhaled deeply. The air smelled like flowers. "Fight for the flowers," she whispered. "Even when that means fighting through a broken heart."

The chicks were nestled into a pile under the heating lamp, asleep and cutely peaceful. She lowered her hand into the trough to check the heat. Toasty and warm. She added some food to the small feeder. "Goodnight, babies," she whispered. "Grow strong."

"Did Noah leave?"

Edith gasped, a hand flying to her chest at the sight of the small boy. He wore an old-fashioned brown suit and had blonde hair and brown eyes. "Toby? Are you Toby?"

He nodded, his expression downcast. "He's gone, isn't he?"

Edith swallowed the lump of emotion that came instantly at the boy's despondent voice. "Yes. Noah is gone. He's with Maggie now."

"She lied to him"

Edith blinked. "What?"

"I heard her, and I think she lied. I don't know for sure but what she said felt wrong."

Edith narrowed her eyes. "What did she say?"

"She told Noah that kissing you pulled on your spirit, but I think it made him real. I think you gave him life and it didn't hurt you."

Edith rubbed at the center of her chest, an echo of the kiss sensations pulsing there. Her mind wanted to wrestle with this idea, but what was the point? "I don't know what happened, but Noah is gone so . . ." She put her hands back in her pockets.

"I will miss him. My tree gets lonely, even when the birds come."

Edith's heart ached. No child should be alone, especially not a ghost child. "You can come visit me. I always need help around the farm."

Toby's face brightened. "Can I help with the chicks?"

Edith laughed. "Anytime."

"Thank you, Edith."

"You're welcome. I'm going out to the fields. You want to stay here or come?"

"I'll stay and protect the chickens."

Edith smiled. "Sounds good. I know you'll keep them safe." Toby beamed up at her and then went to settle by the brooder.

Edith walked out to her flower fields. The neatness of the rows and the hills of white hoop tunnels soothed her raw soul. Soon there would be a new wave of Icelandic poppies with their bobbing heads and pale pastel colors, ranunculus with their layered round pedals and deep colors, and hundreds of friendly white daisies. There'd be sunflowers, zinnias, and loads of craspedia. Cosmos and asters and calendula. Simone's roses and peonies would dazzle with their champion blooms. And Edith would help them all grow and spread them around her corner of the world to bring life to people's days and power to their memories.

That's what I'll do because that's what I love.

Even if I have to do it without Noah by my side.

"Goodnight, babies," she repeated to her flowers. "Grow strong."

Reluctantly, she turned to head back inside.

Noah stood behind her.

Edith gasped, falling back a step. Instantly, she thought she'd imagined him, hallucinated him, but he took a step toward her. "Edith," he whispered, "do you trust me?"

"What? What are you doing here? Noah, what—"

"Do you *trust me?*" he repeated, firmly, all the while moving closer.

Edith's heart beat so fast it hurt. Noah stopped directly in front of her, only a breath away. She put a hand on his chest to be certain he was real. "Yes," she whispered.

In one swift movement, Noah pulled her against him and into a wild, warm kiss. A fevered rush of energy swept over her, bringing with it that free falling sensation. She ignored it, locking her arms around Noah's neck as his mouth moved desperately over hers.

Something in the energy of the kiss shifted but not at all like last time. Edith expected the crippling dizziness. Instead she felt a warm glow in the center of her chest. A pulsing that had nothing to do with her heart. Noah jerked away from her, gasping and clutching at his chest.

"Noah!" Edith tried to reach for him as he stumbled backwards. He hit the dirt hard, falling onto his back. She dropped to her knees next to him, her hands fluttering over him. "What's wrong? What's happening?" Noah had his eyes squeezed shut, his hands in fists on his shirt. She gripped his wrists. "Noah!"

Noah opened his eyes, his breath ragged. He lay puffing for air and looking at her in the most curious way. "My heart," he managed to say.

Edith shook her head, confused. Noah took her hand and pressed her palm to his chest. Edith gasped, a chill rushing up her spine. "Your heart is beating!" She lowered her ear to his chest to be sure. The steady rhythm of a healthy heart called out to her. "Your heart . . . *how*?"

Noah pushed himself up to sit in front of her. He took her face in his hands. "You. Toby was right. You've been bringing me back to life."

"But Maggie said—"

"She lied," he frowned. "She didn't want me to stay and knew I didn't want to hurt you. But as we walked away—when I walked away from you—I *knew* I had to stay. I knew I *wanted* to stay. I want to be here with *you*. I pushed Maggie for the truth, asked her to tell me if there was a way."

Edith shook her head. "I don't understand."

Noah moved his hands down her arms to hold her hands. "Your gift of giving things life, of helping things to grow, extended to me. It's not just your flowers, Edith." He swept a hand toward the fields around them. "Once Maggie realized how much I love you, she told me the truth. I had a choice: go with her and remain a spirit or stay with you and become whole again." He held her eyes. "I choose you."

Edith let out a shocked breath. "What?" she breathed, unable to believe his words or his choice.

Noah smiled. "Edith, from the first day we met you've challenged me and listened to me and loved me. You put life back into me, in every way possible. You saved my soul." He ran his fingers down her cheek. "I love you."

"But Maggie . . ."

"I love *you*, Edith Daniels. In ways I never loved Maggie. What I shared with her ended so long ago. It took me too long to realize it, but what we had was not nearly as amazing as I thought. But this . . ." He held her face again. "This is a miracle. An *actual* miracle." He glanced down at his chest.

Edith laughed, a rush of relief and joy swirling in her chest. "You're staying?"

"For good. Will you take me?"

Edith laughed out loud, her blood alive with energy. "I do need a farmhand. I don't really want to clean out the chicken coop."

Noah scoffed-laughed. "Don't be mean, Edith Daniels."

Tenderly, fingers trembling, she put her hands on his bearded cheeks. She met his stone blue eyes. "I love you, too, Noah Winters."

Noah smiled, pulling her close for a soft, lingering kiss.

Epilogue

August

EDITH SQUATTED DOWN next to an incredible café au lait dahlia, perfectly haloed by the rich, vibrant light of the sunset, and snapped a few pictures. The flower was the size of a dessert plate, and its elegant petals were a luscious creamy pink. It took her breath away, and she knew her Instagram followers would also swoon.

Straightening, she looked out over the acres of flowers. Every growing bed was in bloom, and there was a spectacular amount of color in every direction. "Simone, do you see this?" she whispered. "It's paradise. Thank you for that." Edith felt a pulse of warmth in her chest.

She turned to see Noah heading down the row toward her, a mug in each hand. Tea with the flowers at sunset had become a new ritual. Noah always made the tea while Edith snapped photos. He smiled and she melted. "Here you go," he said, handing her a mug.

"I can't get over how amazing this is," she said, looking over the rim of her mug at the rows of flowers.

"Simone would be very proud." He put his arm around her shoulder. Edith smiled; Noah knew her so well. He reached into his pocket. "Toby, our resident chicken whis-

273

perer, just brought me something. Look at this . . ." He held out a perfectly shaped, light blue egg.

Edith gave a little yelp of surprise. "Our first egg! Look at that color!" She took it from him. "This must be Rhonda's; she's the only Easter Egger. It's so pretty!"

Noah laughed. "It's just an egg."

"But it's *our* egg, from *our* chickens, in *our* coop. Come on, that's pretty cool."

Noah shook his head. "And it's blue. Very appropriate."

Edith gasped again. "Oh, my gosh! Yes! That's just amazing." She handed him the camera. "Take some pictures of it. We have to document this. The Blue Farmhouse Flowers' first egg is *blue*." She laughed, giddy with the magic of it.

Noah snapped a few of the small blue egg nestled in the palm of her hand, the sunflowers in the background. Edith looked toward the barn. "Where is Toby?"

"He couldn't leave the chickens after such an exciting moment." Noah leaned closer and focused the camera. "He said he had to stay and congratulate the girls."

Edith laughed. "Only Toby."

"That's for sure." As Noah handed back the camera, he asked, "You all ready for tomorrow?"

"Yep. I finished the last arrangement right before I came out."

"I can't imagine a better place for a wedding." Noah looked out over the fields. "Speaking of . . ."

They turned at the sounds of Milo and Faye laughing as they approached. Milo waved and called out, "Hey, farmers, can we crash your little tea party?"

Edith shook her head. "No, go away."

Milo laughed. He and Faye stopped next to Edith. Faye said, "This place is so magical, Edith. I love flowers, but this makes me fall in love all over again, every moment."

Edith smiled at her soon-to-be sister in law. Faye looked even more gorgeous than when Edith knew her in New York. She still wore her signature skinny jeans, designer T-shirt, and glasses, but there was a brightness about her for which only Milo could claim credit. "Thanks, Faye. Did you see I finished the arrangements?"

"Yes, and they are incredible. I finished the last garland just now too. That backyard is a fantasy. It should be in every magazine ever."

Milo softly slugged Edith in the shoulder. "Not many sisters get to get married the same day as their awesome brother."

Edith slugged him back, harder. "That's 'cause nobody is as cool as us."

"That's for sure." Milo looked behind her at Noah. "You ready for this, man? Tomorrow we all get married. Not all to each other, of course. You to Edith, me to Faye. It's not weird or anything. Just a *normal* double wedding."

Noah smiled, his hand slipping into Edith's. "I'm ready," he said softly.

Edith lifted her face to him, still in awe of everything that had happened. Still relishing that he was standing beside her, alive and real. He leaned down to kiss her forehead.

With a smile, Milo added, "Well, not that normal, right, sis?"

"Right," Edith answered. "Ours is kind of a miracle."

"For sure."

"I'm so glad we decided to do this."

"Me, too," her brother confirmed with a loving expression. Milo turned to Noah. "Who were you on the phone with earlier? It sounded like book stuff."

Noah nodded. "Yeah, that was my publisher. They're offering me a three-book deal. It's good."

"Heck yes!" Milo held up his hand for a high five. Noah awkwardly returned it and Edith laughed. Noah's new book, his last unfinished manuscript now complete, was his best work yet. She couldn't wait to see it in print and add it to the shelf next to all his others. Of course, the world would never know that Noah Winters wrote this book. He'd changed Anson Lake's name, and his own to a pen name of N.E. Cuthbert, which was a mash-up of Noah, Edith, and Simone Cuthbert.

Edith grinned up at him. "The first of many more new books."

Noah returned her warm smile.

A loud whooping sound made them all turn. Cori waved from the barnyard. David stood beside her, smiling, hands in pockets. "Hey, all you lovers," she called out. "Come eat dinner."

"Coming!" Milo yelled. "Hey, why aren't Cori and Dad getting married with us?" He gasped dramatically. "A triple wedding!"

Edith laughed. "Cori said she wants a Christmas wedding. Also, more importantly, that she didn't want to stand next to you and all your obnoxious muscles in her wedding photos." She wiggled her fingers through the air up and down his body.

Milo slapped a hand to his chest. "That hurts! She's so mean to me and my amazing muscles."

Edith rolled her eyes. She started to move to follow Milo and Faye, but Noah pulled her back. "What is it?" she asked.

He lowered his lips to hers, kissed her gently. When he pulled back, he said, "I have one more thing for you."

"Better than this egg?" Edith grinned and held up the blue egg.

Noah laughed. "That's hard to compete with, but"—he

reached into his pocket and produced a necklace—"I think you'll like this too."

Edith touched the small, unusual charm at the end of a silver chain. "What is that?"

"It's a piece of glass from the Tiffany lamp I threw into the wall."

"Really?" Edith lifted the necklace out of his hand. A quarter-sized teardrop of royal blue glass had been rimmed in silver to form a charm. She held the chain out in front of her and watched the last rays of sun light up the glass.

"It's a reminder of how broken we were without each other," Noah said, his voice quiet with emotion. "A reminder of all the ways you fixed me. And a promise to always be here to fix whatever needs fixing." He smiled tenderly. "Even if it's just that stupid greenhouse fan."

Edith laughed, warmth tingling across her chest. She tucked the necklace into her palm and held it to her heart. "That's beautiful, Noah. Thank you." She kissed him and then put the necklace around her neck.

Noah adjusted it to lay flat on her skin below her throat. "Blue is our color," he said.

"Does that mean you finally admit I was right about the house?"

Noah laughed, shaking his head, "I love you, Edith."

Edith smiled. "I love you, Noah."

"Hey," Milo yelled from the barnyard. "You can make out in the flowers *later*. I *will* eat everything if you don't come *now*."

Edith scoffed and shook her head. "He's such an idiot."

Noah laughed and put his arm around her shoulder. "That's true."

Edith laughed harder as they walked back to their blue farmhouse and their waiting family.

ACKNOWLEDGMENTS

First, thank you, Mom, for introducing me to the 1947 *The Ghost and Mrs Muir* movie, which fascinated me from the beginning and became one of my all time favorites. This book is an ode to that wonderful, romantic story.

Thank you to the amazingly talented farmer florists who I stalk on Instagram and helped inspire this story: Erin Benzakein of Floret Flower @floretflower and The Farmhouse Flower Farm @thefarmhouseflowerfarm. Seriously, start following them now because every picture is heaven.

Thanks to Cristalee Johnson of Blooming Expressions for her helpful florist insights.

Big thanks to Heather Moore and the Mirror Press team.

Family: Love you lots!

And finally, thank YOU awesome reader for taking time to read this book. I hope you enjoyed Edith and Noah's story as much as I do. Let's hang out on Instagram @teriharman.

Teri Harman is the author of *The Moonlight Trilogy*, a witch fantasy series, the magic realism romance, *A Thousand Sleepless Nights,* the magical historical romance, *The Paradox of Love*, and a couple of romance novellas. Her fiction won first place in the "Romance Through the Ages Contest" in 2016 and Kirkus Reviews called her work "unusual and absorbing."

For many years, she's written about books for ksl.com, reviewed books for *The Deseret News*, and contributed book segments to Utah's number one lifestyle show, *Studio 5 with Brooke Walker*. She has taught classes and workshops for writers all over Utah. She works full-time as the National Account Manager for Legends Boxing. Teri lives with her family in Utah, in a blue farmhouse.

Visit her at: TeriHarman.com

Made in the USA
Coppell, TX
30 October 2019